The Color of Frost

KASEY ROGERS

INDIES UNITED PUBLISHING HOUSE, LLC
P.O. BOX 3071
QUINCY, IL 62305-3071

This is a work of fiction. Any resemblance to actual events or persons, living or dead, is entirely coincidental.

Book Cover by K.J. Harrowick

Hardcover 978-1-64456-541-4

Paperback 978-1-64456-542-1

ePub: 978-1-64456-544-5

Library of Congress Control Number: 2022946847

INDIES UNITED PUBLISHING HOUSE, LLC

Acknowledgments

To the Beans. You inspire me every day to try and be a better person.

Writing this book was more difficult than I thought it would be. The first draft came so quickly that I was often convinced it was almost finished. Two people encouraged me to take it further, my editors and dear friends Vicki Lowery and Mary Anne Slack. They prodded and poked me to see how I could revise and edit it into the novel it is now. I'm glad I had the good sense to listen to them and I thank them both for their encouragement.

To connect with Vicki Lowery see her website https://thecozyeditor.com

The cover of this book was brilliantly designed by author and designer K.J. Harrowick https://authorkjharrowick.com

Chapter One

August 1974

NINA SPENT her last twenty dollars selecting the perfect ingredients to make her favorite childhood meal. Of course, that didn't include the Chateau le Tuquet. A wry smile crossed her face as she thought of her papa. He never would have approved of spending as much as she had on a single bottle of Bordeaux. She reasoned it would be a fitting tribute to her life as the final meal she would prepare in her beloved kitchen.

She arranged the sliced veal, prosciutto, and asparagus in the fridge next to the large pan of tiramisu she'd made the night before. Nina removed the fresh pack of Newports and a Bic lighter from the sack and put them in the back pocket of her shorts. The shopping bag was now empty except for a large bottle of Tylenol. She placed that between the toaster and a small transistor radio that was now her only link to the outside world.

She considered listening to some music but had discovered on her drive home that most stations were broadcasting special coverage of Nixon's resignation.

"Richard Milhous Nixon announced last night that he will

resign as the 37th president of the United States. Today at noon Vice President Gerald R. Ford of Michigan will take the oath as the new president of the United States and complete the remaining two and a half years of Mr. Nixon's term," the reporter stated. Every radio station she tuned into had echoed the same news. She had no more interest in hearing about the disgraced, soon-to-be ex-president than she had in thinking about her ex-husband, who shared the same first name. She thought about the irony that it had taken months of hearings to unravel Nixon's secrets, while her ex-husband Richard had openly confessed his. She left the radio alone and instead poured herself a glass of wine.

Not ready to cook quite yet, she wandered into the living room. As she surveyed the empty room, her eyes fell on the mantel above the fireplace. The ghost of an outline remained from a large framed portrait of herself posing with Richard on their wedding day. It was now packed away. Vacation snapshots, framed cards, and assorted memorabilia, all the things that represented the life she once thought was hers—the one that no longer existed—were shoved into boxes, which she had struggled to haul to the basement. She'd been moving most of it into a storage room next to the laundry area since much of what she owned wouldn't fit into the tiny apartment on the third floor where she was moving.

The room where she stood was almost as large as the entire apartment where she lived as a child. Yet she'd grown accustomed to the abundance of space of this first-floor apartment. She and Richard had carved it out of the former mansion that had belonged to his great aunt and uncle long ago. She'd bought into the notion that her life with Richard and his colossal dreams was about them as a couple. But now, Nina knew otherwise. She stood in silence, wondering how her life had come to this. Dismantling her life had reinforced the futility of it all.

Sinking to the floor, Nina sat with her back against the wall. The pack of Newports and lighter dug into her hip. She reached in to take them out of her pocket. Her hands shook as she placed the cylinder of tobacco between her waiting lips, letting it dangle with anticipation as she aimed the lighter at the tip. It had been years since she'd watched a spark envelope the white paper that held it all together—that held her together in moments like this. She pulled the warmth of its flame inside her. The hot acidic taste traveled around her mouth and expanded through her lungs. She savored the rush of dizziness as the smoke escaped from her nose and swirled around her.

She closed her eyes, forcing back the tears that threatened to spill. Until March, she would have described her marriage as happy. Yes, she had been happily married to Richard King, who claimed he adored her. He'd become everything to her. His family, his dreams, his ambitions were all she'd focused on in the almost five years they'd been married. But what she thought was real was merely a reflection of her willingness to push aside the questions that gnawed at her when he was vague or dismissive about her concerns. She let her mind careen toward all the painful memories, knowing it would help her keep her resolve.

She'd met him on a day she'd taken off from work to sit shiva for her old neighbor Mr. Blau, who had passed away. She'd traveled east from Worcester in central Massachusetts to Wellesley, an affluent town west of Boston. Nina brought along a variety of pastries and confections for Mr. Blau's family. She rubbed her sweaty palms against her dress and hoped no one noticed. She hovered near the table where there was an enormous spread of food but turned to leave as someone approached. The man that approached was Richard, who was also a friend of the family. She was entangled before she could retreat. He eyed the last cannoli before he noticed Nina standing close by. He smiled at her.

"Damn! There's only one cannoli left. Would you like it?"

"No, you go ahead," she told him and started to leave.

"Are you sure? I've already had two," he said, with a hint of embarrassment.

"Absolutely sure."

"Hey, do you know where these came from?" Richard asked. Nina turned back. "Let me tell you," he continued, "if I knew who made these, I'd get down on my hands and knees and propose. Well, maybe not if it was a dude. But these are just so good!" He wiped a smudge of ricotta from his chin. "Have you tried one?"

"On multiple occasions," Nina said, as her face flushed.

"I just have to find out and bring some back to my folks in Maine. Do you know where the Blaus got them?" Richard questioned.

"They're from a restaurant in Worcester called Angelo's. Their pastry chef made them."

"Worcester?" Richard said. "That's a haul. How do you know where they come from?"

Nina blushed. "Because I'm their pastry chef."

"You made these?" he said with surprise. "Well, I guess I better make good on my promise. First off, what's your name?"

"Nina. Nina DeMarco."

"You certainly don't look like a Nina DeMarco, but okay." Richard knelt before her with a flourish. "Nina DeMarco, will you marry me?" he teased.

"Could you tell me your name first?" she said, trying to play along.

"Silly me. I should at least have introduced myself before I proposed. I'm Richard King."

"Well, you certainly do look like a Richard King, and while that's an interesting offer, I'll have to turn you down. I only accept proposals from men I've dated at least twice."

"You're tough! Well, I suppose I'll have to ask you out a few times before you say yes?" he continued the banter.

Nina turned away, unable to meet his gaze. His curly brown hair and lanky body gave him a rather professorial look. He was classically handsome, with a square jaw and a broad, Cary Grant smile. But what she found most appealing was his absolute confidence. She tugged on her hair, wishing she could muster even a hint of that.

They dated for almost a year before Richard proposed for real. The couple agreed that they would move into his parents' guest house on their property in York, Maine after they married.

Richard planned to apply to dental school, and Nina wanted to continue her culinary career. Her dream was to open a small bistro or a bakery. Nina hoped that, one day, she would be the one who benefitted from her knowledge and years of experience in creating exquisite meals or desserts, rather than the various restaurant owners she'd worked for in the past. But Richard told her he was eager for them to be on their own, and he was adamant that she take a job his parents offered her as the bakery department manager in their grocery store in Kittery.

"Nina, opening a new business would take time to establish. Why don't we wait a while until you get acclimated to the area. You can pursue your heart's desire when the timing is right. I promise." Nina went along, since at the time it made sense.

While they were dating, however, Richard peppered all their conversations with the idea of buying his late great aunt's estate. The enormous property included not just a stately mansion but an old carriage house and other outbuildings on five acres of land.

"Honey, it's so close to the ocean, we could even walk there. Just think of what we could do with the carriage house. You could use it for a catering business or maybe that's where I set up my dental practice when I graduate. Really, it would be great."

"Isn't it too big for us, even if we used it for a business? It would cost a fortune to heat in the winter," Nina reminded him.

"Well, maybe we could have plans drawn up to use the second and third floors for apartments. That way, we'd have some rental income too. Do you know how hard it is to find an apartment in that area? I bet we could ask top dollar even for the tiny apartment on the third floor."

Eventually, Nina gave in, and they moved forward.

Years passed, and as Richard came closer to graduating from dental school, any time they discussed how to use the carriage house, it turned into an argument. He seemed to have forgotten his promises and even had an architect draw up plans to convert the space into his dental practice without discussing it with her.

Then, in March, Richard had completely shattered her dreams when he had told her the devastating truth about their marriage. The night was etched in her memory. She was dressed in her floral pink nightgown and a terry-cloth robe. She had sat on the couch that night reading the latest novel by Jacqueline Susann, *Once is Not Enough*. She smelled like her favorite lavender-scented soap, and her hair was still damp from her bath. She recalled being sleepy, but she had always waited up for her husband to arrive home from school when he had classes in Boston. She'd gotten off the sofa and turned on the radio, hoping the music would keep her awake. Turning the dial, she heard a few bars of music playing. Rod Argent and his band sang, *"Hold your head up."* She dialed away and found another station playing Helen Reddy's *I am Woman* over the airwaves. The sound was crystal clear.

She heard Richard's car in the driveway but settled back onto the sofa and picked up her book. When he came into the living room, he was quiet and walked straight over to the liquor cabinet in the corner. He'd poured himself a scotch neat and crossed to a chair opposite the sofa where Nina sat. She looked up to say hello and noticed he was pale. She put down her book and studied him.

"Are you okay?" she'd asked him. "You look like you might be coming down with something."

Richard had remained silent for several minutes. "I'm moving out," he finally said.

"What?" She thought she must have misunderstood, and she sat up.

"Our marriage is over."

"Why?"

"I wasn't trying to hurt you, Nina—it just happened."

It took Richard less than ten minutes to strip away the facade of their life together. He confessed that night that he'd been seeing another student at school. The words "our marriage is over" had penetrated Nina's every waking thought for the last few months. Apparently, he was actually with his girlfriend Holly on the nights he claimed to be staying in Boston because of bad weather. He wouldn't tell Nina how long they'd been involved, but she imagined it wasn't something new. Richard moved out the next day and into his parents' guest house. Nothing had been the same since.

At first he acted civil. She assumed it was because Nina still worked for his parents who knew she was an asset to their business. But about a month later, she came home from work and found Richard on a ladder by the window in their apartment.

"What are you doing here?" she asked him.

"Holly wants to redecorate and order some new curtains. Damask isn't quite her style, so I'm taking measurements. I'll be out of your hair in a minute."

Nina shook. "Are you telling me you're planning on living here?"

"That's the only thing that makes sense, Nina," he said, looking at her incredulously. "You don't need this kind of space. It's just you. And this place has been in my family for generations."

"Yes, and it sat empty for years. That's how much it meant to your folks. And have you forgotten, Richard, this is my house, too?" she shouted at him.

The bewildered look on Richard's face told Nina everything she needed to know. He assumed she would just give in to whatever he demanded. He underestimated her desire to keep the one thing that now mattered to her, the place she called home. Shaking his head, Richard left, saying nothing more. But the next day, his father came to her office and fired her from her job at the grocery store. The moment Nina got home, she began searching for a lawyer.

AFTER A FEW PHONE CALLS, she chose a local lawyer named Andrea Goodwin. At their first meeting, she asked Nina, "Where did the money come from that purchased the property?"

Nina's mind raced, recalling the very day she sat in an office at a bank in Worcester, waiting to deposit the check she was holding in her hand. It was for her share of an insurance settlement with her mother's former landlord for negligence. The piece of paper was a horrible reminder of a day years ago that had destroyed so many lives.

When the bank manager came back to his office with an application, he said, "You're so lucky to have this much money at such a young age!" Her hands trembled, and she wanted to tear it up into a million tiny bits. No matter how many zeros there were in the figure, it wasn't enough to erase what had happened to her mother.

"Nina?" Andrea called to her.

"Sorry. It was from an insurance settlement. That money was used to buy the place and pay for all the repairs and renovations while he was off at school."

"Who paid for that? His tuition, I mean," Andrea asked.

"I did," Nina told her, feeling duped.

"Well," Andrea said, "under the laws of the state of Maine, those factors will weigh heavily in the judge's decision over who would be awarded the property. So this won't be a cake walk. Assuming you can document what you're telling me, most likely you will be awarded the property."

Nina barely knew where to begin since Richard guarded their financial records closely. She scoured the apartment searching for them, fearing Richard had already retrieved them. But eventually she found everything buried deep in a closet in his study, a room she rarely entered. In reviewing their bank statements and records of bills and receipts for expenses, she saw transactions that told the story of her husband's infidelity. No wonder he guarded these papers, convincing her this was his contribution to their household chores. Nina wondered why he didn't take these with him and realized he most likely assumed he would only be moving temporarily, so he didn't bother. Soon however, her lawyer had copies of all the records she requested.

On the day they went to court, the judge awarded her the property. Nina was thankful that Andrea's predictions had come true. But as she walked out of the courtroom, Richard grabbed her by the arm and spun her around.

"That house should have been mine, and you know it. You'll

never make it all work without me, Nina," he told her, then sauntered over to Holly, and they hurried down the street. The memory made her blood boil. Nina took another swig of her wine, stubbed out her cigarette on the bottom of her shoe, and lit another.

Initially, her anger had fueled her reaction and made her determined to prove him wrong. When she'd had a few days to think about how to resolve her dilemma, she'd decided to offer her first-floor apartment to Keith Peterson, the tenant who lived on the third floor. He was getting married and had told her he would be moving out. When Nina suggested they swap apartments instead, he readily agreed. With arrangements made, Nina began moving to the third floor while he and his new wife were on their honeymoon. The looming deadline prompted her to pack and begin bringing things to either the storage room in the basement or her new apartment upstairs.

The troublesome move between apartments in the summer heat overwhelmed her. There was little room in the apartment that had once been the maid's quarters. The things she'd accumulated throughout her marriage simply wouldn't fit even though Richard had been awarded all their furniture. The apartment was too small even for the double bed in their guest room that Richard decided not to take with him. Before Keith left for his honeymoon, she'd offered it to him in exchange for his futon couch and the twin bed he used, in hopes of accommodating her new arrangement. He graciously obliged. The only piece of furniture she brought upstairs with her was a rocking chair she'd had since childhood.

She began to wonder why any of it mattered since she couldn't imagine needing any of these things ever again. The future was bleak and she grew more despondent trying to figure out how she would even survive.

That was when Nina began making a mental list of why ending it all made the most sense. First, she'd depleted her money on legal fees over her divorce. She had no job, and no one would hire her because her ex-husband's family had completely sullied her reputation. Both her parents were long gone, and she'd lost touch with just about all of her friends from high school and college when she moved to Maine as a newlywed. The final straw was being forced to give up her home. She realized how much it embodied her life and had become a place of refuge. Now however, it was a place of entrapment, with months of emotional pain and isolation finally pushing Nina over the edge.

It wasn't the first time she'd made this sort of mental list. For years after her mother died, the only thing that kept her going was her job as a pastry chef at a popular Italian restaurant in her hometown of Worcester. There, Nina could shut out the images of her elderly mother trapped by a fire and instead focus on the day ahead.

Each morning, she would get up at five a.m. and let herself into the kitchen. Tucked away from the world she would develop new recipes, order ingredients, manage her inventory, and create. The flakiness of her crust on the sbrisolona and the tart cherries that balanced with the sweetness of her crostata ricotta e visciole tempted the fullest stomachs. Customers ordered her sfogliatelle in advance just to be assured it would finish off their meal. But nothing delighted Angelo's clientele more than Nina's tiramisu. There were multiple secrets to her recipe. She used espresso to soak the spongy savoiardi biscuits and added a tiny drop of Cointreau to the mascarpone cheese. The owner of Angelo's told her that Nina's desserts had become the reason for the restaurant's increase in sales, making her blush.

Nina worked at Angelo's for almost three years before she met and married Richard. She'd hoped to pass along her secrets to the children she would now never have with him. Now all her knowledge would die with her when she ended the despair from which she suffered.

Surveying the living room again, Nina took the last drag of her cigarette and heard a pathetic sizzle as she extinguished it in her wineglass turned ashtray. Her stomach growled. Glancing at her watch, she realized why she was so hungry. It was almost seven, and she hadn't eaten all day.

Nina headed into the kitchen and at the sink, she rinsed her glass. The blood-red wine and ashes fought the current of the tap water. Then she refilled the glass. Opening the fridge, she took out the sliced veal, prosciutto, and asparagus she'd bought earlier, and placed them on the counter. The refrigerator was now almost empty. All that remained was half a bottle of white wine she needed for the saltimbocca, and the large pan of tiramisu. Nina stood there with the door open to allow chilled air to refresh her for a moment against the August humidity. The aromatic scent of espresso wafted up to her nose, making her think of the hundreds of times she'd made tiramisu in her lifetime.

She opened the window, hoping to invite a salty ocean breeze into the muggy apartment. Instead, glancing out the window over the kitchen sink, she noted the shadows encroaching upon the front of the carriage house. It had stood vacant for years at the rear of the property, revealing few of its secrets.

Opening the door to the pantry, Nina took out her most prized possessions, a set of Mauviel cookware Richard had purchased for her twenty-fifth birthday a few years ago. The gift had shocked her because she would have been thrilled with a less expensive set of All-Clad. Eventually, she acknowledged to herself that his extravagance was most likely because she frequently cooked for his family.

Nina preheated the oven and brought the asparagus over to the sink. She remembered the delight it gave her father every time her mother served it. She washed the stalks, breaking off the tough ends before placing them in a bowl. She drizzled olive oil on top and tossed them to ensure they were evenly coated, then spread them in a single layer on a baking sheet. She added a sprinkle of salt and pepper, placed them in the oven, and set the timer.

She leaned against the kitchen counter, sipping her wine, and thought about how disappointed her mother would be. It had never occurred to Nina until that moment how genuinely rebellious her mother, Rose DeMarco, was when, in her thirties, she'd pushed to adopt Nina though her large Italian family had discouraged her. When Nina's father suddenly died when she was eleven, her mother would walk to her job cleaning rooms at a hotel nearby, her feet aching by the time she arrived home at night. Nina would rub them and draw a warm bath to soothe her mother's aging body.

Maybe that was why her mother always told her, *"Devi ottenere un'istruzione." You need to get an education.* She insisted Nina apply to Johnson and Wales for a culinary degree since she wanted Nina to be more independent and be able to support herself.

The earthy smell of the asparagus roasting reminded Nina it was time to fix the saltimbocca. Nina took the veal cutlets and laid them side by side on a sheet of plastic wrap. Then she took a generous piece of prosciutto and placed it on top of each piece. Using her meat mallet, Nina flattened them until they were about a quarter-inch thick. Next, she picked up several pieces of fresh sage and placed them on the veal, securing them with a toothpick.

She dredged the veal in seasoned flour before placing it in the pan. She let it sauté for several minutes then flipped it over before adding white wine to the pan, stirring occasionally to release all the exquisite flavors. As the wine cooked down and burned off some of the alcohol, Nina added the chicken broth and the remaining tablespoon of butter, swirling it around in the pan. When it was done to perfection, she reached for the only plate that remained in the cupboard. She was ready to eat.

Pulling a barstool up to the kitchen island, Nina sat there trying to relish her last meal. But she was too hungry to savor it, and she ate with abandon. The saltimbocca and asparagus quickly disappeared followed by half a pan of tiramisu.

When she was done, she laid her head on the counter and began to cry. Her stomach hurt but it no longer mattered. The fullness in her stomach would never restore the emptiness of her heart. Nina thought back to all the times before when she'd made the list of reasons to end it all. Even before her mother had died, Nina had struggled with destructive thoughts. But in the past, she could often work through them by distracting herself or acknowledging how hurting herself would affect someone she loved or even an innocent bystander. She'd always been able to convince herself to stick around. But this was different. There was no one left in the world that she needed to protect from the loss and grief of her death. There was no one she could reach out to anymore— no one who loved her.

Her love for Richard once kept those thoughts at bay. The belief that he shared her future kept her tethered to the world she often wanted to exit. Nina had resisted overwhelming moments before, but in recent days she found herself making that list and she had no reason to resist her impulses anymore.

Nina looked down at what remained of the tiramisu. It seemed like such a waste to dispose of it. Still, she walked to the sink and scraped the remains into the garbage disposal. She shuddered as the grinding noise reverberated throughout the empty apartment.

After she washed and dried the dishes, she set them on the rack out of habit, even though it no longer mattered what happened to anything that remained behind.

She took the bottle of Tylenol off the counter and placed it in her pocket before filling a glass with the last of the wine. She took one last look around, shut off the lights, and left by the back door. She walked to her VW Beetle that sat alone in the driveway. She climbed into the backseat, opened the bottle, and swallowed as many pills as she could force down, finally feeling the calm she longed for and hoping whoever found her would forgive her.

Chapter Two

Richard stood with his back to Nina as she opened the door. There were others who were in the room, but she couldn't see their faces or hear what they were saying. She floated down the hallway past him, and when she turned to confront him, it wasn't Richard after all. It was her old boss at Ai Fiori's who fired her for revealing that her colleagues were mishandling food in his kitchen —at least Nina thought that's who it was. She couldn't tell for sure because a piece of cloth was covering his face. She continued to wander, entering rooms she never knew existed.

The place was so familiar to her, and Nina realized it was the apartment where she grew up. But instead of being small and homey, it was charred and smelled like dirt. She saw a flight of stairs and headed towards it. When she looked back, everyone had disappeared, and she wondered where they had gone. She continued up the stairs and opened the door at the top. Inside there was a large, bright basketball court surrounded by bleachers. Hundreds of people watched something she couldn't see from where she entered. Trying to improve her vantage point, she slowly made her way to the other end of the court and saw a scoreboard. Polka music played in the background. People began clapping and looked her way. Some stood to applaud her approach.

Her mother was in the crowd. Nina's eyes went to her immediately even though she was the furthest away. She couldn't understand why Mr. Blau was next to her mother since they didn't know one another, but both cheered loudly. She looked down at her hands and feet. They were enormous. She finally understood why it was so difficult to walk—the size of her appendages weighed her down. She tried to lift them so she could continue towards her mother and Mr. Blau, longing for the warmth of their embrace. Each step took every ounce of strength she could muster. Finally, she turned to see why everyone began looking past her. It was Richard again, and this time he had a chainsaw.

She heard a beeping noise. Her eyes fluttered, but each eyelid felt like it weighed a million pounds. Her head throbbed, and her mouth tasted like spoiled custard. Nina began to drift off again when someone spoke.

"I think she's back with us."

She slowly opened her eyes and saw the face of a stranger scrutinizing her. The white lab coat and stethoscope indicated it was someone in the medical profession. She looked no further and shut her eyes, quickly realizing she was in a hospital room. Someone took her wrist. The warm hand checked her pulse. Disappointment and remorse filled her as she realized she was still alive. Tears spilled down her cheeks. She turned her face, hoping she wouldn't be expected to speak.

"I'll let him know that he can take her home in a few days if she continues to improve." Nina heard movement and assumed whoever spoke had left the room.

She was confused. What *him* would be taking her home? Was Richard there? She wanted to tell them Richard wasn't her husband anymore, and he never really loved her. Nina melted further into the bed.

"Mrs. King?" a woman called to her. "The doctor performed a gastric lavage, so your throat may feel sore or you may still feel queasy, but you should be feeling better soon. Your friend stepped away but should be back any moment. Oh! Here he is. I'll leave you two alone."

Nina turned slightly, opening her eyes just enough to see who had entered the room. A man stood there. He looked somewhat familiar, but she couldn't place his face. She struggled to lift herself into a sitting position but was too weak. The IVs restricted her movements. Her body and head ached profoundly. She was disoriented and confused. All Nina wanted was to go back to sleep, but she was intensely thirsty, and her tongue felt like someone had glued it to the roof of her mouth.

"Hello, Nina," the man said, staring at her. She turned her face to avoid his gaze.

An awkward silence filled the room.

"Is there anyone you want me to call? I have Richard's number if that's helpful?"

"No!" she croaked. "Don't call him. Who are you? Why are you here?"

"I'm Ben. I live on the second floor. I've been your tenant for almost a year now."

Nina looked at Ben and studied his unfamiliar face. Richard had always dealt with tenant matters, collecting rent and providing minor repairs when necessary. Nina used to work long hours before her divorce, and since the tenants had their own parking area and entrance at the front of the house, she rarely came face to face with any of them. As a result, any encounter with a tenant was usually at a distance.

The only tenant she knew even slightly was Keith Peterson, who had been renting the third-floor apartment since Nina and Richard had renovated the house on Pepperell Point Road. Having an apartment in this prestigious area of Kittery, close to the oceans and the Cutts Island trails, was hard to give up, so Keith was happy to switch apartments with her since he was getting married and needed a larger place.

Before Nina and Richard settled their divorce, tenants were instructed to mail all rent payments to the escrow account established by the court. She never had to interact with others living under the same roof where she'd lived for years, and she recognized how odd is must have seemed to Ben now that she was forced to think about it.

"Why are you here?" she whispered.

"I found you passed out in the driveway last night. I couldn't get you to wake up, so I brought you here. I'm not sure what your story is, but you scared me. The ground and your clothes were covered in vomit." Ben walked to the window and looked out before turning back to Nina. "I found the bottle of Tylenol."

Nina turned away humiliated. She wished he would go away.

"You were in my driveway?"

"I heard a noise that sounded like a wounded animal. I thought maybe it was the mother cat of the two kittens I found last week. When I went to check, I saw you on the ground. When I brought you in, I honestly couldn't answer most of their questions, and they whisked you away. Today, I learned they pumped your stomach."

Nina turned back and stared at him for a moment. She pushed herself up in the bed.

"I'm not sure what to say. I didn't plan on being here today."

"I wasn't sure if you would be either," Ben told her. "But please, you have to promise me you're not going to scare me like that again, okay?"

"Sure," Nina agreed reluctantly.

"Well, if there's no one you want me to call, I can come get you and bring you home when you're released. Can I bring you anything? Maybe a fresh set of clothing or something?"

Nina thought for a moment. Most of her belongings were already on the third-floor, and that door was locked. She hesitated because it was difficult to choose between leaving the hospital in her soiled clothing or figuring out a way to give him access to her apartment. Noting her hesitancy, he made an alternative offer.

"Don't worry. I'll see what I can find. My younger sister left some things behind when she visited a while ago. I'll be back to pick you up when they call me. Okay?"

"Thanks. I'm sorry.... what's your name again?"

"Ben Comstock."

"Thanks, Ben," she said and sank back into the bed.

Hours later, a young woman wearing the smock of a candy striper placed a food tray down in front of Nina. She lifted a cover, revealing a slice of something that appeared to be meatloaf covered in a thick brown gravy and also smothered a lump of mashed potatoes and an unholy gathering of overcooked green beans. To the side sat a container of bright red Jell-O and a paper plate with a small dinner roll and a packet of margarine. A can of ginger ale rounded the meal out. This was to be dinner.

"Eat up, Miss. I'll be back in a half-hour to collect your tray," the girl told her.

Nina stared at the food. She hadn't eaten anything other than ice chips in twenty-four hours. She was starving, yet she was leery of the food before her. Opening the soda can, Nina pushed a straw into the hole, and drank more than half the can before letting out an enormous belch. She was thankful she was alone in the room, and no one would take offense to the gassy release.

She picked up the fork and piled on some mashed potatoes. Her taste buds told her they were the instant potatoes favored by institutions over peeling large batches of spuds. Nina ate them with more relish than she thought possible, unable to stop once she started. She moved onto the meatloaf but couldn't touch the pile of green beans. Jell-O wasn't a food she had much experience with, but she opted to finish her meal with the dessert, hoping it would help fill her stomach. It surprised her that she would have eaten more if available, which made her think about the night before. She realized it was probably a mistake to eat several portions of tiramisu after consuming such a rich meal and drinking almost an entire bottle of wine. Her overindulgence had most likely made her stomach revolt and caused her to vomit once she'd ingested all the pills. The plan she thought was foolproof wasn't after all. Here she was, alive and right back where she was the night before.

Later, the nurse came in and removed her IVs. Nina climbed out of bed to look out the window. Although only wrapped in a thin hospital gown, it weighed on her limbs.

Aside from being at one of the area hospitals, Nina wasn't even sure where she was. She assumed it was the York Hospital since it was the closest one to her home. It seemed odd to be somewhere and have only a stranger know of your whereabouts.

She wondered what she would do next now that everything else had gone awry. She was still alive, but now she also had to worry about the expenses she was incurring during her stay in the hospital. It all left her feeling more inadequate to cope with the future. She was alive but still had nothing to live for.

Although she was a twenty-seven-year-old woman, she longed for her mother's warm embrace. Tears escaped as she stood there, wishing she could talk to her about her constant thoughts of inadequacy. Nina shivered wishing someone would assure like her mother always did that no matter how difficult life was, it was going to be okay. She gazed out the window wondering if it would ever okay again.

She thought she'd finally escaped the troubles of her past when she married Richard. His charm and adoration had been the antidote to her painful past. It was hard to reconcile that the same man that once told her he loved her with all his heart was now the man that haunted her dreams.

When they first started dating, Nina never really thought the relationship would go anywhere, but it was fun to be out and socializing with someone her age again. After they first met at the Blaus', he showed up one day at Angelo's where she worked. She was putting some desserts in the display case and heard someone calling her.

"Hey! It's my favorite baker, the future Mrs. King."

Nina turned around to see Richard striding through the restaurant's door.

She flashed him a surprised smile. "What are you doing here? It's a far drive just for a cannoli."

"Oh, but yours are the best. But, I admit, my roommate asked me for a ride home, and I said sure if he would show me how to find this place."

"He lives out this way?"

"Yeah. Right near Worcester State. That's not to say I wouldn't drive all this way for one of your desserts, but with everything happening at BU, he wanted to get back home."

Many students at colleges and universities nationwide were engaged in antiwar protests. Things had erupted days before when National Guardsmen opened fire, killing four unarmed students and wounding nine others at Kent State University. Students at Boston University, where Richard attended, had set several fires. There had even been bomb threats. As a result, the school canceled exams and all ceremonies.

"Sorry to hear about commencement."

"Yeah. It stinks. I spent four years at BU, and now we won't even have a graduation ceremony. But this weekend is Mother's Day, so I thought I'd bring something special home for my mom. What do you recommend? What are you bringing your mother?"

His question took her aback. But, of course, he couldn't have known that her mother was dead or about the horrible circumstances that killed her. She turned away abruptly.

"I'll be right back," she said, hurrying into the kitchen.

After gaining her composure, she returned to the restaurant entrance, where Richard was looking into the display case. She handed him a large box of assorted pastries packed into a box.

"I wasn't sure if you were going back to Maine today or tomorrow, so I gave you things that don't need refrigeration. No cannoli, but I promise what's inside won't disappoint."

"Well, that's very kind of you, Mrs. King."

While settling the bill, Nina wondered why Richard was carrying the joke so far. But then, he looked at her intently.

"You know, we should probably think about going on a few dates before we get married. Didn't you say that was your requirement? I'm coming back to Boston next week. What days do you have off from this place?"

Nina wasn't sure how to react. She thought he was merely flirting initially, but his question seemed sincere.

"Well, Mr. King. I usually have Mondays and Wednesdays off."

"Jot down your address, and I'll pick you up around noon on Wednesday and take you out for lunch."

She found herself enjoying Richard's company, but she held her heart in reserve. They went on a few dates. However, Nina wasn't convinced he was a good match, so she never considered it a serious relationship. He bragged a little too much about himself for her liking. When they went out together, she listened quietly as he spoke of his dreams and ambitions and all the wonderful things about himself with an overabundance of confidence. But slowly, she started to think it was more of a facade. And since the hour's drive from Boston to Worcester didn't deter Richard from seeing her, she wondered if she underestimated his intentions.

One day, they sat across from one another in a booth at the Miss Worcester Diner. Nina was still eating waffles, but Richard had finished his hashbrowns and eggs. He chatted away, telling her what she had already heard about Maine and his family's business, how he wanted to be a dentist, and how much he loved to sail. Nina just sat there and listened.

When she finally pushed her plate away, he asked her about her past and family.

It seemed like he was asking more out of politeness since they'd already been out several times, and he seemed to take little interest in learning more about her. Nina began slowing, telling him more general things at first.

"I grew up on Shrewsbury Street in Worcester. If you don't know the area, it's the home of many other Italian families like mine."

"I'm sorry, but you just don't look Italian!" Richard said.

"I'm sure I'm not. I was adopted by an older Italian couple who couldn't have their own children."

Then, she described life in a triple-decker apartment in Worcester. It was the place where she had learned to cook and bake. Papa would lavish praise on Nina's natural instincts in the kitchen and would press his hand to his lips and declare, "Squisito!" Nina would hug his neck, and her mother would laugh and tell him in Italian, "You'd say that if she served you a football." Her father would sheepishly nod his head and eat whatever was before him.

As Richard sipped coffee, Nina told him about all the hours she had spent in the kitchen with Papa preparing meals, especially when their relatives would visit from Springfield once a month. Eventually, however, those visits grew fewer and far between.

"Why's that?" he asked.

"Papa died of a heart attack when I was eleven," she told him. She hoped he wouldn't ask about her mother.

"That's awful," Richard said. After a few moments, he spoke rather intensely.

"When I first met you at the Blaus'," he continued, "I thought you looked right through me when we spoke." He paused and looked at her. "There was something about you that made me want to know more. Those frosty colored eyes of yours make you look rather cold, but I guess that's what I found so intriguing. And now, Mrs. King, I realize your eyes are stunning and unique and quite warm and inviting. The color seems to change constantly. They're not quite a green or blue or grey but all of those colors at the same time. They're truly your best feature."

Nina blushed at the intensity of his stare. He reached over and took her hands and held them tightly. No one had ever said things like this to her before. Richard's comments and flattery struck a chord because she often thought her eyes betrayed her, revealing the loneliness and heartache always close to the surface.

But all those words were spoken years ago, and when they began their divorce, everything he said and did invalidated what she once believed he thought about her. Without work or something else to distract her, her mind became an echo chamber for his repeated rants. She recounted all the times since March when he had arrived unannounced, trying to convince her that any attempt to keep the property was futile.

"Even if you win in court, Nina, you'll never be able to manage this place on your own. I did everything. Without a job, you won't be able to afford it, and trust me, no one in Kittery will hire you ever again. And forget about getting a permit to open any kind of business. You'll have to move someplace new and start all over again. Then what good will it do you to own this place? Holly and I want to move ahead with the renovations on the carriage house, but you're so selfish you can't even see that and let it go. You've always thought more about yourself than you did about me, and that's just one reason I left. I won't go into the others."

Nina searched her mind to think of what he was possibly talking about. Was she that awful a wife? What had she done to make him so hostile to her? She couldn't understand why he was so angry with her when there seemed to be no sign that their marriage was in trouble until the day he announced he was leaving.

Separating the Richard from her past and this new image of him remained hard to understand. She didn't know this person who would shout at her and deliberately try to catch her alone and off guard like the day she found him waiting for her in the driveway right after she got fired from his parent's grocery store.

"I can't believe you're being so unreasonable," he shouted then began following her into the apartment. She turned to prevent him from entering but he wedged his foot in the door. "What's happened to you? You were never this crazy before. Do you honestly think a judge will side with you over my family and me? We've lived in this area for generations. We know everyone.

You don't have a prayer of staying in this place once we go to court, so you should just give up now and end the headaches," he insisted. She stomped on his foot and when he moved, she shut the door and bolted it.

As weeks passed, Nina began to believe what he said could be true. His family did know everyone, and she was merely a transplant who didn't even have a job anymore. She was at such a disadvantage when it came to fighting him. She began to wonder why she was even trying.

Then panic began to set in just like it did long ago after her father died and fears that something would happen to her mother had occupied her teenaged mind endlessly. Out of nowhere, she would become overwhelmed and couldn't manage to calm herself. Her heart would pound. The simple act of breathing was too much. She tried to shake off the feelings of numbness in her hands, and sometimes she became sick to her stomach.

In recent months, she found herself reaching out to her lawyer, Andrea. Nina knew her calls to her would increase the debt she would owe in the end but there were times she needed to hear another human's voice. However, even her lawyer's optimism and reminders of Nina's legal advantages could not assuage Nina's fears that Richard would somehow take the only remaining thing that mattered to her anymore—her home.

Nina heard someone behind her. She turned and smiled weakly at the candy striper who had returned to remove the dinner tray. "Well, you did great! Did you like the meatloaf? Mrs. Walker down the hall raves about it!"

"It was delicious," Nina told her, stretching the truth.

"Can I bring you another ginger ale or something else? I'm off soon but have a little time left before I head home."

"No, thanks," Nina said politely and climbed back into bed. The young woman left while Nina remained behind wondering what tomorrow would bring.

Chapter Three

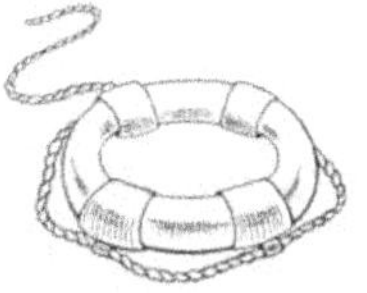

On the day Nina was to be released, she stood in the bathroom looking at herself in the full-length mirror on the door. She was still exhausted and had become frighteningly thin. The clean T-shirt Ben had brought when he arrived hung on her slight frame. She wore a pair of jeans his younger sister had left behind on a visit, and Nina had to ask the nurse for something to hold them up. She tried not to care that her dark blonde hair, usually streaked with gold, was unkempt, dull, and dirty. Her unwashed hair and fuzzy teeth didn't bother her yesterday. She hadn't expected to be alive today. Nevertheless, Nina couldn't help but think that the frosty green eyes that Richard once claimed were beautiful were the same eyes that looked back at her, frightened and wary and full of pain.

Once she was dressed, she moved to the chair next to the bed and sat looking out the window waiting for Ben to come back to her room. She was anxious to be discharged and to be anywhere but the room where she sat. Yet Nina also wished there was another way to get back to Pepperrell Point Road. She agonized over the anticipation of the ride home with this stranger.

She was relieved that when he arrived, Ben was quiet as the nurse wheeled her out of the room and to the exit of the hospital.

She gently waved his arm away and lifted herself out of the wheel-chair even though it took all her strength. Nina followed him and they walked to the parking lot without speaking. He opened the passenger door and held it for her while she reluctantly climbed inside.

As Ben drove south towards Kittery, Nina looked pensively out the window. There were moments where she could glimpse the sea. Waves rolled onto the shore. Gulls floated effortlessly above each crest, ever watchful for whatever morsel they could extract from its bounty. She admired their tenacity, knowing the fury of the waves could beat back even the strongest of men. The gulls must be after the delicate sea creatures, mussels, clams, crabs and the like. With their hardened shells they could cling to rocks to protect themselves. Nina closed her eyes and wished she had a rock to cling to.

Ben tried some small talk, but Nina couldn't respond. Uncertainty kept her from conversation of any kind. She was still sure she had no reason to go on, and his kindness complicated her resolve.

Close to the house, Ben turned left instead of going straight. "Hey, where are we going?" Nina asked him.

"I know I'm being presumptuous, but something tells me you aren't ready for this, so I'm heading to a beach near home. We can take a walk and talk if you'd like. Or not. Your choice."

The locals knew all the places to access the ocean where they could avoid the tourists that flocked to the beaches of Maine, especially in August. Ben navigated to a secluded area close to the ocean and stopped the car.

"Are you coming?" he asked Nina. She stared blankly ahead for a moment then reached for the door handle and dislodged herself from the seat.

She sensed Ben was trying to find a way to say what was on his mind. Hoping to avoid any unpleasantness, she moved farther away, giving him a wider berth. She tried to dart ahead but his long strides were no match for her. Instead, she navigated towards an outcropping of rocks and sat down, believing it might discourage him from getting too close.

She watched as the waves crashed onto the endless shoreline. The sea made her uneasy. One minute, it appeared calm and warm; the next, it was cold and restless. Nina had never learned to swim and even the thought of being close to it made her queasy. When she first moved to Maine, Richard encouraged her to go swimming or sailing with him. Sometimes Nina wanted to cast aside her fears and join him. She would dip her toes but was afraid to go all in knowing she could easily get over her head. Most of the time, she stayed as far away from the water as she could and read or sunned herself instead.

"You don't know what you're missing," he often told her once he emerged from a swim.

"I'd rather not find out," she'd reply and continue to read whatever novel or magazine she'd brought along.

Ben approached and sat on a rock next to Nina, who silently wished him away. She wasn't ready to be confronted with the words she anticipated him uttering. But, nevertheless, after several moments, he cleared his throat and spoke.

"Look, we both know that what happened the other night wasn't an accident. I can't bear the thought of bringing you back home if you're still in that really dark place. Not to get into too much personal history, but my twin brother committed suicide in college. Finding you the other night in the driveway..."

Nina shot up, breaking away from her perch. She swiftly retreated towards the car unwilling to hear what Ben had to say. But he caught up with her quickly and tugged gently on her forearm, trying to coax her to listen.

"Nina, please hear me out." His voice trembled. She stopped, turned slowly to face him, and saw the pleading look in his eyes.

"I'm sorry to be this blunt, but I can't go through this again. Every time I look in the mirror, I see my twin brother, Byron. I wonder what I could have done or said to make him want to stay alive and be here to celebrate our birthday. I will never understand why he took his own life. That look of despair in your eyes is too familiar, and I don't know how to help. What can I do to make whatever you're thinking of doing go away?"

"You don't even know me! Why should you care?" she said with bitterness.

"Because you're a human being and you're hurt. Isn't that enough?"

Ben's sincerity cut through the gloom of Nina's despondency, and she gave into his kindness and compassion. She sat down on the warm sand, trying to collect a tidal wave of emotions. Ben sat down next to her. Nina opened her mouth to speak, but she couldn't meet his eyes.

"I don't want to put this on you," she said when she finally gathered her thoughts. "It's hard to explain it to someone who is normal and hasn't grown up thinking about dying all the time."

The two sat in silence until their attention was drawn to a couple setting up beach chairs far from the water.

"They must be Mainers," Ben commented.

"How do you know?" Nina asked him.

"They're putting their chairs far enough away from the water so they won't get wet when the tide changes. Maine has two low and high tides about six hours apart every day. If they got too close to the water now, they'd just have to move them soon when the tide comes in."

"I've pretty much ignored the ocean since I got here. Richard and I went to the beach a few times but I don't know how to swim and I rarely agreed to tag along. Eventually, he just stopped asking me to go. I know this place isn't far from the house, but I've never been here. I love the smell of the ocean air, but otherwise, I never seem to acknowledge it."

"That's interesting. I come here all the time. Not to swim but to walk. It's either here or one of the trails close by."

"Another place I've never explored," Nina said, looking out toward the sea. "For years I've been so busy either working or fixing the house I've rarely taken time to enjoy all of this."

"The sunsets are magnificent, especially in the fall. Sunrises too, but I never seem to get up early enough to see them. My work schedule, I suppose."

"Oh? What do you do?"

"I'm a cellist for the Portland Symphony."

"That's the music I keep hearing!"

"I hope my practicing hasn't bothered you?"

"Not at all. I really enjoy hearing you play."

Silence descended between them again, and again Nina's mind churned. She picked shells off the beach and arranged them in a circle. She wanted to talk but had no idea where to begin. Then she heard Ben clear his throat, and he started to speak.

"When Byron died, I tried to believe it was a sudden decision. I told myself he did it on the spur of the moment because something happened at school, or maybe it was an accident. He was so funny and intelligent that it was easy to ignore the moments when he seemed overwhelmed. I had so many things to keep me busy that I couldn't focus on the stuff that could have led me down the same path. And believe me, I had plenty of reasons in high school that were, shall we say, challenging. But Byron was different. No one ever imagined he would be dead at eighteen. I don't know what demons he kept hidden from us, but it's made me very aware that sometimes people find themselves in a bad place and don't know how to cope. I don't know if I did the right thing by coming to get you from the hospital, but I hope I did. Please tell me I made the right decision."

"I'm really sorry to hear about your brother, but I can't say what he thought since I didn't know him."

Nina had a chill even though the August day was sunny. She wrapped her arms around her knees as her mind raced, unable to express her own internal storms. Everything in her life seemed to change shortly after her father died. The last memories of her father were etched on her heart and often took over her mind as she tried to will a different outcome. But no matter how much she wished she could change things, her memories always brought her back to that same Sunday morning when Papa was at the table reading the Boston Globe.

Nina stood at the stove in her night gown making him pancakes. Something dripped down her leg. She looked and saw a small pool of blood on the floor. She screamed and threw the spatula across the room in a panic and ran into the bathroom. That dreaded thing her mother had warned her about had arrived. She sat on the seat of the toilet, crying, unsure of what to do. Her mother wasn't home. She'd gone to visit her sister in Springfield and wasn't expected back until later that day. Nina forgot all about the pancakes and the stove but not about Papa. She was embarrassed that she'd have to face him and try to explain herself. After she removed her soiled clothing, she took a bath, stalling for time. She threw on her mother's robe that hung on the back of the door and emerged from the bathroom, then snuck into her room. She changed clothing and finally walked slowly to the kitchen, not sure what to expect. As she entered the room, Nina found her father slumped on the floor in front of the stove. She rushed to him shouting, "Papa! Papa! Wake up!" over and over again. She ran to the phone and dialed the operator. She gave her address and asked for an ambulance like her mother had taught her to do in case of an emergency. Then she ran downstairs to get her neighbor.

Nina looked over at Ben. She realized he was waiting for her to speak. She swallowed and said, "My father died when I was eleven. I was alone with him when it happened. After that, I began waking up every day wanting to die. For years, the only thing that held me back was knowing how much it would hurt my mother. And then she died too."

"Oh, Nina. How awful!" Ben said.

Nina stopped for a moment. It was a part of her past she rarely spoke about. She didn't even tell Richard about much of it until they began talking about their wedding and putting their guest list together. By then he knew about the money she had stashed in a savings account, as he'd helped her pick out her new VW. Richard's parents wanted a huge affair, and since it was customary for the bride's parents to pay for the wedding, she was at a loss for how to proceed. Most of her aunts and uncles had passed away, and the only people she wanted to invite were a few of her friends from college and her colleagues from the restaurant and Angelo, who had agreed to give the bride away.

Nina looked at Ben closely. His brow was furrowed, and when he leaned his head towards her, their eyes locked momentarily before she glanced away. There was a pain she could see in Ben's eyes, as though he had been there with her years ago. It made all the feelings she'd suppressed for so long bubble to the surface, and she began to reveal things she'd never dared to talk about to anyone before.

"After my mother's funeral, I was, well, broken. The hotel where my mother worked offered to let me stay there a little while so I didn't have to travel back and forth to Wellesley. But eventually I had to go back to my apartment. I just felt trapped. Do you know what I mean?" Without waiting for Ben to respond, Nina urgently continued. "It was torment just being alive. That was the first time I thought really seriously about ending it all."

Ben hung his head, visibly disturbed. Nina sat silently beside him, but her mind roiled with thoughts she tried to bat away. They slipped through anyway—one after another. Each recollection brought back the minutes, the hours, the days that had followed after she had returned to her apartment in Wellesley.

"The only way I was able to cope with it all was to sleep," she said. "Days went by. Sometimes I ate, but even that was almost too much. I didn't have contact with anyone. Sometimes the phone rang, but I just let it ring. If there was a knock at the door it went unanswered.

"One day, I heard someone knocking and it woke me. I thought it was the landlord looking for overdue rent, so I crawled out of bed and opened the door. But it wasn't the landlord. It was a young woman. I just stared at her. I couldn't think of anything to say. But it didn't matter. She told me her name was Sarah. Her grandfather lived across the hall from me. He had suffered a heart attack but was being released from the hospital the next day. She said she was just reaching out to a few of his neighbors to see if they would check on him from time to time. There was something so kind about the way she spoke."

Ben looked at her. The genuine interest she saw in his eyes warmed her and compelled Nina to continue.

"Sarah slipped me a fold of paper with her phone number and that of her parents. She thanked me and then went on her way."

Nina remembered how Sarah had seemed oblivious to Nina's unkempt appearance that day. It brought to mind her greasy hair and the oversized clothes she now wore. Ben seemed not to notice either, and it allowed her to relax and take in the warm breeze blowing from the sea.

"So?" Ben asked. "What happened? With Sarah's grandfather, I mean."

"I made him some cookies," Nina told him smiling.

Ben grinned and nodded his approval.

Nina recalled that for days, she had avoided going over to check on Mr. Blau. But she'd continued to think of the loving way Sarah spoke of her grandfather and how she desperately wanted him to live. The thought that she could bring a tiny amount of joy to another human being stirred something inside her. And so, she did what she did best. She baked.

Day after day batches of cookies came out of Nina's oven. The intoxicating aroma served as a tonic to her soul. She'd been so devoted to the complex desserts at the restaurant that she'd all but forgotten how scrumptious a simple shortbread or oatmeal raisin cookie could be.

At night she took relaxing baths to ease the muscles that had become stiff from being idle. She exhausted herself each day and so began to sleep better. When Nina finally mustered the courage to knock on Mr. Blau's door, she handed him a batch of hermit cookies and was touched when her neighbor beamed back at her. He invited her into his home.

They began to interact daily, and Nina's fog began to lift. She had something to look forward to. Mr. Blau never made assumptions about her life or asked questions she wasn't ready to answer. It was as if he already knew the depths of her pain, and she knew the blue inked numbers on his forearm meant he, too, had things buried deep in his past.

Mr. Blau marveled at her baked goods, and soon she brought him lunch and supper a few times a week. He always insisted she stay and eat with him, and he gave her money to buy groceries. They played rummy and hearts and watched *Hogan's Heroes* and *The Dick Van Dyke Show*. They went to Warren Park and out for coffee. She fed his cat, Mittens, and got to know his children and grandchildren when they came to visit. Nina wasn't lonely anymore. The Blaus made Nina a part of their family, and the loneliness lifted, even if it never entirely disappeared.

Nina's thoughts were interrupted when a small sand-colored, sparrow-sized bird common along the shore landed close by and begin pecking at something in the sand. She watched it for a moment before looking over at Ben who seemed to be waiting for her to continue.

"The Blau family were wonderful people and so good to me. Long after the fire that killed my mother, the cause was determined to be faulty wiring," she told him. "The inspector held the landlord responsible since the other tenants had lodged repeated complaints. It was Mr. Blau's son Adam that suggested I join the lawsuit against the landlord. Sometime after that, I got a large settlement. Then, Mr. Blau passed away, and at his funeral, I met Richard and moved up here. The end."

"Not the end, Nina," Ben said firmly. "Definitely not the end."

She rested her chin on her knees and stared at the sea while Ben sat silently next to her. The high tide was coming in, progressing toward the coastline. Nina suddenly breathed in deeply and exhaled, mimicking the rhythm of the sea.

She pointed to the few swimmers who yielded playfully to the surf. Ben laughed at a man trying to teach the small child he was holding to swim. He patiently held him tight before letting him try on his own.

Nina got up off the sand and extended her hand to Ben. She brushed the sand off her bottom and the two strolled side-by-side down the beach. She picked up a shell and pressed it hard between her fingers. Ben reached over and took it, forcing her to look in his direction. She tried to smile, then looked out at the ocean and saw someone hang gliding.

"That looks like fun. Maybe I should give that a try," she told him.

She thought of the lightness of the engineless aircraft and how peaceful it must be floating freely above the fray. There was a hopefulness in achieving such heights while maneuvering to one's destination on a current of air. It inspired her to think that maybe there could be better tomorrows.

"Not me," Ben assured her. "I'm terrified of heights."

"Well, who said you had to come along?" she teased.

"Damn, straight. But I'll watch you if you really want to do it."

"Not now," she told him. "But maybe in the future."

Chapter Four

Ben pulled into the long driveway. He parked in the front, avoiding the rear of the house.

"Hey, I want to show you something," He told her when they got out of the car.

"What?"

"Do you like animals?"

"I guess so. I thought about getting a dog or a cat because it was lonely when Richard was in Boston, but he squashed that idea. He's allergic to fur."

"Well, you're in for a treat."

They entered the front foyer of the house and Nina followed him up the staircase, passing the door to her new apartment. As he walked down the hall and opened the door to his apartment, two kittens immediately accosted him, climbing up the leg of his jeans.

"Well, they're sure excited to see you!" Nina exclaimed.

"Yeah, I probably should have fed them before I left to pick you up. I thought I'd be right home."

"What are their names?"

"I haven't named them because I didn't plan to keep them. About a week ago, I heard this crying and found them huddled together under the bushes. I don't know what happened to their mother. I haven't found the right home for them yet because all the local shelters are full."

"Well, you rescue creatures of all varieties," Nina said with a smile. "Do you want me to take them off your hands?"

"What? You want them?" Ben asked incredulously.

"I've never had a pet before, and who knows? They're pretty cute."

"Well, that would be great. I'm already attached, but I just can't see taking this on at the moment. The other day, one of them tried to climb into the hole in my cello while I was practicing. So I'll donate the supplies I've already accumulated. That will keep them going for a while. Also, Nina, if it would help, I'm happy to pay you a few months' rent in advance if it will get you back on your feet. I didn't know Richard was such a jerk."

"Ben, I don't know what to say. Let me think about that part, okay?"

"Well, don't stand on ceremony if you need help. I have few expenses and a decent salary from the orchestra, so I'd rather help you than see it sit in my savings account."

"You're something. I don't know if I deserve your kindness, but thank you."

"You're welcome. Now let's get these two upstairs to your apartment, shall we?"

When Nina opened the door, the heat hit her as though she were opening an oven door. The windows were closed, and the curtains were open, allowing the sun to stream through them unabated.

"This isn't good. It's too hot in here. I thought about bringing up the small air conditioner Richard and I had for our guest room, but it didn't seem necessary."

"Let's bring the kittens back downstairs, and I'll help you get the A/C unit. In the meantime, let's open some windows."

ONCE THEY GOT the air conditioner in place, they returned to Ben's place, and he offered to fix her something to eat.

"You must be hungry. I know I am. I'm not a great cook, but I made some Hamburger Helper yesterday, and there are plenty of leftovers. Or, I'd be happy to grab a pizza or something."

Nina was hungry but not hungry enough to endure Hamburger Helper. She was reluctant to order pizza since she didn't feel right having him pay for dinner, and she had nothing to offer him.

"Would you be okay if I poked around in your fridge? I'm a pretty good cook," she grinned.

"By all means. I always order out or make something that doesn't require much skill. A home-cooked meal would be a treat."

Nina accompanied Ben to the kitchen, and after staring into the largely empty fridge, she took out some bacon, eggs, butter, and some Kraft Parmesan cheese. In the freezer, she found a box of frozen peas.

"What can I do to help?" Ben asked.

"Do you have any spaghetti?"

Ben reached into his cabinet and pulled out a box of Prince spaghetti.

"How about you fill a pot with cold water and add a pinch of salt?"

Ben obliged.

"Once the water is boiling, just add the spaghetti to the pot and stir it gently so the strands of pasta sink to the bottom. That way, they won't stick together. What does it say on the box regarding how long it takes to cook the pasta?" Ben examined the box. "Whatever it says, time it for about a minute less, okay?" Nina told him.

It was strange to be cooking in Ben's kitchen but even stranger to be cooking with someone. The only thing Richard ever offered to do was taste something for Nina. She liked the air of cooperation that Ben brought to the situation.

"It was interesting to see your apartment. I've never been up there and couldn't figure out how it was configured from the outside," Ben said.

"The only way the architect could carve out a kitchen for the attic apartment was to use a room on the second floor. It is rather strange, but I guess I'll make do. Richard got all the furniture and in some ways, that was a lucky break because as you saw, there would be no room for any of it up there."

Nina imagined trying to move some of her furniture up the stairs to reach the modest living room, bathroom, and bedroom on the uppermost floor of the house. But unfortunately, the narrow staircase that accessed the upper level was so tight she could barely get her rocking chair up there. She was lucky there were drawers and even a closet built into the eaves in the apartment. She presumed it was because those who lived there in the past had little furniture of their own.

As she and Ben chatted, Nina began cooking the bacon. When it was crisp, she removed it from the pan and turned down the heat.

"I'm curious. If you work up in Portland, why did you get an apartment in Kittery? Especially with gas prices so high," Nina asked.

"I was traveling quite a bit to Boston, and Kittery was the halfway point," he said and quickly changed the subject. "Can I get you something to drink? I have some iced tea or several flavors of tonic."

"I'm good for now, but I'd love something with dinner. When the pasta is done, can you drain it but save me about a cup of the pasta water? And you'll need to steam those peas."

Once Ben had finished draining the pasta, he handed it off to Nina, who added it to the pan with the bacon fat. She whisked the eggs, salt, pepper, and Parmesan cheese in a large bowl and slowly added it to the pan while tossing the hot pasta quickly to prevent the eggs from scrambling. She finished it off by adding some pasta water and the peas before topping it all with bacon.

"That smells amazing!"

"Well, it's got Hamburger Helper beat. No offense."

The two sat at Ben's kitchen table and ate in a comfortable silence.

After dinner, they went into the living room to relax. The kittens were running around the room chasing one another. One ran up the front of Ben's cello case, and the other scrambled onto the chair before flying onto Ben's jeans as he went to sit down.

"I wish I had that kind of energy," Nina said, smiling. Ben took the orange tabby and placed it on the floor. Nina grabbed the one with the tortoiseshell pattern and scratched it under the chin before returning it to the floor.

"Mind if I put on some music?" he asked her.

"Not at all."

"Hey, on second thought, nature is calling. Why don't you look through my albums and pick out something you'd like?"

Nina loved the thought. She had grown up with music, but Richard never seemed to like any of the music she listened to, so after a while she avoided playing it. Ben, however, appeared to have very eclectic tastes, and Nina noticed he had quite a few cast albums of various Broadway musicals. As interested as she was in some of them, she didn't want to overstay her welcome and avoided choosing such recordings as *The Three Penny Opera, Follies,* and *Applause* because it would be hard to listen to only a part of those types of recordings. She picked up a 1953 recording of Maria Callus in *La Traviata* and clutched the album to her.

"Did you find something?" Ben asked as he came back into the living room.

"I can't believe you have a recording of *La Traviata*! I grew up with all of the Italian operas. My father and I listened to them endlessly on Sunday afternoons when my mother visited her sister."

"I'll tell you what. Why don't you borrow it? I haven't

listened to it in a while, and maybe you can introduce me to others. Do you have other albums?"

"I put them all in the basement."

"Maybe we can bring those upstairs as well."

"I'd like that." Nina smiled.

"Here, let me play one of my favorites. Have you ever heard *The Capriol Suite* composed by Peter Warlock? It was originally written as a piano duet, but Warlock later scored it for both strings and even full orchestras. Someday, I'll play Warlock's 'Serenade for Strings.'"

Nina sat back in the overstuffed chair in Ben's living room and closed her eyes to listen to the music. Soon, she was fast asleep.

Chapter Five

Nina shifted the box of cookbooks onto her hip as she opened the door to her apartment. She placed the box on the kitchen floor along with a small selection of albums and the pots and pans she'd left in the pantry of the first-floor apartment. Keith and April were coming back, and she wanted to make sure she removed everything before they arrived.

Her new kitchen was about the size of the pantry in her old apartment. There were a sink and stove, a small amount of counter space, and cabinets set up galley style. She'd placed a bistro-style table in front of the window to make the kitchen more functional. She had no idea where she would put all her cookbooks and kitchenware, but she decided not to worry too much about that at the moment. Having them close by was somehow comforting. Nina heard a frantic meowing coming from upstairs. She climbed the stairs to investigate. Cinnamon greeted her, but Ginger was nowhere in sight. She heard intermittent meows and stood in one spot to listen, trying to determine the direction, but the noise of the air conditioner made it hard to hear in the small apartment.

Out of the corner of her eye, she noticed Cinnamon going toward the bathroom and assumed she was about to use the litter box. Following her, she saw the calico kitten duck under the fabric apron of the sink and disappear. Nina hurried over to inspect. Under the sink and to the right of the drainpipe there was a door that pushed inward. It was ajar. It looked like whoever plumbed the bathroom installed the sink right in front of it without thinking how difficult it would then be to access. Nina got down on her hands and knees to investigate, but it was impossible to see exactly what was inside the darkened space. She reached up and took the apron off the sink to get a better look. The heat being thrown off by the small attic space was fierce. Fear crept into her heart hearing the plaintive cries of the kittens.

Nina rushed to the kitchen to find a flashlight, but many things were still packed away and she couldn't locate one. Instead, she grabbed a saucer of milk hoping to lure the kitten out of the space and ran back upstairs. She bent down and pushed the small door further inward and placed the saucer inside the space. Cinnamon scurried towards her with cobwebs on her whiskers and her tri-colored fur. Nina grabbed the kitten and moved her to safety. She could still hear Ginger crying, and it was clear that the poor kitten was in distress. Sticking her head as far into the attic crawl space as possible, she saw green eyes staring back at her at the far end of the enclosed space, about ten feet from the opening.

Nina got back down on her belly and inched herself into the room. Sweat began dripping down into her eyes from the intense heat in the enclosure. She wanted to back out but knew it meant leaving Ginger behind. As her eyes adjusted, she could see years of dust and cobwebs. Images of mice and slithering insects invaded her mind and panic mounted, but she forced herself to move further and further inside. The hairs on her neck raised involuntarily, but she continued to make her way towards Ginger.

"Here, kitty." She tried to coo but her voice trembled and sounded more frightening than soothing. As Nina moved ahead, she wondered why Ginger couldn't extricate herself.

When she finally reached her, Nina saw that Ginger's claws were embedded in a wooden beam and she seemed unable to retract them on her own. She gently unhooked her claws and pulled the frightened kitten to her. She slowly turned herself around and headed towards the opening to return to the bathroom. As she crossed the space, thin whisps of sticky threads clung to her face. These silks were menacing and sinister, but she focused on escaping rather than imagining the creatures that could weave them in an effort to lure the prey into their web.

Struggling to hold the squirming kitten, she inched closer to the cubby door. Nina noticed dusty stacks of shoeboxes not far from the entrance to the space and another set further in the corner. When Nina reached the opening, she placed Ginger safely onto the bathroom floor then freed herself from the suffocating area. She shooed Ginger into the living room and quickly closed the bathroom door. Covered in grime, she perched herself on the seat of the toilet for a moment trying to recover before attempting to close the door to the cubby so the kittens couldn't reenter the space. On her hands and knees again, she saw the dusty shoeboxes within reach. She grabbed the closest stack and began backing out of the space. As she got up, all the dust made her sneeze, and she banged her head on the sink.

Nina howled in pain and ran her fingers along her scalp and discovered a large welt. She left the bathroom and sat on the futon before she mustered the energy to go downstairs to get some ice from the fridge, only to realize she'd never made any. Despite being covered in grime, she reluctantly headed to Ben's to ask if he had any available.

She knocked on his door, but he didn't answer, and she remembered he had told her he had to go to a rehearsal and would stop by later. As she was about to head back upstairs, a woman in her early twenties peeked her head out of the other second-floor apartment door.

"Oh! I thought someone was knocking on this door," she said, about to close the door quickly.

"Hello? Maddie?" Nina called to her. "I'm Nina from downstairs. Well, now upstairs," she stammered.

"What's up?" the young woman said, keeping the door ajar.

Nina sensed she had interrupted something. "Look, I am so

sorry to bother you, but I hit my head and don't have any ice, and it really hurts. I'm wondering if you might have some," Nina pleaded.

The slight young redhead seemed relieved.

"Sure. I'll get you some. Would you mind waiting here?" Maddie asked her gently.

"Not at all. Thanks so much," Nina said, rubbing the top of her head.

Moments later, Maddie returned with a tea towel full of ice. "Here you go," she said, handing her the ice. "Hope you feel better," she added and closed the door quickly.

BACK IN HER APARTMENT, Nina made her way upstairs and rested on her futon sofa with the ice pack on her head. She sank onto the futon, trying to find a comfortable position to rest her head while applying the ice to her wound. Cinnamon crawled up on the futon with her and began kneading a pillow and purring loudly. Ginger joined her, not to be left behind. Within minutes, the three of them were asleep.

Nina woke up with a slight headache. Her immediate reaction was to go into the bathroom to get some Tylenol. The thought gave her goosebumps. She closed her eyes, trying to wish away the images that were brought to mind.

Wet from the melted ice, Nina got up to find a fresh T-shirt. Ginger was scratching at the bathroom door and Nina realized the closed door meant the kittens had no way to use the litter box. Reluctant to let them in there, she would have to secure the cubby door soon and remove the dusty shoeboxes that were still scattered on the floor.

Nina snuck into the bathroom, closing the door behind her. Once she secured the cubby door, she removed the cover to a shoebox. Inside were stacks of neatly folded letters. Each box contained the same thing. One of the kittens began meowing and scratching at the bathroom door, so she let them in and took the shoebox out to the coffee table.

Ginger climbed up and began investigating some of the dusty boxes. Moments later, Cinnamon joined her and started to sneeze.

"Yup, they're dusty, girls."

NINA WENT DOWNSTAIRS, emptied the box of cookbooks onto the kitchen counter, and returned upstairs to transfer the contents of the shoebox into something cleaner and dust-free. She tried to stack each pile of letters in the order she took them out of the boxes. When she got to the third box, an old photograph had been placed on top of the first pile of letters. Nina studied the picture of an attractive man sitting on a chair with two small children on his lap. They all beamed from the past.

"Hmmm... Who are you?" Nina wondered aloud. She found herself excited to examine things more closely but only after she had a chance to take a bath.

Clean and refreshed, Nina propped herself on the futon and carefully untied the bundle of letters with the picture on top. There were no dates or names on the back. She unfolded the letter and began to read.

June 12, 1955
Dearest David and Elizabeth,

I'm thinking of you, especially today, because I know it is Lizzy's birthday. Happy birthday, sweet child. I hope one day to say that to you in person. Today, as I stare at the pictures of you both, I am reminded of all the good times we shared together. You loved my uncle almost as much as I loved him, and my favorite picture is of him reading you a bedtime story.

I will never forget the first time I met him--

Uncle Billy, that is. It was in early June 1930, and I was living with Mrs. Peck and her daughter Emily at the time. My parents, grandmother, and Mrs. Peck's husband, Albert, had all been killed in an automobile accident while she was caring for me. I ended up staying with them for years.

My parents had moved to the West Coast in the mid-1920s after my grandfather died and my grandmother needed help with the farm. We lived about three hundred miles north of Los Angeles in Mariposa. It wasn't a big farm, less than a couple thousand acres, I imagine, but it was a homey place with plenty of space to play. Albert was one of the farmhands, and he and his family lived in a small house across the street. The Peck family was a part of our regular lives, and I often played with Emily or stayed with them if my parents were off in town shopping or such.

My dad was the oldest of three boys, but only two were alive, my father Earl and his younger brother William. No one spoke of William very much when I was a child. The only way I knew he existed was that Mrs. Peck insisted I take the family Bible the day I retrieved my belongings from our house, days after my parents' and grandmother's funerals.

While my parents were alive, Mrs. Peck seemed

like a pleasant woman. I'm not sure if she changed after the accident or if the fact my parents employed her husband caused her to treat me kindly. But when I started living with her, life was pretty horrible.

In those days, children weren't protected very well. I was frequently punished for minor things by Mrs. Peck. She would slap my face, or take a stick to my bottom or legs. Worse were the days she said I was full of wickedness, and she would force me say the Lord's Prayer while I knelt on the kitchen floor covered with dry kernels of corn until my knees bled. I truly hated her with all my heart, but one misstep meted out more punishment, so I learned to hold my tongue and act as though I had repented.

One particular day, I had to remain locked in my room upstairs while she and Emily went to church. That wasn't the worst way she punished me because I really didn't mind being alone.

That was the day my Uncle Billy showed up. I was glancing out the window of my second-floor bedroom. I had been reading a book and needed to hide it again before Mrs. Peck came home.

I noticed a bright green automobile parked in the driveway of my old house and a tall man on the porch looking through the windows. The place had remained vacant for years because, as I later learned, no one could locate William, the sole heir to my grandmother's estate. With the country sliding more and more into the Great Depression, no one wanted a farm anyway.

I watched this strange man with great curiosity, and then he disappeared into the barn. Just then, Mrs. Peck arrived home with Emily in a small horse-drawn buggy.

I quickly hid the book I'd borrowed from Emily, called Anne of Green Gables. I was determined not to let Mrs. Peck find it and steal away from me. My heart raced at the idea that my hiding place would be discovered, so I moved away from the window and hid it under the blankets in the chest at the end of the bed. When I looked out the window, the stranger was standing in the driveway petting the horse and talking about something with Mrs. Peck. There was something so familiar about him, but at first, I couldn't think of what it was. Then I realized the tall, sandy-haired man looked just like my father!

I couldn't hear what Mrs. Peck was telling him, but he seemed to be turning away. Before he got too far, I opened the window and shouted to him, "Are you my uncle?"

He turned so quickly that he almost stumbled

and looked up at me with the broadest of smiles.
"I sure am!"

And that, dear David and Elizabeth was the
first time I met him.

NINA UNTIED one bundle after another, reading for hours. By the time the light faded in the room, she was too tired to head downstairs to get something to eat, so she drifted off to sleep, trying to imagine the woman who wrote them and why she had left her personal letters behind.

Early the following day, Nina arranged herself on the futon couch with the box of letters on the coffee table. With her cup of coffee she began reading where she left off.

April 9, 1957

My dearest David and Elizabeth,

I have taken a position in Kittery that includes room and board. The couple I'm now working for seem nice, but I can imagine the position will be fairly demanding. The house is enormous, and I will be responsible for both cleaning and cooking. There is an apartment in the attic that I can call home.

There is no kitchen, but I'm allowed to eat some of what I will be serving the Hirsts, or Ida and Henry, as they prefer me to call them. They're part of an old Kittery family, but they've fallen on hard times. So I will be the only person tending to their needs now, though they have had more household staff in the past. Still, they don't entertain these days, so that should cut down on the amount of work.

This house is truly magnificent. I've never lived in a place this elegant. The kitchen alone is the size of half our apartment above the restaurant in Portland. I know I am assuming you both remember all that. It was so long ago. I can only recall your faces as I study the photos I keep with me. I wonder what you look like now and long to see your sweet and cherished smiles.

I have some sad news to report. My Uncle Billy passed away several months ago. I am at a loss to express my sorrow. He was ill for quite a while. His declining health began shortly before your father came to retrieve you — no, steal you both from me. His declining health was largely responsible for my being unable to search for you earlier. He suffered a stroke within days of your departure and never fully recovered.

I struggled to care for him once he returned home, while also tending to all the daily needs of the restaurant. I ended up selling it to prevent putting him in a home. He would have hated that. While he did improve some over time, he was never the same. His speech, in particular, was affected by the stroke as it paralyzed the right side of his body, including his face and arm. Teaching him to dress and care for himself took a long time, and I believe he found it humiliating since he was always such an independent person. However, I did not mind caring for him in the least.

He passed in late January, and I will forever mourn the loss of this gentle and kind man. Other than your Uncle Jake, he was one of the most important people in my life, including you both, of course.

I buried him in a graveyard outside of Portland. When I finally find you, I can take you there if you want to pay your respects. I am determined more than ever to keep searching for you. My love for you has never wavered. I will write again soon as always.

Love to you both, Auntie Lilia

NINA PUT down the letter and wiped the tears from her eyes. The heartache Lilia wrote of permeated the pages. The trove of letters to Elizabeth and David were touching. She couldn't fathom how and why this man Jesse took these children from her. At first, she wondered if Lilia and Jesse were married. But then she learned Lilia's husband was a man named Jake. There were no letters exchanged between Lilia and Jake among those she'd found so far, but there were sketches in books and on scraps of brown paper. Some looked as if they were drawn by a child at various stages of development, as some were barely stick figures while others were clearly done by someone with developing artistic talents. Under one, she found the words,

"*It's been my experience that you can nearly always enjoy things if you make up your mind firmly that you will.*"

There was a face of a young girl drawn in pencil and one of a man Nina guessed would be Lilia's Uncle Billy. Hours slipped by as Nina read through them, trying to figure out the relationships between all these people.

NINA REALIZED it was long past lunchtime. She forced herself to put down the latest letter and went downstairs, stuck a piece of bread in the toaster, and slathered on some peanut butter before returning upstairs.

She carefully opened the next envelope and was happy it seemed to fall in close succession to the previous letter.

August 10, 1955

Dearest David and Elizabeth,

I have been unable to write for some time now, but the longing in my heart remains, and I am still determined to find out where Jesse took you. I want to find you both again. I have reason to believe your father may be living somewhere in the Portland area. So, the next opportunity I get, I will continue my search.

The last time I wrote to you, I believe I was telling you about my uncle. When he saw me in the window upstairs, he demanded Mrs. Peck allow him to see me. He assured her that he only wanted to visit and would be leaving town shortly, so she reluctantly complied.

He charmed her into letting him take me into town for ice cream at Driscoll's Pharmacy, and I willingly jumped into his automobile that was parked behind my old home. Once we left the farm, he told me how sorry he was that he hadn't come sooner. He was devastated when the news finally reached him about his mother and my parents. While he was fairly vague about why he was away and out of communication for so long, he was genuinely concerned about my well-being, especially after I told him about the treatment I received at the hands of Mrs. Peck and showed him my various scars.

For the next hour, we chatted over ice cream sundaes. By the time he had to return me to Mrs. Peck, I had begged him to take me with him. His troubled eyes told me it would cause him great difficulties, but he said he would think about it only if I promised not to discuss it with anyone. I laughed at the suggestion because my only friend at that time was Millie, Mrs. Peck's milking cow.

When we returned to Mrs. Peck's, he thanked her for her cooperation and said he would be leaving in a few days after taking care of some business in town. He asked if he could see me one more time before leaving, and she was surprisingly eager to comply, smiling graciously at his request. On Sunday, there was a church bazaar Mrs. Peck planned to attend, and he arranged to meet us there. I was on pins and needles for days. Finally, he gave me specific instructions about what to do when we got there.

That Sunday, I stuck a small sack with my overalls, a shirt, and my shoes in the boot of the buggy. My uncle met us at church and sat with us in the pew, squeezing my hand. After that, we all joined those strolling around on that beautiful Sunday. The bazaar was quite crowded as people came from miles around to have an opportunity to socialize.

Mrs. Peck allowed me to go off with my uncle while she strolled around with Emily. About an hour later, I retrieved my sack and went into the outhouse set off at the back of the church and not visible by those attending the bazaar. I dressed in the boyish clothes and stuck my cap on and casually strolled out of the outhouse and disappeared into the woods behind the church.

There I waited for my uncle to pick me up. In the meantime, a small crowd of people milled around the tables selling baked goods and other items to raise money for the church. Shortly after I made my escape, my uncle found Mrs. Peck

and said his goodbyes. When she asked where I
was, he announced that I was rather upset and
had run off in the direction of the outhouse.

He got into his automobile and drove off, stopping at the point where we agreed to rendezvous. I
hid on the floor of his roadster until he believed we
were safe. Off we went, heading north towards
San Francisco, where we stayed for a few days.
He cut my hair really short and bought clothing so
I could dress as a young boy and began calling
me Louis. My uncle told me that once we hit
Sacramento, we would be heading east towards the
coast where he'd lived for the past few years. So
we traveled across the country as father and son,
and I never felt one minute of regret leaving California and the Pecks behind.

It took us more than a month, but it was such
an enjoyable venture. We stopped to see the sights
and met some nice people who thought my uncle's
son was such a well-behaved little boy! He gave
me a kind of sketchbook and diary. He said it
was so I could write about our journeys. I think
it was his way of keeping me busy while we traveled. I still have those somewhere. Once we were
on the east coast, my uncle rented a house near Old
Orchard Beach in Maine and arranged to have his
belongings moved from his home in Provincetown to
our new home. And that dearest David and Eliza-

beth is where I met my husband, Jake, and your father, Jesse.

Nina put the letter down and nibbled on the toast, now cold and hardened with peanut butter. Thoughts swirled around her head as she imagined Lilia dressed up as a boy traveling across the country with her uncle. Nina's biggest adventure was a high school field trip to Washington, DC. After that, she'd rarely ventured even as far as Boston.

She was about to dig into the next letter when the phone rang, startling her. She couldn't imagine who was calling her, and for a moment, she just stared at the phone before picking up the receiver. A voice from her past greeted her across the telephone wire.

Chapter Six

"Nina?"

It took a moment for Nina to recognize the voice of her college roommate. "Julia?"

"It's so nice to hear your voice! I've been thinking of you for so long, but now, I just had to call," she paused. "Are you all right?" Julia asked.

Julia's question seemed odd. Nina hadn't spoken to Julia for quite a while so she couldn't know of the turmoil that had plagued Nina recently.

"I'm fine. How about you? Where are you working these days?" Nina asked, trying to stay with safe subjects.

"I'm still at the front desk of the Copley. That's why I thought I had to call in the first place."

"Why is that?" Nina asked.

"Jeez, Nina. I'm not sure how to tell you this, but I saw Richard here the other day. He was with another woman."

It took a moment for Nina to respond. "That would have been Holly, Richard's new girlfriend. Or should I say current girlfriend since I have no idea how long the two have been seeing one another?"

"What? You know about this?"

"We're divorced. Richard started seeing her while we were married."

"That's awful, Nina! Wait. Where are you living, then? This is the same number I had from before."

"I'm still in the house. I moved up to the attic apartment and had the telephone company relocate my phone to the upstairs apartment so I didn't have to change numbers."

"Oh! I'm surprised he let you keep the house."

"He didn't *let* me. I had to fight him tooth and nail. I swapped apartments with the guy who was renting the third-floor apartment. He was getting married—I was getting divorced. It seemed about right."

"It sounds like so much has happened since we spoke last."

Nina closed her eyes and massaged her temple. "Yes, we have a lot to catch up on."

"Hey, why don't you come for a visit? Can you get away from work?"

"That shouldn't be a problem," Nina told her without further explanation.

"When do you want to come?" Julia asked.

"You're still in Boston, right?"

"Sure am."

By the time they got off the phone, Nina had hesitantly made plans to visit Julia in Boston. But every time she started thinking about a trip she became anxious. She fretted about leaving the kittens alone for an entire day. What if they knocked over their water dish and didn't have anything to drink? They could tumble down the stairs. Or what if she did something foolish, like leave the stove or the iron plugged in? While Boston was only an hour and a half away, to Nina it was as if she'd agreed to visit the moon.

She almost convinced herself that it was too soon to venture out, especially such a long way. But Julia's call made her realize how isolated she'd become since she moved to Kittery. Once Nina began working at King's Groceries, she rarely had two consecutive days off, and many of those were filled with matters related to the house's renovation. Richard had discouraged her from becoming friendly with the other employees she worked with. He convinced her that doing so would undermine her authority as the bakery manager. So much of Nina's life was wrapped up in Richard and his family that she barely had contact with anyone who wasn't a part of that world.

Over the week that followed, the *what-ifs* threatened to crowd out her desire to reconnect with her college friend, and she picked up the phone a dozen times to tell Julia she couldn't make it after all.

On one occasion when Ben stopped in to see her, Nina told him about her proposed trip to visit Julia.

"I don't know if I'm ready to venture out, especially all the way to Boston," she commented.

"I think something like that is just what you need," he encouraged. "You told me yourself you've had little contact with anyone since you moved to Maine. Seeing an old friend might be a way to start reconnecting with things that are unrelated to Richard and his family."

"But what about the kitties? Ginger got into a small cubby in the bathroom the other day. What if something like that happened again?"

"First of all, I can check on them while you're gone. Now, what happened to Ginger?" he asked.

Nina filled him in on what happened and showed him the cubby and the letters. They sat in the kitchen drinking tea and poring over them.

"Well, whoever this Lilia is, it doesn't sound like her life was very easy," Ben remarked after a while.

"That's for sure," Nina agreed.

ON THE DAY of her scheduled visit, Nina picked up the phone yet again to call Julia and cancel. But she finally convinced herself to go through with it. Shoving her fears aside, she looked over at

Ginger and Cinnamon. They were playing with the fringe of an afghan her mother had crocheted for her as a child. It was one of the only things Nina had left from her childhood, so she gently took it from them. The kittens' closeness suddenly made her feel lonely, and she reminded herself that Julia was once a close friend. Nina checked on their food and water one last time, gave them each a kiss, and headed downstairs with a bag of scones she'd baked.

EVEN THOUGH IT was bright and early, there was already a flow of traffic heading south when Nina reached the I-95 corridor towards Boston.

Trying to avoid the congestion, she got off the highway and drove over to coastal Route 1, but it was almost as bad. Nina decided to call Julia, knowing she would be late. She saw a payphone outside Cumberland Farms just north of Seabrook, New Hampshire. Digging around in her purse for change, she found she had none. She decided to buy something to drink so she could get change for the phone.

She plucked a bottle of Snapple Iced Tea out of the cooler and brought it to the check-out counter to pay. A large display of cigarettes loomed behind the counter. She stood there looking longingly at a column of Newports, debating what to do. The almost fifty cents per pack seemed too extravagant. Nina talked herself out of buying it, paid for her drink, and quickly left the store so she couldn't change her mind. She dialed Julia's number on the payphone and told her she would be later than expected.

As she drove, her body tensed. Pains formed in her neck and back. She shifted in her seat, trying to get more comfortable. The short daily drives to work and back were so routine she rarely worried about getting behind the wheel anymore. However, it had been years since she'd traveled any distance alone, and all of the reasons she avoided it came back the further south she drove.

The honking cars and other distractions began to overwhelmed her almost as much as the expressway. Even the slower pace of Route 1 left Nina wishing she had canceled after all. She even thought about turning around. But whether she went north or south, she was surrounded by traffic, so she allowed her mind to drift to the last of Lilia's letters and what was becoming an increasingly comfortable diversion.

Nina thought back to the last letter she read and couldn't help but wonder where David and Elizabeth's father took them and if Lilia ever found them. The pain of their absence was apparent. Lilia's letters indicated she was their aunt, and the children had lived with her and Lilia's Uncle Billy for some time. She decided maybe she should start keeping notes to help her keep track of details the letters provided.

But more than anything, Nina wondered why it mattered to her so much. Maybe it was because it was a safe distraction? Spending time reading the letters made it possible to ignore reality for a bit. Whatever the reason, Nina was too intrigued to stop reading now.

WHEN SHE FINALLY ARRIVED CLOSE TO Julia's apartment, Nina squeezed her VW into the closest parking space she could find. She sat in her car for a moment trying to marshal enough courage to get out and walk the few blocks to her friend's Brighton apartment. She closed her eyes and imagined Julia breezing along the streets, stopping at the small shops as she made her way to her apartment on Commonwealth Ave. She finally opened the car door and grabbed the bags of scones while trying to anticipate a joyful reunion.

Nina knocked lightly on the door to Julia's apartment. When Julia opened the door, the two friends embraced for a long time. Then, they each took a step back to look at one another.

"Oh, my god! You grew your hair out! And how the hell you do stay so thin working around food all day?" Julia said, laughing.

Nina was momentarily embarrassed, but she tried to recover. "Well, I don't work around food anymore. And, I can't believe you stopped dyeing your hair," Nina said, looking at Julia. "I was still expecting to see you as a blonde. But, I like you better as a brunette."

"Has it really been that long? I stopped doing that a while ago. That's right, the last time I saw you was when I came up to Kittery with Matt. We broke up about six weeks later, but before I took the job at the Copley. I think the time before that was at your wedding, right?"

"I'm sure you're right." Nina handed Julia the brown paper bag. "Well, I hope these are still your favorite."

Julia opened the bag and took a deep sniff.

"You remembered!" she said, extracting a lemon ginger scone. Then, with her mouth full, she offered one to Nina.

"No, thanks. I baked them for you. How is your job going?"

As Julia filled her in on work, Nina studied her friend closely. The two college roommates couldn't have been more different. Nina grew up an only child, while Julia had four brothers. Nina grew up in a triple-decker in a crowded neighborhood in Worcester, while Julia grew up in an affluent part of Natick, a small town west of Boston. While Nina was tall and slender, Julia was barely five feet tall and had a voluptuous figure. She was raised Jewish but had abandoned her religious upbringing. Nina was raised in a Roman Catholic Italian household but now avoided religion altogether.

In college, the two roommates had spent hours discussing their backgrounds and sharing insights into life and the world around them. Julia was one of the first real girlfriends Nina had had. While many of their friends switched roommates after their freshman year, Nina and Julia stayed together until Nina dropped out of college right before starting her junior year. Both experienced significant tragedies in their lives two years later, with Julia losing her boyfriend Patrick in a car accident, and Nina losing her mother in the fire. Although they always maintained their friendship, life pulled them in other directions, and calls and visits became infrequent, especially after Nina got married and moved to Maine.

The two women walked past the small kitchen into the living

room before Julia flopped on the leather sofa, smiling. Nina looked around with admiration.

"It is so nice to see you. I love this apartment!"

"Well, let's face it. It's nothing compared to your house," Julia said with certainty.

"Well, my house is very grand, but my new digs aren't nearly as elegant. I told you I moved up to the third floor, right?"

Julia nodded, as her mouth was again full.

"Well, where I am now is hardly roomy or elegant. It's tough to adjust. The kitchen is barely functional, and it's probably a good thing that Richard got all the furniture. I never realized how unappealing the rest of the house was compared to our apartment. Richard always wanted to keep costs down when we went to carve out the upstairs apartments, and I guess I never thought about what it would be like living in one of them. But I'm getting by."

"Can I get you some coffee? I made a fresh pot," Julia asked.

"Sure. Hey, are you still in touch with Molly or Heather? I lost touch when I quit school."

"Well, let me fill you in," Julia said, bringing in a coffee for Nina. "Do you still take your coffee black?"

Nina nodded, and Julia crossed the living room and pulled out a small photo album. "I was at Molly's wedding. She married that guy, Doug, she was dating senior year. Don't get excited, though. They divorced, and she remarried—a guy named Arnie. They're living in Providence, close to Johnson and Wales. She never pursued hospitality but became an elementary school teacher. Go figure. I never thought she'd graduate from school, never mind pass the licenses needed to teach," Julia added.

Nina looked through the album slowly. She never imagined that the people who were such an important part of her daily life at one time would be so absent from it now. She had to search her memory to even remember the names and faces of all these people she knew so well in college, while Julia seemed to have kept track of everyone.

"Do you remember that guy Danielle was dating in school?" she asked Nina.

"Not particularly," Nina told her. "Wait! Was he the one who always called us ladies? Hello, ladies. What's up, ladies? Good afternoon, ladies?"

"That would be the one!" Julia confirmed. "Well, you'll never believe this, but after you left, he and Danielle dated for a little while, and she ended up getting pregnant! Remember, we couldn't even get her to go see *Diary of a Mad Housewife* with us! She said it was too immodest, and she heard there were 'bedroom scenes.'" Julia gestured air quotes. "After seeing that, I had the hots for Frank Langella for a long time. As a matter of fact, he reminds me a little of your Richard, but of course, your ex acted more like the Richard Benjamin character. What a creep."

"You have a good memory."

"Not really. It's just that I'm still here in the area so I tend to run into our old friends from time to time."

For a moment, the two friends seemed to run out of things to say. It left Nina thinking about one of the things that discouraged her from staying in touch with Julia in the first place. She seemed to take great pleasure in gossiping about their friends behind their backs and was quick to point out others' faults but never wanted to examine her own.

"How are you handling it now that you're divorced? Are you dating anyone?"

"I can't even think about that right now," Nina fumbled. "Richard was my first longtime relationship, and I'm not about to jump into another one. I just have to focus on getting back on my feet and figuring out what to do now that I have no job."

"What happened to your job? Aren't you still managing the grocery store?" Julia asked her.

"I only managed the bakery department, not the entire store. That ended the moment Richard thought he could use it as leverage to get the house. His father came into the store and humiliated me in front of all the employees. He said my 'services' were no longer needed and told me to leave right there and then.

He watched me as I gathered up all the stuff from my office as though I would steal something. I couldn't believe how quickly everything went downhill after that. I was stupid enough to believe they would be fair since Richard was the one breaking up the marriage. When I went in to collect my last paycheck I heard that my ex-father-in-law insinuated they had caught me stealing, and that's why they fired me. No one at the store believed him but it's made finding a new job nearly impossible."

"That really stinks. I can't believe what a dick he turned out to be. Well, if you're not working, what have you been doing to keep busy?" Julia asked.

Nina thought before she spoke. She decided to keep matters light, and she told her more about moving up to the attic apartment and finding the letters.

"Lilia was caring for Richard's great aunt and uncle who owned the building long ago. So that's how she came to live in the attic apartment. From what I've learned, she was married to a guy named Jake, who died in World War II. Apparently, he came from a rather strange family. Lots of brothers and a mother who wasn't exactly the greatest. There's no mention of his father so far. One of his brothers, Jesse, showed up at a diner Lilia ran with her uncle, Billy. He pretended to be visiting with his two children. He told Lilia he was going out to apply for a job, but he never returned. So Lilia and Billy raised the kids, David and Elizabeth. Years later, Jesse showed up again and took the kids back."

"What? Could he do that?" Julia asked.

"Lilia really didn't have a choice but to let them go. Right after Jesse showed up, her uncle had a stroke, and she was busy caring for him, and managing the restaurant. She had to sell it and when her uncle passed away, she immediately started looking for them."

"But I don't get it. What are all the letters for then?"

"I'm not really sure. I think Lilia was used to writing things down because when she was little, her uncle gave her sketchbooks and a diary to keep her busy when they were traveling east after he rescued her from this woman named Mrs. Peck."

"What? Why was she living with her uncle and who is hell is Mrs. Peck?"

As the afternoon passed, Nina filled Julia in on the details she'd gleaned from the letters.

"Well, this Lilia woman had a rather peculiar life."

"She was certainly interesting. That's for sure."

"You said 'was.' Do you think she's dead?" Julia asked.

"I think she must be," Nina told her. "I still have boxes of letters to read, and there are more boxes in the attic that I haven't reached. I can't imagine that a person who took so much time to write these would have just left them there."

"Wow! This is fascinating! So much so, I forgot my manners! Do you want some more coffee?" Julia offered.

"I'd love some, especially since it's too early for wine!" she laughed.

The two friends continue their chat until early afternoon. Nina started to feel antsy but agreed to have lunch since Julia had already prepared the meal. Julia set a plate of small biscuits on the table and ladled soup into two bowls.

"This looks yummy!" Nina said.

"I've been preparing a lot of recipes from a vegetarian cookbook. Can't say I'm a total vegetarian, but I'm leaning that way."

"Well, I might have to steal the recipe for these. Not that I have anyone to cook for these days, but maybe I can talk you into coming up for a visit," Nina said, the words popping out of her mouth before she realized what she'd said.

There was a lull in the conversation, and Julia seemed compelled to fill the silence. "I'm really sorry I haven't been in touch. My job has kept me really busy, and I'm exhausted when I get home. This is the first full weekend I've had off in six months. However, I have some vacation time coming, so maybe I can take a few days off and visit."

"That would be nice. Maybe when the leaves turn, we can do the whole touristy thing," Nina suggested.

"Are you going to look for a new job?"

"I need to try again soon, but I might have to look outside of the area."

"What about opening the catering business you always talked about?"

"I don't have a place to do that right now. My kitchen in the first-floor apartment might have been an option, but starting out is hard. Especially in a town where I barely know anyone not somehow related to my former job, and don't forget, my references have been tainted. Money is really tight."

"What do you mean?" Julia asked.

"Everything is gone. We spent most of the insurance money buying the house and renovating it. And of course, I paid for Richard to go to Tufts."

"I don't know what to say," Julia told her. "On the surface, he seemed like such a catch! Incredibly handsome. Funny. Charming. Now it seems like he was a monster!"

"I don't know about monster, but it all caught me off guard. Now I barely have enough money to survive. The only thing that will keep me afloat is the rental income, but that only covers the expenses."

"Can you sell the place?" Julia asked her.

"The market is horrible right now. Besides, this is my home, Julia. I have no place else to go," Nina told her with a catch in her voice.

"Life certainly took some unexpected turns, didn't it? First, we all thought I would be married to Patrick, and you would be working as a sous chef or even a head chef somewhere until you could open your own place."

"Not exactly what happened," Nina said quietly. "How did you cope with Patrick's death?" she asked then quickly grabbed Julia's hand and squeezed. "Was I wrong to bring it up?"

"Not at all," Julia said warmly. "I actually appreciate a chance to talk about him because most of my friends act like he never existed. That makes it even harder. He will always be a part of me, and they try to erase that."

"I get it—believe me. Even though I was young when my

father died, I miss him every day. And memories of my mother are so hard because I don't want to forget her, but recalling how she died is mixed into all the good memories too," Nina told her.

"Yes! That's it exactly. I didn't want to even think about him at first because I always connected thoughts of him with the car accident. I buried so much of my grief. I think that's why I stayed here in Boston, so I wouldn't have to cope with being at home and being told to get over him. He was only twenty-two, Nina. Far too young to die. One day we're planning a graduation party and talking about getting married, and weeks later, I'm attending his funeral. It makes little sense, and the pain doesn't magically disappear either."

"Well, I'm sorry if I haven't been more available to you," Nina said. "I guess I've been inside my own head, and that's not always a good place to be."

"Not to worry. I know you've had your ups and downs, too. Anyway, I've been seeing someone, and it's really helped to get past all the emotional entanglements of Patrick's death."

"You mean a new boyfriend?" Nina asked curiously.

"No, silly! A therapist." Julia laughed.

"Really? I don't know if I could ever do that."

"I went through quite a few of them before I found the right one. My mother insisted I keep trying," Julia said, rolling her eyes. "But, even though I was angry with her at the time, I'm glad she badgered me because I really needed to talk with someone, and it truly helps. Especially because my folks still pay for it. You should try it."

Nina quickly changed the subject, not wanting to remind Julia that she couldn't afford a therapist, even if she managed to find someone appropriate.

When lunch was finished, they gathered up the dishes and placed them in the sink. Nina excused herself to use the bathroom, and when she came back, she grabbed her purse.

"Are you leaving so soon?" Julia asked her, surprised. "Can't you stay for a while longer?"

"I really feel like I need to get home. You know—traffic and all. I really am glad I came, though. Let's not let so much time pass before we see each other again, okay?" Nina said, holding the door and slipping her purse over her shoulder. "I don't have a lot of space, but there's enough room for you to visit. As long as you don't mind Cinnamon and Ginger purring in your ear."

"I would love that," Julia assured her.

Nina slipped out the door. An onslaught of city noise assaulted her as she rushed towards where she'd parked her car. She bent her head and kept navigating toward the safety of her VW. An enormous sense of relief washed over her when she finally unlocked the car door. The heat engulfed her like an oven. Even so, she sat and baked for a moment, content. She rolled down the windows and started the car, pleased with herself that Julia didn't seem to know how overwhelmed Nina was during most of their visit.

Chapter Seven

Nina inched forward in the bumper-to-bumper traffic on I-95. The lane slowed to a stop, and the warm breeze coming through her car window felt more like it might be coming from the truck that was perilously close to the rear of her car. She turned on the radio trying to take her mind off the cacophony that surrounded her, but all the songs remind her of something she wanted to avoid thinking about. As car horns blew and drivers tried to change lanes, she gripped the steering wheel so tightly that all the blood drained from her fingers. She wanted a cigarette badly and regretted not buying a pack earlier.

She reminded herself how nice it was to see Julia again and how much she had enjoyed the company of her friends in college. It saddened her that after she left school, she'd lost touch with so many of the people who once meant so much to her. They seemed long forgotten by the time she moved to Maine. Her mind drifted to Lilia and how often she had moved around as a child and into her teen years. Maybe that was why she clung to the hopes of finding David and Elizabeth. They were her connection to Jake.

As Nina crawled along, she got so caught up in her distraction, she almost plowed into the car in front of her. She slammed on her brakes and decided it would be best to once again take Route 1 the rest of the way north.

By the time she reached Salisbury she was famished, so she made a detour to one of the many seaside ice cream stands. She bought a boat of fried clams and ate them as she walked along the boardwalk. It prompted her to think about one of Lilia's letters in which she described the day of her first encounter with her husband Jake when she met him at the beach.

It must have been fall, Nina thought because Lilia wrote that it was after the tourist season had ended. Nina could remember the story almost as if Lilia was telling it to her as she walked along. Lilia had ridden her bicycle along a roadway in Old Orchard Beach. The streets had been pretty empty, so when she heard a commotion towards the water, she headed that way. Lilia put down her bike and approached several young boys, one of whom was crying. An older boy, about Lilia's age, was lying on the beach and clearly had been injured. Blood gushed from a cut on his foot, and he looked like he was about to faint.

"What happened?" Lilia asked one of the younger boys.

"Jake cut himself on a broken bottle buried in the sand," he told her.

"Do you live close by? Is someone getting help?" Lilia asked them.

"Jesse went to get Mum, but she's probably still sleeping. I don't want to get in trouble. She told us to stay close to the yard," another of the boys added.

"Well, let me see if I can help. So your name is Jake?" she asked, directing her question towards the injured boy.

"If you grabbed your bike, maybe I could get on, and you could wheel it to my house? This hurts really bad," he said, ignoring formalities.

"Sure." Lilia ran and got her bike. She looked away from his blood-soaked foot. Once he was on, she let him put his arm around her shoulder and guided the bike as they moved slowly towards a motel in the distance.

"You're probably going to need stitches," Lilia told him.

"Can we cut out the chit-chat? I feel bad enough already," he said through gritted teeth.

As they approached the motel, Jesse came out, followed by a blonde woman in her late thirties. She had a shawl wrapped around her shoulders and a cigarette dangling from her mouth.

"Jesus Christ," she yelled to them as she approached the beach. "I can't lie down for a minute without you idiots getting into trouble."

"You can get lost now. Just beat it," the woman told Lilia and took over. They all disappeared into the motel without even a casual so long.

Lilia was so shocked at the woman's behavior that she stood there a moment longer before gathering her composure and turning for home.

Nina remembered that days later Lilia had gone to the beach again, but this time on purpose. She had been curious to see what had happened to the one named Jake. She didn't have to wait long before seeing him with a large bandage around his foot, close to the seaside motel where she had last seen him and his brothers. He looked up and waved to her, motioning for her to come over.

As she approached, she noticed how different he looked now that he wasn't in excruciating pain. Her letter to David and Elizabeth described how his sun-bleached brown hair and tan were fading as the season changed, but how he looked healthy and so ruggedly handsome that it took her breath away. He was watching the younger boys play in a tiny courtyard area next to the motel. The one they called Jesse was nodding off in a beach chair and woke only long enough to acknowledge Lilia before going back to sleep.

"Hey, I'm really sorry. I never had time to say thanks the other day," Jake said as she approached.

"Well, it looks like you survived, so that's good," she grinned at him.

"I never got your name, though. I'm Jake, and these are my brothers, Jesse, Lucas, Michael, and Nicholas."

"Nice to meet all of you," Lilia said, nodding her acknowledgment as the younger boys smiled at her. "I'm Lilia"

"Do you live around here?" Jake asked.

"We just moved here a few weeks ago. Are you all staying at this motel?" Lilia asked, to steer the conversation away from herself.

"We live here. My mum manages the place," Jake said. "What grade are you in? I haven't seen you at school."

"I'm not enrolled yet."

"Wow, not going to school. That must be great."

"I actually wish I was in school. I get bored sometimes. I read and draw a lot, but I would rather be in school."

One of Jake's younger brothers came over to them as they stood there chatting. Lilia crouched down to address him at eye level, which prompted him to hug Jake's leg.

"Hi, there! Which one are you?" she asked the tike.

"Nicholas," he said, looking away with a shy smile.

"Well, you're just about the cutest thing I've seen in a while," she said, poking him teasingly in the tummy. Nicholas smiled and tried to melt into Jake's leg.

"How old is he?" Lilia asked.

"He'll be three in a month," Jake said, looking down at her.

"Well, I have to get going," she told him. "I'm sure Billy is wondering where I am," she added wistfully.

"Who's Billy?"

"He's my uncle. I'll see you around," she said, looking over her shoulder as she left the beach.

The letter indicated that Lilia never did see Jake anymore, at least not for many years. Lilia and Billy didn't stay in Old Orchard Beach. Shortly after she met Jake, Lilia and her uncle moved to Portland. Nina wasn't sure how they reconnected, but she was looking forward to finding out.

WHEN SHE FINALLY GOT HOME, after checking on the kittens, she wanted to crawl into bed. She resisted, afraid it would make it more difficult to fall asleep later, and being alone at night was somehow worse. So instead, she decided to begin unpacking more of the mystery of Lilia's life.

Since the letters were never mailed, they had no postmark. She wondered why were there no letters from Jake among those she found. Maybe there were, she thought, but they were in the boxes she had yet to retrieve.

As Nina's evening wound down, she still had not answered one question that persisted. Why did Billy and Lilia move so frequently? Nina assumed it was because of their unorthodox exit from California. However, she imagined that, as her uncle, Billy would have had more right to custody than that old Mrs. Peck would. Even after Lilia was eighteen, they still seemed to move frequently. She hoped to answer that and many more questions. Plus, her curiosity and her need for a distraction drove her to keep reading.

OVER HER MORNING COFFEE, Nina began reading a letter that caught her eye the night before. It was again addressed to David and Elizabeth, but it was written on March 21, 1953. So far, it was the earliest of Lilia's letters that Nina had found, and it seemed to have been penned before she moved to Kittery and the house on Pepperell Point Road.

March 21, 1953

My Dearest David and Elizabeth,

I can't begin to express the depth of my sorrow. I've been on my own for a week here in Portland while Billy is in the hospital. You have been gone for two weeks that seem like an eternity.

You must know I have no way to fight your father since he is blood and I am not.

He left no information about where he was taking you, and if I could have, I would have begun searching for you the moment I realized he wasn't bringing you back. But my uncle needs me, and I have to stay close by. I can only hope your father has changed and treats you both like he should. He was with a woman I saw through the window after he ushered you down the stairs. She greeted you pleasantly, so I hope she will be kind towards you.

When Billy is recovered, I promise I will do everything I can to find you so I can know you are safe and cared for. And if Jesse is an inadequate father, I will do everything I can to fight him. I was so happy caring for you both, and I hope you know how much my uncle and I loved making a home for you here in Portland. I thought I had finally made it through and was on the other side of our chaotic life. But having lived with Mrs. Peck for several years, I know how easy it is to have all the love and security a child needs suddenly erased. Someday I will tell you both more about how my own life was upended. And just as my uncle came and rescued me from that nasty woman, I will do whatever I can to find you.

Nina turned the letter over. The other side was blank. She opened the envelope again to search for more pages but found it empty. It made no sense that Lilia would stop writing the letter when she did; there had to be more. She wondered if she'd accidentally left a page when she transferred them into clean boxes. There were no loose pages in any of the boxes she looked through. She wanted to know more.

Days passed and Nina always found a reason to sit and read more of Lilia's letters. Although she had vowed to go out to look for work after the holiday weekend, sometimes it was the rainy weather that made an already daunting task worse. Other times she got up too late or too early, or she simply wasn't in the mood.

Each night, Ben would stop by to say hello and visit with Nina and the kittens. Every night, Ben asked her the same question.

"How the job hunting going?"

Every time he asked, she sheepishly admitted she hadn't started looking. She realized she was stalling and she didn't know why. After visiting with Julia, she knew more than ever that her isolation worked against her. But her fear of failing got the best of her and she managed to convince herself it was futile to even try. Ben continued to encourage her, and she would once again promise to start looking. But for the moment, all the lingering questions about Lilia's life propelled her out of bed each morning, searching for more clues. That was a significant accomplishment considering that weeks earlier, she never wanted to get up ever again. So, for the moment, she decided it was okay to keep reality at bay for a while longer.

Chapter Eight

Several days later, Nina decided she had to apply for work. It wasn't just Ben's gentle reminders each time she saw him. Her dwindling bank account was the biggest motivator.

The clear skies and cooler weather made it easier to commit to getting up early to begin the arduous tasks of job hunting. She sat drinking her coffee trying to envision filling out applications at restaurants that were hiring. The question kept coming back to where? Where should she look? Nina wanted to preemptively eliminate any place the Kings had obvious connections. But Richard and his family were well-known all over Southern Maine.

Kittery and York were of course out of the question because of the Kings' prominence in both these communities. She thought about going to South Berwick, but then thought about the fact that Richard had attended a private school there when he was growing up. The Kings were everywhere, at least Nina thought so. She decided maybe the best thing to do was to go to the library and get some newspapers to look at the want ads. That would be her first task.

Locating the phone number, Nina called the Rice Public Library to find out what hours they were open. She'd often passed the beautiful old Romanesque Revival building when she worked at King's. She'd had few occasions to visit the grand building that had been recently listed on the National Register of Historic Places. It was only a few miles away, but she was glad to learn they were open until five so she would have plenty of time to look through several area papers for their classified ads.

On her way there, Nina drove past many historic homes along the shoreline and the First Congregational church where she and Richard got married. She followed Whipple Road and turned left onto Wentworth. As she pulled up to the stately brick building, she found herself enjoying her adventure.

Inside, the woman at the desk pointed to a small set of steps that led to the circulation department, which held daily newspapers from around the area. She browsed through them looking to see who was hiring. There were few listings for anything but waitress jobs. She'd never held a waitress job before and her knowledge of how hard and demanding the work was made her shy away from noting any of them on the note pad she'd brought with her. There were plenty of restaurant jobs listed in the Portland Press Herald but Nina was leery of traveling to Portland in the winter. Plus, even though her VW was good on gas, prices had almost doubled in just a year and she was concerned they would only go higher.

Then she noticed that there was a job as head chef for a nursing home in Dover, New Hampshire. She'd never thought of other places where she could use her culinary skills, like schools, nursing homes, and anywhere else food had to be prepared. *Maybe one of those places would be easier to apply to?* Nina knew all too well how competitive the kitchens of upscale restaurants often were, and few employed women. She jotted down the names of a few places that were hiring. Since she was already at the library, she decided to do some research on Lilia and the Hirsts. She had no idea when she'd ever be in this much command of her time, so she decided to make the most of it because she didn't know when this all would end.

Nina already knew some of the history and ownership of the house because the property itself was quite distinguished. She assumed some records of ownership and occupants would be listed in some official documents.

She walked briskly to the front desk and asked the librarian how to retrieve information about the various individuals that lived at the address in the past. She pointed Nina towards the second floor, where she could speak with the research librarian who had access to records, including census records dating back to the early 1900s. Nina climbed the stairs, hoping to glean something more from official records.

From what she learned, Lilia Michaud was not living at the house when the 1950 census was taken, confirming what she had learned from the letters to Elizabeth and David. Neither Ida nor Henry were listed on the 1960 census. She assumed they'd both passed away by then and was going to try to find the exact date each of them had died.

The place had been vacant for almost ten years after Ida King Hirst had passed away. Most people were still experiencing economic hardships from the recession, and large homes were not wise investments. As appealing as the 12-foot ceilings and grand fireplaces were to Nina and Richard, they had been a negative selling point for many years. Besides the deferred maintenance, the size of the almost 4,800-square-foot house was just one more reason the place had stood vacant in the struggling economy.

Earlier records further indicated Henry and Ida weren't the original owners but that the house was originally a private academy built in 1902. The academy closed during the Great Depression, and the Hirsts purchased it and converted it into a large, single-family home. However, much of the building's architectural details remained.

When she and Richard first visited the property, she was struck by the multi-paned windows that overlooked the flagstone patios and overgrown gardens. Richard envisioned escorting guests into the grand foyer with the impressive staircase, whisking them past the massive fireplace that graced the entrance. He dreamed of holding elegant parties in the large dining room and serving after-dinner drinks in the library. None of that impressed

Nina, but her heart was won over the moment she walked into the extraordinary kitchen lined with expansive cabinets and with an attached butler's pantry with open floor-to-ceiling shelving.

NINA HAD BEEN at the library for hours. A gnawing hunger pain grew, and her optimism began to slip away. Feelings of frustration crept in as she headed home to have some lunch. It suddenly seemed like such a waste of time to search for information about Lilia and her beloved David and Elizabeth.

Why does it matter so much to me? Nina wondered. *Maybe I need to let this whole thing go. What happened to this family was long ago and doesn't really matter anymore. Lilia was just a woman who cared for these two children who weren't even hers biologically.*

As she drove home, Nina realized something about the entire situation that struck a chord.

On Nina's eighteenth birthday, her mother had asked her to come into the kitchen. She seemed nervous, which was out of character. She brought a wrapped gift to the table after dinner. Nina opened it to find a macrame purse with a savings passbook inside. Her mother told her to keep it safe. It was for when she went off to culinary school. Nina hugged and thanked her then dug into her panna cotta. She noticed her mother wasn't eating and looked at her closely. Tears streamed down her face.

"It's alright, Momma. I'll come home every weekend," Nina reassured her.

"I know," she stammered. "It's not that. I've been trying to think of a way to tell you something for a long time, but it is hard to know what to say," her mother explained.

That was when her mother revealed that Nina was adopted. Nina almost laughed when her mother told her. It was something she had assumed for a long time. One look in the mirror told her she was either adopted or genetics worked much differently than she learned in biology. She towered over both her parents by the time she was ten. Her straight, dark blonde hair, the sprinkle of freckles across her nose, and her bluish-green eyes were all clear indications she was not born to her parents.

Her mother's admission opened up a conversation between them and Nina learned that her mother was unable to have children and had adopted Nina when she was almost two. It reinforced the feelings Nina had whenever they visited with members of her mother's extended family. She knew she was different than her big Italian family. Once the "secret" was revealed, it confirmed that those feelings weren't a part of her imagination.

Months later, Nina expressed an interest in finding her biological parents and talking to them now that she was older. Her mother told her that her birth mother had died in childbirth and her father was unable to care for her on his own. Nina never raised the subject with her mother after that. But still, she always wanted to know more.

Once she went to college, she rarely thought about the matter anymore. When she first learned about David and Elizabeth, she had to think that these two children might also wonder what happened to Lilia, the woman who had cared for them in their early childhood. They might not realize that Lilia wanted them very much. Nina shared a kind of kinship with them even though she had no idea who they were and what their lives had been once their father came to get them. There was this invisible bond between her and these unknown people in her life. She justified her indulgence by acknowledging that learning more about Lilia wasn't the worst way she could spend time.

ARRIVING HOME, Nina made herself a quick lunch and climbed the stairs to check on the kittens since they hadn't greeted her. She found them cuddled together sound asleep and thought about joining them.

Nina thought about her day. Her trip to the library didn't yield much new information about Lilia, but she had found some possible jobs to apply to. And she had to admit Ben was right. It was nice to spend time outside of her apartment and get back into the world. It wasn't her job at the grocery store that she missed. On the contrary, at King's she missed the creativity that had enlivened her work as a pastry chef at Angelo's. But interacting with others and using her skills to promote the family business had made her feel valued.

When she first took over the bakery management position, everyone knew that she got the job because she married the owner's son. But slowly, she earned their respect because she treated the employees fairly, gave them a voice, and truly listened to ways to improve their department. Small things added up to big things.

Nina set up tables for customers to sample items and began cultivating a base of clients that relied on the store for desserts and pastries. Nina studied the area's demographics. In one meeting with the store manager, she spoke out about catering to those living closest to the store to motivate them to shop closer to home instead of traveling to the bigger stores miles away.

Nina's bakery items were a big draw. She expanded the idea of sampling and ran specials on items that seemed non-essential at first. But as sales increased, she learned that specific patterns emerged. Repeating the sales at regular intervals allowed her to entice customers to shop on days the store was usually slow. The manager received much credit for the idea, but Nina was happy to share her thoughts, especially as they helped those she thought of as her family.

Chapter Nine

Views out a small dormer window in her apartment lured Nina outside to begin to explore her own backyard. She traversed the slate walkway that led to the parking area behind the house and noticed that Keith and April had placed some outdoor furniture in the enclosed porch attached to the first-floor apartment. Nina had spent hours of her life in its sunny space reading or doing crossword puzzles. When she chose to move upstairs, she didn't consider that she would be losing access to this special area behind the house as well. She was glad Keith and April would be enjoying it, even if she was a little sad that it was no longer a place she could use as a retreat.

As usual, there were no cars in the back driveway. The newlyweds, for some reason, still parked in the front of the house. *Maybe they're just used to using that entrance,* Nina thought. But it was also a weekday, so they were likely at their jobs.

Whenever she drove in and out of the driveway, she passed several small outbuildings and an abandoned greenhouse to the left of the carriage house. But for years, she had ignored them. They were now so fairly overgrown they were easy to miss.

Approaching the area to the left of the carriage house, she marveled at the fact that there was an old stone wall that ran the entire length of the rear of the property, and she had never known of its existence. She quietly watched various groups of birds gathered to feed. A robin with its rust-colored breast and charcoal back feathers landed on a branch of a plant with an eye-popping shade of purple berries. Sparrows munched away on a plant nestled in the shade of the greenhouse. It grew next to a long row of hydrangeas turning from white to pink with the cooler fall weather.

Further back at the edge of the property, a small clearing was framed by borders of purple asters scattered among white and yellow coneflowers. Nina interrupted the musings of a crow sitting on a low hanging branch of a pine tree and making an obligatory series of loud caws followed by a mixture of hoarse grating coos, rattles, and clicks, warning its murder of her intrusion.

The smell of the pine had been obfuscated by the strong scents of the ocean, but the clean, sharp fragrance intensified as she walked closer. She heard a persistent tapping noise and looked up to see a small black and white woodpecker working to extract its prey.

Nina wandered around, trying to find the place where Lilia might have planted her garden, but nothing pointed to an obvious location. Still, she discovered several places that might provide the right conditions for one sometime in the future.

As she came back towards the carriage house, she stopped. Sweet notes of a cello wafted through the air telling her Ben was practicing. She wondered why she had rarely heard him play before and why she never thought about going to the symphony. Surely it was something she could do on her own someday. It would be yet another thing that would bring back her joy. Nina was so grateful for this new friendship.

When she reached the carriage house, she stopped to examine the building more closely. The old stone structure was solidly built and, considering its age, it looked like it was in excellent condition.

From outside the building, Nina viewed the three heavy, arched wooden doors used to access the area of bays where Nina thought carriages, then cars, had once been stored. Above the doors was a row of dormer windows. *Those would have to be for the loft,* Nina thought. Richard told her that it would make a great space for his office since it was flooded with sunlight. While the slate roof might need to be repaired, Richard said much of the work that would have to be done to renovate it to accommodate his practice was cosmetic rather than structural.

Ida and Henry had done little for the property even before Henry's death. She knew Lilia probably had her hands full tending to Ida, so the carriage house and its contents hadn't been a priority for some time.

When she and Richard negotiated the divorce settlement, his lawyer brought up the contents of the carriage house and those of the main house. Even though Richard tried to claim that he should get all the carriage house contents in the settlement, Andrea, her attorney, had scoffed at the idea that Nina should part with anything other than what had already been agreed upon, namely, the furniture in their apartment. Richard had tried to suggest it was because he had fond memories of playing in the carriage house when he was a young boy when his parents came to visit Henry and Ida. He described imagining he was a pirate and searching for the treasures his father told his young son that Henry must have buried somewhere. Fortunately, the judge had disagreed with him. Nina had been convinced at the time that much of what Richard was told was merely his father's way of keeping his son busy while he spent time with the elderly couple.

She'd only been inside the carriage house once before they'd purchased the place, and her impression was it had become a dumping area for old furniture and belongings too nice to part with but no longer needed in the main house. Thinking back now to Richard's comments, Nina's curiosity was instantly piqued. She wondered if there was something valuable inside after all.

It was both fun and daunting to think about how the space could be utilized now that she alone possessed the property. She could see why Richard was adamant about using it for his practice. The stonework gave the building an earthy elegance. There was plenty of room for parking, and the proximity to the house was appealing.

There was a door with an overhang in the front of the building to the right, but she had no key to open it, so she hoped the back door that accessed the kitchen was unlocked. She approached it cautiously, fearing there might be animals living inside and imagined it full of cobwebs and insects.

Before she entered the building, she pulled the hood of her light jacket up over her head and tried the door. It was unlocked, but it took some time to push open, as it seemed to have swollen over time. She noticed a pane of broken glass in the door, which made her curious if someone had entered the building without her knowledge. Nina wondered if Richard had ever attempted to extract anything from the building.

The dirt and grime told her that if someone had broken in, it was most likely a while ago. Still, she decided once she could, she'd have the pane fixed and keep the door locked since it was not visible from the house.

She pushed the door to open it, but it wouldn't budge. Even ramming her shoulder against the solid frame was of no use. She almost gave up, worried she would get hurt. But one more try finally dislodged it.

Once inside, Nina inspected the large room with beamed ceiling and concluded that this part of the building was being used for storage just as she'd remembered. Heavy canvas cloths were still draped over curious piles stacked almost to the ceiling at the end of the large open room.

To the right of the entrance was a small kitchen area with a Mamie Eisenhower pink counter and cabinets that were reminiscent of her childhood. Her aunt had had a kitchen right out of that era. It gave her a clue when the last carriage house renovation had been done. Could Ida and Henry have been more attentive to the building more recently than Richard realized?

Nina made her way towards the back of the room and peeked under the drop cloths. She couldn't determine if there was anything of value, but she guessed some of the pieces were most likely antique. As she turned and looked right, she saw a door leading into the garage bays, and close to that was a set of stairs that led to the loft on the second floor.

She meandered over to the kitchen and was about to let herself into the bay area door when she noticed one of the smaller kitchen cabinets above the sink appeared to be coming loose from the wall. Directly behind it was a recessed area neatly carved out of the plaster. She decided to investigate but without a step ladder of some kind, she couldn't reach it to get a closer look.

There was a barstool lying on its side on the floor, so Nina used it to climb on top of the counter. Straddling the sink, she could reach the cabinet itself but from her position she still couldn't see behind it and into the hole. She was afraid that if she grabbed the dangling cabinet, it might come loose and cause her to fall backwards. It was hard to keep her balance from her vantage point as it was, so she got back down from the counter puzzled about what would possess someone to create such a space.

She reached up to open the door to see if anything was inside the cabinet when, without warning, the whole thing came crashing down, landing on the counter. Nina jumped back, completely startled as dust and debris flew at her. She coughed and spat and stared at the space in the wall behind where the cabinet was moments ago.

The space itself was roughly a foot in diameter and perhaps six to eight inches deep. When she thoroughly recovered, she moved the fallen cabinet out of her way to inspect the area. Then, feeling brave, she gingerly climbed back up onto the counter, trying to get a better look inside. But even with the poor lighting it was clearly just an empty space carved into the wall.

From that vantage point, however, she noticed something in

the sink, covered with dirt and grime. She got down off the counter and lifted it out of its resting place. Wiping it off, she saw an odd-looking one-dollar bill. Nina hesitantly put it in her pocket to examine it more closely in the sunlight.

The mysterious hole behind the cabinet and the odd bill piqued her curiosity and she sauntered over to the door to the garage bay and opened it with a heightened anticipation. The darkness made it difficult to see so she waited a moment to allow her eyes to adjust. The architect had suggested removing the doors and replacing them with windows as the room was gloomy without the benefit of sunlight. Now she understood why.

A smug smile tugged at the corner of Nina's mouth as she imagined Richard's disappointment. *Oh, well*, she thought.

As she turned to leave, a noise behind her made her jump. The hair on the back of her neck began to prickle. She turned quickly just as something flew at her. She tried to duck but wasn't fast enough. It clutched the top of her head, then bounced off the wall and seemed to land on top of something further into the bay. She screamed and fell forward on her knees trying to escape. Desperate to get free of her attacker she scrambled to her hands and feet. Sprinting to the door, she slammed it behind her. Shivering, she shook her hands out, flaying them against her body, the remnants of the unknown assailant still with her. She was sure that there would be blood from the claws that had impaled her scalp, but there was none.

Even with the door closed, Nina could hear a loud chittering from the garage. She had invaded the home of another creature and this outburst served as a warning. The distressing chirps brought images of a swishing tail and the utter confusion of a cornered animal. She knew the feeling.

Nina looked down at her knees and saw her jeans were caked with dirt from her encounter with the cement floor of the garage. Despite the momentary scare, she felt a rush that she couldn't explain. She was alive and thrilled that there were more mysteries for her to uncover.

WHEN SHE RETURNED to her apartment, Nina took a quick shower and changed out of her grimy clothes. When she exited the bathroom, she saw the flashing light on her answering machine.

Nina tousled her hair with a towel, then hit the play button and heard Julia's cheery voice.

"If the invitation is still open, I could visit on Columbus Day weekend," Julia said.

Nina reached for the phone, but the kittens were meowing incessantly, so instead she headed downstairs to feed them. She couldn't wait to tell Julia about the carriage house. Nina wondered about the significance of the loose cabinet and then remembered the single dollar bill she discovered. Retrieving it from her pocket, she examined it more closely.

The paper was more of a tan color than green, and the print was blue, not black. While George Washington still featured prominently in the center, she knew there were other differences, so she got her wallet and extracted her one remaining single to compare them. Nina read the words, "This certifies that there has been deposited in the treasury of," which were printed directly above "THE UNITED STATES OF AMERICA" printed in capital letters. Below Washington's picture were the words, "ONE SILVER DOLLAR." Underneath that, she read, "Payable to the bearer on demand." Nina didn't know what to make of any of it but knew there had to be something unique about this bill. She decided perhaps another trip to the library would yield some answers. She climbed the stairs again, the kittens bounding close at her heels, and tucked the bill into the drawer of her nightstand for safe keeping.

Ginger began crawling up the leg of Nina's jeans. She picked up the kitten, careful not to pull too hard as Ginger's claws were firmly stuck in the denim. The orange cat nuzzled into her neck purring so loudly that Nina laughed. It didn't seem possible that such a tiny creature could make so much noise. She scooped up Cinnamon as well and deposited the two onto the futon, then crossed to the phone to call Julia.

"Hey, Jules! It's Nina."

"Well, hi there! Glad we finally connected. So, is Columbus Day Weekend okay?"

"I would say so."

"Great! I'll put in for the long weekend," Julia agreed.

"It will be so much fun. You can meet the kitties, and maybe we can splurge and go out for dinner one night. Or better yet, I can make you something special and spend the money on wine."

"I'd rather come early on Saturday morning rather than contend with Friday night traffic. Would that work for you?" Julia asked.

"Sure would!" Nina told her friend excitedly. "Give me a clue as to what you're eating these days. Are you still doing the vegetarian thing?"

"I'm still moving that way. I just read *Diet for a Small Planet*. It really made me think about what I'm putting in my mouth," Julia said.

"I'm not familiar with the book, but I'm always up for experimenting in the kitchen, and veggies are cheaper than a good cut of beef. I can even see if they have some cookbooks at the library. I spent several hours there today," Nina told her.

"What were you doing there?"

"I was looking at the classifieds, then tried to get more information about the house and Lilia. Remember, that woman who left the letters behind? I would never make it as a detective!"

"What is it that you want to accomplish with all this?" Julia asked.

"I guess I'd like to find David and Elizabeth and give them all of Lilia's letters. Since Lilia left them behind, I'm assuming that she's dead, but I'm sure she would want the two kids to have them."

"What information do you have now?" Julia asked.

"Just their names and approximate ages, along with a general location of where they were living when their father came to get them."

"That's not a lot," Julia said. "Have you tried looking in the phone book?" Julia's question took Nina off guard.

"Oh my god! Why didn't I think of that? I only have the Kittery phone book, but there are phone books at the library that cover the entire state. There is a chance that Elizabeth has married and her last name has changed, or they're in another state, but I could begin by looking up David Michaud and seeing what I could find. You're a genius! I can't believe I never thought of that."

"Well, I didn't read all those Nancy Drew mysteries for nothing. Glad I could help."

When the receiver was back on the cradle, Nina went down to the kitchen to search for her phone book.

Chapter Ten

Nina finally found her phone book sandwiched between a few cookbooks she'd piled onto the counter. She opened it with excitement only to discover there was a column of Michauds but nothing for a Lilia, David, or Elizabeth.

Discouraged, she started to wonder once again whether it was all a waste of her time. Her connection with these strangers filled a void and gave her something to look forward to each day. But the reality was that she had to find a job soon or risk everything. She decided to tackle her job search in the morning, and if she had time, she'd stop once again at the library. But until then she felt free to continue reading since it lifted her spirits. Reading the letters kept her occupied and left her feeling in control of the only thing she had control over—her time.

Ben had stopped by after his rehearsal, and when he left, Nina climbed into bed with a shoebox that contained more of Lilia's letters. At the bottom, she discovered a journal as well. She flipped through it and found it full of pen and ink sketches of David and Elizabeth. These were not the drawings of a young child but of a gifted hand that sought to capture a beloved subject. She touched the pages, and tears fell down her cheeks. It saddened her to think of Lilia's heartache at not being able to find the children she so clearly loved.

Cinnamon joined her on the bed and began purring as Nina stroked her fur. Moments later she heard a meow, and she smiled as Ginger hoisted herself up onto the bed and lay next to her sister.

Passages, poems, and what appeared to be idle scribbling covered the pages between the sketches of plants, flowers and the sea. But the most haunting were the faces of the two young children Nina knew were David and Elizabeth. Under one drawing, there was a thought...

"Every day, I see you in the faces of the children I come across in the grocery store, in the pews at church, or in my dreams. I have to wonder what your life is like now and if you miss Billy and me.

Another read,

I thought the heartache of losing Jake was bad. But, unbelievably, that was almost eighteen long years ago. Maybe because he's been absent from my life for so long, the memories of his arms around me have all but faded. But your sweet smiles, hugs, and kisses erased the sorrow that had enveloped my heart. I will continue to search until I find you.

The raw emotion of Lilia's words began to seep too deeply into Nina's heart. She was about to close the journal when she noticed a piece of stationery Lilia had used in previous letters sticking out from the back. Penned in Lilia's now familiar hand, Nina read another letter addressed to the children.

I just got back from Gorham. For some reason, I thought just maybe Jesse had relocated there. My uncle Billy and I lived in Gorham, close to Portland when I was reunited with Jake decades ago. Billy was working at a little diner at the time; I can't recall the name right now. After graduating from high school, I started a part-time job waiting tables there. One day, I approached a table and took an order from two young men sitting in a booth in the corner. As I was taking their order, I felt there was something familiar about one of them. I looked at him momentarily, trying to figure out how I knew him.

By that point, Billy and I had moved so many times, faces and memories blurred together. I was about to leave the table when the young man grabbed my arm and said,

"You're that girl—the one from the beach."

"Pardon?" I said, turning to look at him.

"The beach. I cut my foot, and you helped me get back home," Jake said, sure of himself.

It took me a minute to recall the event, but then I remembered. Billy and I had stayed in Old Orchard Beach briefly when I was sixteen. It was the boy I helped back to the motel where they lived. He told me he was taking some courses at Gorham State Teachers College.

Young men left the state in droves because of the Depression-era employment conditions. But Jake had stayed to help his younger brothers, who depended on him since his mother had died years earlier. He came in almost every day after that and asked to sit at my table. We'd chat, and he seemed to linger as long as possible and sometimes brought some books to read while I waited on other customers. I wasn't sure what to make of it all. I'd never really had a friend before. Because Billy and I moved around so much, I didn't exactly have the typical social interactions that teens experience. As I got older, I shied away from making friends because I always had to leave those friendships behind. In retrospect, I think that's why Jake was so precious to me. He wasn't just the first man I ever loved—he was my first real friend, too.

While my uncle and I were close, he was of a different generation and cared for me much like an older brother would. About the only interest we shared was cooking. We might not have lived at the same address for very long, but we always had a kitchen wherever we moved. So, Billy and I would experiment with all kinds of cooking and baking, and that was how I spent those years living with him and trying to make it to adulthood.

Jake and I married in June of '39, when I was nineteen. Your uncle Jake became my world, especially after Billy announced one day he was going to head back to the Cape. It was strange to be apart. He was so much more than my uncle, and I missed him dearly. So I kept myself busy and continued working at the diner with the woman that owned the place. She offered me Billy's job as the cook, and I accepted.

Jake and I moved into a small apartment in Gorham so he could continue taking courses. He worked part-time at a shoe store that hired him full-time later that year. The extra money helped us save up enough so I could open up a small diner in Portland. Not long after we opened, something happened on the Cape, and my uncle moved back to Portland and started working with me at the diner.

It was a glorious time. Finally, we saw an end to the Depression, and Jake and I had high hopes for our future. But our joy was short-lived because every day the newspapers informed us of the upheaval in Europe with the Germans' invasion of Poland and Great Britain and France declaring war. Yet it all felt so far away.

Jake left his job at the shoe store and came on board at the diner. The three of us worked like a well-oiled machine, serving many of the workers that were employed by federal or state programs meant to boost the Maine economy. But as you know, Jake didn't stay put. He enlisted after the attack on Pearl Harbor and never came back to me. Even now, so many years later, it is painful to think about the many long days and nights I waited for him to walk through the door and take me in his arms. His death framed my life until your father came to the restaurant one day with the two of you in tow.

I had little contact with any of your uncles, even before Jake died. Jesse was out of the picture until almost five years later. I wasn't even sure how he found me.

When this tall, gaunt man came in holding the hands of two small children, I didn't recognize him. At first, I thought he was one of the many people in Portland who were down on their luck, and he was looking for a free meal. When he said, "Hello, Lilia," I realized who was standing in front of me.

Jesse was always an extremely handsome man. But when he came into the diner, he looked much older than he actually was, and his hands were shaking. He smelled of stale cigarettes and needed a shave. The Depression was not any kinder to Maine than to other places, but we had the added disadvantage of being too stubborn to seek help. Many survived by leaving the state or returning to the many rural farms that existed outside of larger cities like Portland.

You were too young to recall much of this, but when he brought you both in, you sat at a table clinging to him while we spoke. He told me your mother had died and asked me if I could watch you just for a few hours while he went to apply for a job at the naval yard. I was so flabbergasted I barely knew what to say. His sudden appearance was just shocking. Jesse handed me a bag that contained a few homemade toys and headed out the door. Billy took over for me in the kitchen, and I brought you both upstairs and waited for your father's return. That day was the last time I saw him for over five years.

Nina looked on the other side of the paper to see if there was more, but the letter ended abruptly, prompting her to dig under the other letters to see if there was a page missing. One envelope at the bottom of the box seemed different from the rest. It was heavier and she heard a jingle. Her hands trembled as she started to open it.

Chapter Eleven

Many of Lilia's letters were written on an assortment of beautiful stationery and enclosed in their appropriate but unsealed envelopes. The envelope at the bottom of the box was nothing like the others. It was a brown kraft envelope similar to ones used for business. It was also sealed.

Nina's hands shook as she peeled it open. She gasped in sheer disbelief as she lifted a stack of crisp bills of various denominations out of the envelope. She began doing a mental calculation in her head. Mortgage, insurance, groceries, gas, utilities—the weight of all these worrisome expenses began to float away—at least for the moment.

She was so flustered, she had to count again and again, as she kept losing track. The kittens started pouncing on the bills so she got out of bed and used the coffee table to organize the cash. As the piles increased, so did the width of the grin on her face. Three hundred and fifty-one dollars and twenty-nine cents was the exact amount.

Suddenly, she stopped smiling. Nina realized that if Lilia left this money behind, she must be dead. Why else would someone abandon such a considerable amount of cash in a shoebox, tucked away in the crawl space of an attic?

THE NEXT DAY, Nina distracted herself with thoughts about Julia's visit. She wanted it to be special and the money she'd found would certainly help her achieve that goal. She'd never given much thought to a vegetarian diet and wasn't even sure how to approach a menu for the weekend. She scanned many of the cookbooks still stacked on her disorganized counter but nothing struck her as being quite what she was looking for, a recipe that featured vegetables but would make her mouth water.

Then she thought of one of her favorite pastimes, browsing the shelves of the used bookstore she once frequented. It was where she'd found many of the cookbooks she now owned. *Surely one more wouldn't hur*t, she thought.

An hour later, Nina pulled up directly in front of the store and squeezed her Beetle into a space only a small car would fit. She walked to the door, anticipating another fantastic find. Signs guided customers to the selections of books within each section of the store. However, Nina didn't need to look at them. With unbridled delight, she headed to the far left corner of the back row of the store, touching the spines of each book as she walked down the aisle towards a multitude of colorful books in various sizes.

Many of these were copies of things she already owned, or they contained recipes for dishes she'd already mastered or wasn't interested in trying. Julia's new vegetarian diet intrigued her even though she wondered how long Julia would stick with this one, as it seemed like she was constantly changing her eating habits and rarely stuck with one diet for very long. Still, Nina wanted to support her friend, and it was interesting to think about cooking in a new way.

She picked up a yellowish-colored book from the top shelf. There was a playful illustration of a woman lying in a garden with various plants. The blurb on the cover read, "262 recipes that bring vegetarian cooking to new gastronomic heights with talk about good food, the art of making fine bread, and menus designed to make every meal a delight and a celebration of life."

As Nina began flipping through the pages, she thought, *That's a pretty tall order.* But she was delighted with what she found inside. The beautiful illustrations reminded her of Lilia's drawings in the journals she'd left behind. The pages spoke to her with recipes of all kinds for dishes that featured many of her favorite fruits and vegetables. Now that she was cooking for herself, her meals often featured eggs, salads, pasta, and grains. She found a slew of recipes she was eager to try. Tucking the book under her arm, she was convinced she had found another treasure. She purchased *The Vegetarian Epicure* cookbook and left the store eager to try the potato curry and spiced dal recipe for dinner.

WHEN SHE ARRIVED HOME, Nina worked on organizing her kitchen. She finally placed her pots and pans on a rack that hung above the stove and made space for a baker's rack she'd stored in the basement long ago to hold the cookbooks stacked on her table and counter. It was so much better to have them all on display. It made her tiny kitchen homey.

Nina made a list of items she needed to buy for Julia's visit. She decided to make an eggplant parmigiana prepared with wheat germ instead of bread crumbs. She couldn't decide if she wanted to make an herb and onion bread and a vegetable soup for lunch or perhaps a zucchini quiche. Regardless, Nina was once again excited about cultivating her love for cooking.

Cinnamon and Ginger joined her in the kitchen, and she gave them each a little milk. Once her list was complete, she assured the kittens she would be back soon and headed out the door.

Nina drove to a small grocery store further from home to avoid shopping at King's. The colorful array of fresh vegetables boosted her spirits. Cruising the aisles, she selected the best produce she could find. She was thrilled to see small eggplants, knowing they would be sweeter and have fewer seeds than the larger ones. She was so lost in her shopping it took a moment to register that someone speaking to her.

"Hey, Nina," a voice called.

She turned and found Ben standing behind her. "Oh, Ben! What are you doing here?"

He grinned. "Probably the same thing you're doing."

"I'm sorry. That was a silly question. My old college roommate is coming over for the weekend, and I'm doing a bit of cooking."

"That sounds like fun. What are you preparing for the main course?" he asked, looking at her grocery basket.

"These are for an eggplant parmigiana. My friend Julia recently became a vegetarian, so I'm trying to think of things to make."

"Well, that pasta dish you made for me was excellent, but I guess you couldn't make that unless you made it without the bacon," he said playfully. "I really should learn how to cook more. My mom taught my sisters, but she always shooed me out of the kitchen."

"Richard never even learned to boil water," Nina told him. "Not that you're anything like Richard." Nina found herself overtalking, something she did when she was nervous. Would you care to join us?" she blurted out. "I'm sure Julia wouldn't mind."

"That's very nice of you," Ben said. "I'd love to, but I have to work tomorrow evening. Maybe I could stop by for dessert."

"That would be great! I haven't even thought about what I'm making for dessert, so thanks for reminding me."

Wanting to move on, she tried to extricate herself.

"Well, I don't want to hold you up. I'll see you at home," she said and realized that too was an awkward statement. "You know what I mean."

Embarrassed, she turned and left the produce aisle even though she still needed to buy some ingredients for a salad. As she was about to turn the corner and head to another aisle, she turned back to look at Ben and found he was looking at her as well. She smiled and waved glad he wasn't close enough to see she was blushing.

ON THE DAY before Julia was to arrive, Nina lounged in bed with the kittens curled up beside her. She stroked Ginger's back, rubbing her hand back and forth over her orange fur, eliciting a loud purr. While she lay there thinking, Nina decided that right after Julia's visit, she would have to apply for the places she learned were hiring. She chastised herself for not being more diligent and reminded herself that her recent windfall would only supply a momentary reprieve. She even wondered if she was entitled to the money.

"Time to get up, right, girls?" she told her furry companions.

She plodded down the stairs and put the kettle on to heat some water for tea. She looked around, pleased at all the work she'd done over the past few days preparing for her guest. The kitchen was much more organized and friendly with the baker's rack. It really added so much space, and the bright red color livened up the room. Finally placing her various pots, pans, and utensils on the wrought iron pot rack over the stove left her counters clearer than they'd ever been and she was able to put out the set of blue and white canisters adorned with flowers so she had easy access to them. Admittedly, it was a hodgepodge of decorative styles, but it made Nina smile despite the lack of cohesion.

She wanted to avoid cooking during Julia's visit, so she began preparing some of their meals ahead of time. She heard music, presumably coming from the apartment across the hall. She hummed off-key while Aretha belted out *Respect*. "All I want you to do for me is give it to me when you get home Re Re Re Respect."

The tightness in her neck dissolved as she tossed zucchini shreds for baked eggs with zucchini. She added a few teaspoons of salt and let them rest while she heated some butter and olive oil in a skillet. After squeezing the excess water, she placed it in a piece of cheesecloth to further drain out the liquid. The butter and oil browned in the pan, so Nina sautéed some scallions she had cut earlier until they were tender.

She turned up the heat and added the zucchini and a dash of freshly ground pepper. When everything was done, she placed it in two oven-safe dishes to warm later before making a hollandaise sauce that would go over the eggs. Then, Nina assembled the eggplant parmigiana and baked a loaf of fresh bread. The smells wafting from her kitchen delighted her, and she continued to hum off-key as she moved around the small space. With lunch and dinner mostly finished, she debated what to serve for dessert. She knew Julia loved a dish she frequently made when they were roommates, and she decided to surprise her with some chocolate rugelach for dessert. Pleased with everything she had accomplished, Nina headed upstairs, exhausted but happy.

THE FOLLOWING DAY, Nina woke up early. Julia expected to arrive somewhere around 11 a.m., so Nina wanted to pop out to get some wine or beer before she came. Slipping on her jacket, she started down the stairs and heard Ben practicing his instrument. She remembered their odd encounter at the grocery store and wondered if he had a girlfriend. She never noticed extra cars around, but that could be simply because he stayed at her place occasionally. After all, that's what Richard did with Holly, and Nina was never the wiser. The thought colored her mood, and she stopped listening to him play and hurried down the stairs to get to the liquor store. However, as she reached the end of the driveway, Julia pulled in. Nina rolled down the window of her car as Julia pulled up beside her.

"Hey, you must have made good time!" Nina said.

"You're telling me! All the traffic was going south. But I have to confess, I had a hard time sleeping last night, so I left a little early. I hope that's okay. Where are you headed?" Julia asked.

"I'm off to the liquor store. Why don't you park around the back of the house and hop in?" Nina offered.

"I actually brought several bottles of red, but if you think we need some white, I'm game," Julia told her.

"Well, I like either, so you tell me. Should we get more?"

"Always!" Julia teased. "I'll go park my car."

When she returned, Julia hopped in Nina's VW. She told Julia about inviting Ben to dinner, while driving to the closest liquor store.

"Is he cute?" Julia asked.

"He is. But more importantly, he's very nice."

"Do you like him?" Julia pestered.

"Yes, but not in the way you're trying to insinuate. What do you want to do today? Any ideas?" Nina asked changing the subject. "I made lunch and dinner already, so we can eat in," Nina replied.

"I haven't been to see a movie in ages. Are you game?"

"That would be perfect because I've been dying to see *Blazing Saddles* but everyone I know has already seen it. Do you think we could see if it's still playing anywhere?" Julia suggested.

"Absolutely! There are a bunch of places that play second-run movies, so I'm sure we can find it somewhere. It's not that old."

The two young women entered the package store and looked around, going their separate ways. Nina scanned the liqueur aisle, looking for something special for an after-movie cocktail.

"Hey, look what I found to go with dessert!" Julia said, holding up a bottle of Baileys Irish cream. "My treat. Did you find what you want?"

"The Baileys works for me," she assured her. "Maybe I'll just grab a six pack of Heineken for Ben. I think he likes beer better than wine."

"Oh, he does, does he?" Julia teased.

Nina ignored her and went to the back cooler to grab some beer.

Once the two friends were back in Nina's apartment, she introduced Julia to Cinnamon and Ginger and then went downstairs to finish her lunch preparation. She smiled, hearing Julia playing with the kittens and cooing over the adorable pair. When lunch was ready, she called her downstairs.

As they ate, Julia spoke openly of life's challenges, telling Nina she was going to look for another job.

"I love the work I'm doing, but it's so hard to work for my boss, Brad. The man is a pig. There is not one day that goes by that he doesn't accidentally touch my ass or comment on my boobs. I am just so sick of it," Julia complained.

"Is there anyone you can go to and file a complaint?" Nina asked between bites of her new favorite zucchini dish.

"I doubt they'd take me seriously," Julia told her. "You would think things would have changed in this day and age with women's lib," she lamented. "All I want to do is go to work, do my job, and come home at night not needing to scrub myself from head to toe to get the disgust off. Is that too much to ask?"

"I was lucky I didn't have to go through that in my job," Nina said. "I don't know what I'd do if I had to endure that all the time."

"Well, at least I don't have to contend with working for my husband's parents. Boy, that must have been tough."

"I didn't really have to deal with them too much because they focused on their bigger stores, especially the one in York. And I have to say, I guess because I had a track record for increased sales, they let me do my thing. But I worked more hours than I was paid for, and whenever they had a party or family gathering, I served as their own private chef. 'Oh, lovey, can you whip up something?' his mother would say. When she needed me, I became her favorite person in the world. I can't tell you how many events I catered for them when Richard and I were married.

"Of course, when Richard announced he wanted a divorce, things eventually got ugly. I'm sure he convinced them it was all my fault to justify cheating on me. I don't know what he told them, but I could have been frostbitten the last few times I saw them."

"You should have sued them," Julia told her passionately.

"They can't just fire someone because their son is a dick!" she added.

"Actually, I'm rather glad they did because I probably would have quit. At least I was able to collect unemployment for a while. But that ran out months ago, and now I really have to think about looking for work. I did find a few jobs I'm planning on applying for soon."

"You're lucky you don't have a mother breathing down your neck about having kids!" Julia said, then gasped. "Oh, Nina! I'm so sorry. I didn't mean that the way it sounded. I forgot for a minute."

"I understand. I imagine that my mother would be wondering about that too. We're practically old maids by today's standards," Nina said.

"Every conversation I have with my mother begins and ends with, 'When are you going to settle down and start a family?' I always say, 'Yeah, Ma. I'll get right on that.' I think that's why my parents are willing to pay for my therapist. They think there is something wrong with me because I'm not married and don't have a steady boyfriend. I admit I wonder if I'll ever find the right guy, but maybe that's not the right thing for me. I rather like my life. I would like it better if I could work and not worry about my sorry-ass boss hitting on me. But at least I don't have to worry about taking care of a mess of kids or if my husband is being faithful. That must have been awful, Nina."

What Nina said and what she wanted to say were two different things. She wanted to tell Julia how much of her life had been wrapped up in her marriage and, when it was over, she was devastated. Richard and his family had become her entire world once she moved to Maine. Nina wanted to tell her old friend that even before the divorce, she missed her mother every moment of very day and that she worried she wouldn't be able to pay the tax bill when it came due or that she feared the upcoming winter months because she didn't know how much her heating bill would be. She wanted to tell her how angry she was sometimes recalling how much Richard had hurt her. Did he mean all those horrible things he said?

Instead, Nina left all those thoughts unsaid and simply shrugged. "It's been really hard but I'll get through it." She was grateful when Julia changed the subject.

"Do you still plan on using the carriage house for your catering business someday?" Julia asked.

"I don't have the money right now. Maybe one day though. After lunch, we'll take a stroll out there, and then you can see why that's not a very practical solution," Nina told her with a hollow laugh.

Chapter Twelve

Julia sat at the kitchen table riffling through a stack of Lilia's letters while Nina was making some tea.

"Hey, listen to this," Julia said.

> My dearest David and Elizabeth,
>
> I am alone for the first time in days as I've spent much of my time downstairs with Mrs. Hirst. Henry died of a sudden heart attack in June. Henry was Ida's everything. He took care of all the financial matters, and Ida does not know how to run this household, so I've taken over much of that responsibility since leaving it to her would end in disaster.
>
> When I operated the restaurant up in Portland, I took care of all the financial transactions for my uncle and me, but we were family. As much as I like the woman, Ida is not kin. It makes dealing

with her intimate financial matters difficult. But there is no one else to attend to her needs. The only relative she has left is her nephew, Donald King. While I don't have or want access to any of her bank accounts and such, she's confided in me about how to deal with the matter, as she has other financial resources.

"What do you think she meant by that?" Julia asked.
"Can you read that again?" Nina instructed.
Julia obliged.
Nina turned towards Julia, and the two exchanged a perplexed look.
"Whoa! Give me a minute. I have something to show you," Nina told her. As she went upstairs, Nina debated whether she should tell Julia about the cash she found but decided against it. Instead, she retrieved the dollar bill.
"Keep reading. I can hear you," Nina called.

I've stopped taking my salary since I don't want there to be questions about my compensation or for anyone to think I'm taking advantage of this awkward situation. While I am working so much more than I ever was when getting paid, I feel horrible taking a cent from this woman. It makes me uncomfortable. Every once in a while, she hands over some money. I've joked with her about having a hidden printing press, but she slyly smiles and places it in my hand or sometimes leaves it on the table.

I honestly don't need the money. When Billy

passed away, I inherited his entire estate, which, to my surprise, was considerable. In addition, he had all the money from the sale of my grandmother's farm in California put in a trust for me and now that all those matters are finally settled, I don't have to worry as much as I did when I first took the job.

I guess I will have to continue caring for her since she's told me often enough she has no other option since even her nephew doesn't seem to have the time On the rare occasions he and his family visit, he walks throughout the house, touching things like he's sizing the place up. It shocked me when she said he's not very trustworthy. Still, she knows him better than I do, and my instincts tell me that Ida is right.

So, my Dizzy darlings, I am now caring for Ida full time. You wouldn't think that one elderly woman would require so much care, but she is mourning the death of her beloved Henry, to whom she was married for much of her life. She barely eats and often just sits in the living room by the fireplace, staring off at who knows what. Every conversation begins with, "When Henry was alive..."

I wish there was more I could do to comfort her. She hates to be alone and wants me to move to the first floor. While it might make life easier, I am used to my solitude. I haven't written to you in weeks because I'm never alone. I tried to take her to see a movie to distract her, but we left halfway through. So now I'll never know what happened to Humphrey Bogart or Katharine Hepburn in African Queen!

Well, dear David and Elizabeth, I must close but will write again as I can. I love you both and hope to find you soon. Auntie Lilia.

"I can see why you find all of this very interesting." Julia handed the letter to Nina who rejoined her at the kitchen table.

"See what I mean? It's all so mysterious."

"It is indeed, Ms. Nina. It is indeed!"

"Well, if you think that's interesting, look at this," Nina said, showing her the old dollar bill.

Julia's eyes widened as she looked at Nina.

As the two finished their tea, they speculated about the odd-looking bill and where it came from, wondering if it tied into Lilia somehow.

Before heading to the carriage house, Nina grabbed her flashlight. She suggested Julia put on one of her old sweaters on over her blouse. Because Nina was so much taller, it swam on her. But Nina assured her it was best not to enter the carriage house in anything that could get ruined and told Julia about the incidents with the squirrel and the hanging cabinet.

Once appropriately equipped and attired, the two headed out to explore the building.

"Here, you take the flashlight," Nina said, handing it to Julia.

"Is it really that dark in there?"

"No, you might need it to beat off a squirrel," she joked.

They entered the carriage house through the back door into the kitchen and cautiously looked around.

"Well, you're right! It is a mess. But boy, if it could be cleared out, I think you'd have enough space to start your business," Julia remarked.

"Yeah, but how do I get rid of all this junk?"

"Are you sure it is junk?" Julia asked. "Have you taken a look at what's under those covers?"

"I took a brief look. But, I keep imagining a colony of spiders breeding under them," Nina said, shivering.

"Think of it this way," Julia assured her, "until you know what's under there, you have no way of knowing if it's just old, worn-out furniture or something you could sell to raise money for some renovations to this place. So, let's take a look."

"Alright. But, let me roll up this shade and see if we can get more light in here." Nina navigated between large, covered pieces of furniture to reach the window and approached the shade with trepidation. Julia poked around in the former kitchen area.

Nina pulled the decaying string on the old roller shade, which sprung up so suddenly she jumped back reflexively.

"You okay?" Julia asked, laughing at her friend's timid response.

"Well, I'll survive, but boy, this isn't my favorite thing to do. But the light helps. Imagine how much more light there would be if there weren't several layers of dirt on the window."

Nina gingerly made her way across the room, and Julia followed. The two women approached the pile hidden under the canvas cloths. They each took an opposite end of the canvas and began to lift. The weight and filth of the fabric made the task difficult, but they persisted, revealing what lay underneath. Several chairs, desks, and even an ornately carved bed frame were pushed against a floor-to-ceiling stone fireplace. Nina was struck by a beautiful rustic table that seemed to be the last item added. There were chairs piled on top that looked like part of a set. She looked closely and saw the table was made of five wide planks that could be teak. The tapered legs were sturdy and appeared to be hand-carved. There were even two drawers that pulled out on each end. Perhaps because the cloth had shielded it from the grime, it still had a warm sheen. The women exchanged glances of wonder.

"Holy cow!" Julia exclaimed. "I'm not even remotely qualified to say these might have value, but everything seems to be in excellent condition."

"Yeah. I can't imagine why these were kept in here. And something tells me there's more in the bays of the garage, but let's avoid going in there for now and check out the upstairs."

"I'm game!" Julia grinned. "What are we waiting for?"

Julia's adventurous spirit emboldened Nina. She was happy to have a companion who was willing to explore. It made tackling the unknown exciting instead of frightening.

Julia crossed to the staircase leading to the room above the first floor of the carriage house.

"Be careful," Nina warned her.

They cautiously navigated each step, but the staircase wasn't decayed at all. The second story of the carriage house was disappointingly empty except for a small wood stove presumably used to heat the space.

"Well, this is surprising!" Nina said. "I expected treasure chests filled with pirate's gold brimming from one end to the next." She laughed.

"I wasn't sure what we would find, but it never occurred to me it would be empty. I wonder why there's nothing up here. Maybe Lilia's letters will give you a clue."

"There's another stash of letters still in the cubby but I can't reach them."

"What?" Julia replied, startled. "Did you tell me that?"

"I think so. I saw them before, but they were further back and out of reach. I have one of those things that you can use to grab cans from the top shelf, and thought while you're here, I might be brave enough to crawl under the sink again," Nina told her.

"What's that, under your foot?" Julia asked, looking down.

Nina jumped. "Where?"

Julia burst into laughter. "It's just some kind of paper, silly goose. What did you think it was, another killer squirrel?"

Nina chuckled with embarrassment and removed a piece of paper stuck to the bottom of her left boot. She saw it was yet another dollar bill.

"Well, well. It's another one," Nina showed Julia. "Let's go back to the house and compare it to the one I found earlier."

As the two women made their way up the stairs to Nina's apartment, Ben came down with his cello.

"Hi, Ben! Heading out?" Nina asked.

"Yes, I'm off," he replied, smiling. "Is this your guest?" he extended his hand. "I'm Ben, Nina's tenant—and friend. Nice to meet you."

"Hi, Ben. I'm Julia. Nina tells me you play for the Portland Symphony."

"Yes, I do,"

"Have you been with them long?"

"Only a few years. Before that, I was with the VSO, Vermont Symphony Orchestra."

"Are you still coming for dessert later?" Nina asked him.

"Sure am. Well, it was nice meeting you Julia. See you both later," Ben made his way around them and headed downstairs.

Once the women were inside Nina's apartment, Julia looked at her with a wide grin.

"He's the type of guy that grows on you," she said. "He's not classically handsome, but that brown curly hair and enormous smile are very appealing."

"Well, I'm not in the market now, and unless you want to date him long distance, neither are you," Nina teased. "Besides, he probably already has a girlfriend. Guys like that always do."

NINA RETRIEVED the can grabber and flashlight, scooped Ginger up from the kitchen chair and headed upstairs. She found Cinnamon already in the bedroom, so she closed the door, and signaled to Julia she was ready to explore the space behind the sink.

"You hold these while I get down on my belly, okay?" Nina said.

"Sure, thing. I'll pull you out quickly if you scream," Julia teased.

"Don't laugh. I panicked the last time and hit my head. Boy, did that hurt. I feel better that you're here, though. If I get stuck and die there, I know someone will take care of the kittens."

Nina pulled her hood over her head and got down on the floor. Julia handed her the can-grabbing device and the flashlight. Nina crawled in and saw what she was looking for— three additional shoeboxes, plus a small wooden chest she'd overlooked previously. She carefully extended the can grabber and manipulated it to bring each box within reach of the opening and backed out of the cubby. Nina handed Julia both the flashlight and grabber and pulled the shoeboxes and wooden chest out to the bathroom floor. Dust covered each, and soon she was sneezing. She stood up cautiously to avoid hitting her head.

"Let's take a look," Julia said.

"Believe it or not, there's more. I can see something in the very far corner, but let's save that for another time. It's probable more pictures or letters," she said getting to her feet.

Nina and Julia brought everything out to the coffee table in front of Nina's futon couch. Nina looked at Julia with a large grin.

"Well, here goes!" Nina said, lifting the cover to the wooden chest.

The two women peered inside.

"Lilia, perhaps?" Julia exclaimed.

Nina lifted up an old photograph on top. The face of a lovely young woman with a radiant smile looked up at them from a candid photo.

Sandy-colored hair escaped from a bun at the nape of her neck, while a "Rosie the Riveter" red bandana restrained the rest of her long, curly locks. She stood in front of a sink piled high with white dishes and appeared to have turned around when someone caught her by surprise. Lilia beamed back at whoever had taken the photo.

Nina turned it over. On the back, there was an inscription.

"Lilia, 19."

She handed it to Julia and turned away. Nina was overjoyed as if she'd been reunited with a lost friend. The image liberated weeks of longing, and a single tear fell. She moved toward the rocking chair in the living room and took a moment to compose herself. She became overwhelmed by her deep, inexplicable connection to this stranger. Julia didn't seem to notice, as she was preoccupied with naming each item contained in the chest.

"Here's a set of old keys... looks like one of the kid's baby teeth, a broken watch, a few old coins and a locket." Julia was silent for a moment as she struggled to open it. A poignant sting came over Nina as she thought this small wooden box was possibly all that remained of Lilia's life, and it had been hidden in a dark space.

"Look at this!" Julia said. Nina, who rejoined her on the futon and stared at a picture of two young children inside the locket.

"This has to be David and Elizabeth." Nina looked at the tiny picture. "I recognize them from the other sketches in Lilia's journals. She really captured the essence of each of them," she said.

The cut out of the black and white photograph provided more details to fill out her imagination. Seeing the tiny humans solidified her determination to continue her search to find them to give them Lilia's letters.

"Let's look in the shoeboxes," Julia suggested.

"They're pretty filthy. Give me a moment, and I'll run downstairs and grab a clean box."

"I admit, I peeked inside," Julia told her when she returned with a clean box. "It looks like more journals rather than letters."

Nina transferred them into the larger clean box. She flipped through one and saw drawings she knew were from Lilia as a young girl.

"Can you imagine traveling cross-country back then?" she asked Julia. "I could barely stay content for a ride to my aunt and uncle's, an hour or less from Worcester, at that age. But then again, she was motivated by leaving behind that Mrs. Peck. I guess her uncle tried to make it fun for her," she concluded.

"Well, as interesting as these are, if we're going to the movies, we need to get cleaned up and head out the door. Otherwise, we will miss the next showing," Julia advised.

"You're right," Nina said. She picked up the photograph of Lilia and the locket and brought them into her bedroom and placed them, along with the two one-dollar bills, in the drawer of her nightstand for safe keeping.

Chapter Thirteen

For the next couple of hours the two friends ate popcorn and watched *Blazing Saddles* at a second-run movie theater in York. They finally came out, both laughing hysterically. Julia did her best Madeline Kahn impression. "I'm tired. Sick and tired of love," she sang off-key.

Nina dabbed her eyes. She couldn't remember the last time she had laughed this much. Or at all. They returned to Nina's apartment in high spirits, and shortly after they'd eaten, Ben joined them. Instead of crowding into the kitchen, Nina brought their coffee, Baileys, and dessert upstairs. Nina sat in her rocker while Julia made herself at home on the futon next to Ben. They gave him an update on what they found in the attic crawl space and showed him the picture of Lilia, the locket with David and Elizabeth, along with the two one-dollar bills.

With a mouth full of pastry, Ben motioned to the Baileys.

"Are you trying to tell me you'd like some?" Nina teased.

He nodded. "Sorry! That was rude, but Nina, these are so good."

"How about you, Julia?"

"Yes, I'd love some too. Ben's right. These are wonderful."

Regardless of how many times Nina had been praised for her skills, it was nice that they acknowledged their delight.

Nina poured some coffee into her cup but abstained from adding the Baileys. She was getting tired, and the wine was going to her head. She told Ben more about the movie and the plans she and Julia had made for the next day.

Around midnight, Nina began getting very sleepy but didn't want to interrupt Ben and Julia, so she sat quietly, trying to stay awake while the two talked about Boston and other things they had in common. Julia seemed quite interested in Ben, and Nina wondered if she was flirting or if she was imagining it.

About a half-hour later, she could barely keep her eyes open and asked if they minded if she went to bed. They apologized for keeping her up, and Julia offered to gather up the dishes and bring them downstairs so that their conversation wouldn't keep Nina up. Ben grabbed things, gave Nina a goodnight peck on the cheek, and joined Julia, who had already headed downstairs.

Nina tried to fall asleep, but all the coffee she drank to keep her awake suddenly kicked in. She stared at the ceiling in the dark. The whole day whirled through her mind as she thought of the wonderful fun and excitement of the day. It had been a long time since she'd enjoyed a day going to a movie and hanging out with a girlfriend. Then there were the treasures they'd discovered and seeing the faces of the strangers who had somehow become dear to her. Her mind raced to the odd money she found. Getting more information about that would have to wait until Tuesday, after the holiday, when the library would be open. Nina was confident there had to be some reference book on antique money.

All the thoughts that prevented her from slumber bombarded her, and the things she normally did to try shutting off sleepless nights were unavailable without being in her kitchen. She quietly got up to get a drink of water from the bathroom sink when she heard Ben and Julia talking in low tones through the register on the floor as she entered the room. She hesitated for a minute and stopped to listen when she heard Julia say her name.

"It doesn't surprise me. All our mutual friends thought he was out of her league when they started dating. She's adorable in an earthy sort of way, but Richard could work as a model if he wanted."

"Well, I think she's more than cute, and Richard is a jerk for treating her like he did," Ben told Julia. "Besides, what she looks like isn't the point. He clearly took advantage of her, and she's suffered for it."

"I know. You're right. All I'm saying is I wasn't as surprised as I pretended to be over the phone when she told me Richard divorced her. They always seemed like a mismatch from the first time she introduced him."

Nina left the bathroom without using the toilet and escaped into her bedroom. She never imagined that Julia thought Richard was "out of her league." Julia often told Nina that she was too good for Richard and he didn't deserve her. Now, she wasn't sure what to think. She lay awake for hours.

Despite a restless night, Nina got up early. Julia was sprawled on the futon, snoring. Both kittens slept beside her, having deserted Nina sometime in the night. She wanted to snatch them up, feeling wholly undermined by her friend. Unconvinced that she could conceal the impact of Julia's comments, she quickly got dressed and left the apartment, heading to a trail she'd previously passed by. Her staccato steps echoed on a wooden boardwalk that cut through a marshy area. She walked for almost an hour before turning around and returning home.

Julia was still sleeping when Nina got back. She busied herself making breakfast. She banged the pots and pans around as she cooked, letting them bear the brunt of her resentment. Lost in thought, the kitchen closed in around her as she remembered the things Julia had told Ben. The sharp whistle of the tea kettle releasing its steam cut though her thoughts. As she poured water into her teacup, she wished she too could let off steam.

When Julia finally got up, she came downstairs and sat down at the table.

"You're pretty quiet. Is everything alright?" she asked as Nina placed a plate of hashbrowns and poached eggs smothered in hollandaise sauce in front of her.

"I have a massive headache," Nina told her before suggesting they spend Sunday at a local apple festival. She imagined that attending the outdoor event would make it easier to mask her irritation than if she was sitting across from Julia, watching her eat the meals Nina herself had painstakingly prepared. Even so, now that Nina knew what Julia thought of her relationship with Richard, she wished she could hurry the day along.

After they returned from the festival, the two read through Lilia's journals and letters. But this time, when Julia mentioned how quiet Nina was, it was true—she did have a massive headache. Her head throbbed, so she excused herself and retreated to her bedroom.

When Julia left early Monday morning, Nina was relieved to see her go. She gave her a limp hug and watched her pull out of the driveway, waving to her as she headed towards Boston. Hurrying inside, she ran into Ben on the stairs as she headed back to her apartment.

"Hey, are you okay?" he asked, stopping to stare at her.

Nina couldn't speak and tried to move past him. He stopped her and forced her to look at him.

"I was just about to go get some breakfast. Why don't you come with me? My treat."

Nina paused for a minute but said nothing. She simply followed him and got in his car.

As he drove, Nina looked out the window, not even curious about where Ben was taking her. He parked his car at the same beach he'd taken Nina to when she was released from the hospital. Nina tried to make light of it.

"Is this your therapy office?" she asked.

"Kind of. Whenever I need to sit quietly and figure things out or even blow off steam, I come here. It happens more often than I care to admit."

"I somehow doubt that. You always seem in control," Nina told him.

"That's because you only see me occasionally and when I'm at my best. But I have my moments." They headed towards the beach and sat down to watch the ocean.

"So why the glum face? Did you and Julia have a fight or something?"

"No."

"Well, something clearly happened. When I saw you yesterday, you seemed really happy."

Nina laid her head on her knees.

"Julia and I have had our problems in the past, and last night, I heard you two talking downstairs in my kitchen. I found out what she really thought about my marriage to Richard. I'm furious she seems to think somehow I'm beneath Richard."

Ben was quiet for a moment, digesting Nina's revelation. "She didn't say you were beneath him exactly, but I can understand why you're hurt. Somehow, people seem to think men like Richard, those men who are exquisitely handsome and charming, are above treating others with respect and kindness. Believe me, I know how you're feeling more than I want to admit."

"It's really hard because I had started to trust her again. To be frank, it was one of the reasons I dropped out of school. It wasn't just that I had a hard time keeping up with tuition payments. But she wanted to stay roommates, and I just couldn't do it because I'd heard from others what she said about me behind my back."

Ben looked over at her with curiosity. He got up and reached out to Nina, who allowed him to pull her up to walk while talking. They strolled down the beach arm in arm.

"She was a real party girl at college," Nina continued. "She and her boyfriend Patrick organized keg parties just about every weekend. She thought I was making up excuses when I didn't participate because I had to get home to see my mother. But we lived in two different worlds. My mother needed me to take her grocery shopping and to the laundromat. I had to help her pay her bills and balance her checkbook. She'd never learned to do things like that before Papa died, and since she only spoke broken English, she was embarrassed to even try to reach out to anyone else but me. So what was I to do, go to one of Julia's keggers, or go home to care for my mother?"

"Did you tell her that?"

"Oh, yeah. We even fought about it once. But Julia couldn't seem to put herself in my shoes. She grew up never having to worry about any of those things. She used to tell me I was too young to be hanging out with my mother all weekend. But, of course, I wasn't hanging out. I was caring for the woman who needed me. Later I found out she discussed it with a few of our other friends behind my back. She seemed to want to prove a point that I was too sheltered or something. And then—there's the whole Patrick thing."

Ben looked at her quizzically.

"Patrick was a guy she met freshman year and dated throughout college. He was a nice guy, but like I said, they both partied way too much. He was killed in a car accident. It was really tragic, but the thing is, she would never talk about the fact he was drunk and killed a mother and two kids as well. It was as if the only thing that mattered was that *he* died, not anyone else. I mentioned that on the phone once, and she got really angry with me. We didn't speak for quite a while until Richard and I ran into her in Boston, and she invited us to double date with her and this guy Matt she was seeing. Somehow, after that, things were all smoothed over."

"I know you went to visit her a few weeks back, but before that, you two haven't seen each other for a while?" Ben asked.

"Only when I went to Boston over Labor Day. I guess we both got really busy, and after I married Richard, I didn't get to Boston very much unless it was for some kind of event he wanted to attend. She and Matt did come to our wedding, though. She was one of only a handful of people I invited. Now I'm really torn over whether I want to remain friends with her at all. The sad thing is, I really enjoyed her company. She seemed to like you a lot too so I hope I'm not spoiling something for you."

Ben grew quiet and withdrew his arm.

"Did I say something wrong?" Nina said, alarmed by his response.

" No, I..." Ben stammered. After a moment or two, he finally responded. "This is hard."

"Oh, you do like Julia, don't you?"

"Oh, no! That's not it." Ben took a deep breath before he continued. He stopped walking and sat down on the beach, put his arms around his body, and laid his chin on his knees. He was silent again, looking out over the ocean as if looking for answers to his deepest questions.

"I haven't dated anyone for a long time, and trust me Julia isn't my type."

"I hope you don't mind, but that's a relief. Can I ask why? I mean why you haven't been dating?"

Ben's brow furrowed and looked over at Nina searching her eyes. He cleared his throat before he began to speak.

"So, a long time ago, I was in love with someone like Richard. It kind of did a number on my head."

"Why? What did she do?" Nina asked.

After a moment, Ben told her, "It wasn't a *she*, Nina. The person I was in love with was a man. I'm gay. I fell for a guy just like Richard, and he almost destroyed me."

Nina was quiet for some time, processing what Ben had just told her. Finally, she took Ben's hand and held it tight. "Do you mind telling me about it? What happened?"

Ben squeezed her hand. "It was shortly after Byron committed suicide. I was so lost without him. I had signed a contract with the VSO and moved to the Burlington area. I didn't know anyone, and I was in so much pain; I couldn't stay by myself because the thoughts of what had happened to my brother haunted me. I wasn't out yet to anyone, not even myself. I knew I wasn't like Byron, but I couldn't admit that I had these feelings I couldn't understand. Then I met this man at a bar, and I was completely under his spell."

"In what way?" Nina asked.

"Well, when we first met, everything was so intense. From the moment we met, he wanted to know where I was at all times. But if I questioned him about where he was going or what he was doing, he acted as if his life was this big mystery. He insinuated he had some high-level position within the government and his life in Burlington was part of some secret mission. When I say that now, it seems ridiculous, but at the time I needed to get outside of my grief and confusion; I bought right into his tales. But more than that, he would show up at places like my job and pretend he was from another orchestra, scouting talent for a conductor or something. When I asked him why he did that, he tried to claim it was true."

It took Nina a moment to take in all that Ben had shared with her.

"May I ask, what was his name?"

"Allen," Ben took a deep breath. "Trust me, Nina, there is so much more I could tell you, and some of it reminds me of the way Richard treated you. But the details of my experiences with Allen are still painful even though it happened when I was young. I eventually found out he was married and had a wife and three kids. He told me he wasn't gay. He claimed he just liked to experiment."

"That's awful," Nina said.

"Look, I didn't mean to dump all this on you, but it's nice to confide in someone. I don't really talk about this to other people." Ben stood up. "Anyway, I was taking you out to breakfast, and now it's almost lunch. Let's get out of here. We can chat more at my favorite diner."

Nina got up and gave Ben a hug. "You're on," she told him gently.

Chapter Fourteen

The High Tide Diner was in nearby Portsmouth, New Hampshire, a few miles across the bridge on Route 1 and only a few miles from Kittery Point. As Ben drove, the two chatted easily.

"Well, Nina. Besides being an excellent cook, what else do you like to do?"

"That's a good question." Nina paused to think. "Cooking is the only thing I've ever been good at, and I've never considered other options. My parents were thrilled when I began cooking with my father when I was little, but I guess it was something I did to please them initially. But when others praised me too, it became a way to win people over."

"I know you and Julia met at Johnson and Wales but did you go there specifically because you wanted a culinary degree?"

"My high school guidance counselor recommend it to my mother. After my father died, Momma wanted to make sure I could care for myself."

"Was it hard being adopted?" Ben asked.

"Sometimes. I always knew how much my folks adored me but that didn't make up for the fact my mother's sisters and brothers weren't also thrilled they adopted me. My uncle used to tell my mother that I was really peculiar. I towered over my father by the time I was ten. Momma would say, '*Lei è la famiglia.*' She's family. I think my uncle finally accepted me only after he tasted my version of an old family recipe. Then, he came up and gave me an unexpected hug and said to Momma, '*Lei è la famiglia.*'"

"That's interesting. I remember walking in on my mother and my oldest sister, Theresa, one day when I came home from college. She was married by the time I graduated from high school and she wanted kids desperately. I think she must have had several miscarriages. I heard her asking my mother what she thought about adopting. But other than that, I've never given the subject much thought. I know all she ever wanted was to get married and be a mom. Now she has three boys and I think there might be days she wished otherwise. Especially because my nephew Micky is really a handful."

"So you have more than one sister?" Nina asked.

"Yeah, I have a younger sister, Emmy. She's in med school. I think each made the right choice for herself. They both seem happy, anyway," he told her.

"Med school? That's interesting. I've never had a woman doctor," Nina told him.

"Top of her class."

"Where does she go to school?"

"She wanted to stay close to home, so she's at the University of Vermont College of Medicine. I'd love for you to meet her someday. I don't get to see her often, but maybe I could invite her down when I have some time off."

"I would love that," Nina said.

BEN PARKED ON MARCY STREET, blocks from the Piscataqua River, and they walked south toward Prescott Park before reaching the diner. They took a booth in the corner and studied the menu while waiting for the waitress to bring the coffees they ordered.

"I'm starving. What are you going to have?" Ben asked Nina.

"I'd like something I wouldn't normally make for just myself, so maybe some Belgian waffles. The ones that come with strawberries, blueberries, and raspberries sound amazing. How about you?"

"They make the best sausage gravy and biscuits I've ever had. It's what I order every time I come here," Ben told her.

After the waitress took their order, there were a few moments of awkwardness before Nina got up the courage to ask Ben about something that had been bothering her.

"Not to go on and on about Richard, but you said something that has me curious, and I'm wondering if you could explain what you meant," she asked, wringing her hands.

"What was that?"

"I can't think of your exact words, but you said something like, you fell for a guy just like Richard. What did you mean by that?"

"I guess it's just that neither Allen nor Richard were initially what they seemed to be. While I didn't witness the two of you together very often, I have to admit the first time I saw you interact with one another, I was rather shocked," he told her. "It was after I moved in last November—around Thanksgiving as a matter of fact. I'd just come home from Vermont. I'm assuming you were with Richard's family?"

"Yes, I made the entire meal, of course."

"I was just about to go to bed and crossed the living room to shut off the lamp near the window when I saw the two of you in the back driveway."

"I remember that night well," Nina said. "I spent the whole day cooking for his family, and his father gave Richard a nice bottle of wine as a thank you as if Richard had done all the work."

"Is that what broke? What he was so mad about?" Ben asked her.

"No. I got out of the car and had my arms full of stuff to bring into the house. He went ahead of me, carrying nothing. I went to grab a bag, and I accidentally dropped it. The wine miraculously survived. It was a bottle of scotch that broke—Richard's favorite," she told him.

"At first, I didn't even see him there, but I saw you drop something. So I raised the window in my apartment and was about to call out to you to see if you needed help when Richard came into view and started yelling at you."

A crimson stain rose on her cheeks. "I'm glad I didn't know you saw all that." Nina looked away.

"These things happen, and marriage is hard. But I did think it was a pretty petty argument that night. To be honest, though, there was another time; it must have been before he moved out, and it showed what I suspect is his true character."

Nina looked back, determined to learn more.

"It was a time when he came up to collect rent. I had just come out of the shower and still had my robe on when I heard him knock at the door. When I answered the door, he asked if I could give him the rent because he was heading to the bank."

"What was so unusual about that?" Nina asked, confused.

"Nothing, really. It was more about his reaction when I told him I'd left my checkbook in my car. He got all huffy because he said he had to leave and couldn't wait. It's like I'd inconvenienced him on purpose. So I told him I could drop it off and leave it with his wife, and he rolled his eyes and said something like, 'Don't bother. I'll come back later.' It was strange."

"I'm learning new things about him every day. First, Richard betrays me, and now Julia."

"I know this is hard, but I don't think Julia betrayed you in the way Richard did. Julia seemed surprised that Richard would be attracted to you, based solely on your looks. But you have much more going for you, Nina. I think you are very attractive, but, more importantly, you're kind and strong and smart and talented. As Julia said, Richard is very handsome. But there's nothing deeper. He lacks integrity, and to me, that makes him very unattractive."

"I was always kind of uncomfortable with how some women fawned over him. Sometimes when we'd go out, I felt invisible."

"You are a natural beauty."

"If you say so," she said, smirking. "When we were in college, Julia often called me Twiggy because I'm tall and thin and wore my hair short. I can't help my body type any more than she can, and the only reason I wore my hair short was because I just got tired of it getting in the way when I was working."

"I honestly don't think that's what bothers her. Just look back a decade or so at who men considered sexy. Women like Marilyn Monroe graced the covers of all these magazines. Suddenly someone like Twiggy is taking over. I think Julia is jealous that suddenly the standards are quite different. Julia's pretty, but I wouldn't be surprised if she spends hours in front of the make-up mirror. There's nothing wrong with that, but I've observed that some women seem to think that's preferable to being more naturally pretty. Maybe because they feel like they have more control over their appearance. I'm not sure. But I wouldn't say her rather drunken confessions last night amount to a betrayal of you, but more of a betrayal of herself because apparently, she's pretty shallow."

Nina laughed so hard she spewed some of the coffee she was drinking.

BY THE TIME Ben dropped her off, Nina was sure she wanted to spend the day outdoors. It was such a beautiful fall day, with unseasonably warm weather. She practically sprinted up the stairs to her apartment. Once inside, she found Ginger asleep on the chair in the kitchen while Cinnamon was playing with a scrap of paper, tossing it like a ball in the air. As she went up to her living room, she noticed a message on the machine. Nina decided to ignore it for the time being because she was afraid it might spoil her good mood.

She heard the toilet running and went into the bathroom to jiggle the handle. She knew it was something she'd have to address soon because it was a waste of water. She wasn't sure how to fix the problem and didn't want to get caught up in worrying about it.

She returned to the living room, trying to decide what to do with the afternoon. It was futile to job hunt on a holiday week-end, but many other activities were off-limits financially. She decided to go for a drive. The first place that came to mind was the hour drive north to Old Orchard Beach.

Since moving to Maine, Nina had spent little time visiting the places tourists flocked to in the summer months. But her sudden decision, inspired by Lilia's letters, pleased her. She liked taking control of the day and would at least be doing something other than indulging the habit she'd fallen into of reading more letters. Nina gathered a warmer jacket and an old blanket and made a peanut butter and jelly sandwich before leaving her apartment.

As she opened the door to her VW, she looked up at the back of the house, towards the windows in Ben's apartment. It had never occurred to her that her private life with Richard would be visible to anyone else. She could understand how easy it was for Ben to look out and observe that night. A flash of fury overcame her for a moment as she remembered that night and Richard's lack of concern for her well-being. But she was determined not to allow thoughts of him or Julia to get in the way of enjoying the day.

Her thoughts were interrupted when she turned and noticed someone at a window in the other second-floor apart-ment. The girl had long, dark hair and seemed pretty young. When she realized Nina had seen her, she disappeared from view. The window belonged to Maddie McInnes's apartment. Since moving upstairs and taking over as landlord, Nina had noticed how elusive Maddie was. Other than the day Nina had knocked on the apartment door looking for some ice, she'd only encountered her when rent payments were due and once in the basement while doing laundry. She rarely heard noise of any kind, even coming from the room directly below her own bedroom, except for some music from time to time. It made her wonder who this young woman was and why it was always so quiet.

As she pulled away, she glanced up at the window and saw the young woman looking out again. *This place is full of mysteries,* Nina thought.

OLD ORCHARD BEACH was a place Lilia had referenced several times in her letters, and Nina wanted to see it first hand. Since Lilia wrote that Jake's mother had managed a motel right near the beach, she hoped to at least see the place where the two had met— if she could find it. So much time had passed since then, her chances of locating any helpful information were slim. But unlike Portland, the town of Old Orchard Beach was small and historical. Even if she couldn't locate anything that might seem familiar based on Lilia's letters, she could at least walk the beach or visit the pier.

Nina avoided the highway again. Richard had always driven when they traveled together, but she preferred the slower Route 1 rather than the hectic pace of the highway. She tried to convince herself it was because it was more scenic, which was partly true. In reality, however, there was a nagging realization that driving on the highway made her anxious, and that was something she was trying to avoid in her life right now.

She wished she had a map. Though she knew the general direction, she wasn't sure how to navigate to the beach itself. But she wasn't going to let that deter her. As she got closer, signs would surely direct her toward the beach.

Nina couldn't help thinking about all the things she and Ben had talked about earlier. She'd never met anyone else who was gay. Or at least she didn't think she had.

"They often punish men who are gay through sodomy laws," he had explained. "Some argue that these laws protect public morals and decency."

"But I thought all that changed, didn't it?" Nina asked.

"Unfortunately, no. Many still think of homosexuality as

sinful and reason enough to disown a person," Ben said quietly, looking around. "The law sees consensual sex as more of an issue of privacy, but we face a lot of discrimination even now."

Ben's revelations were interesting, and something Nina would never have considered. It made her appreciate the risk he took opening up to her and how much he trusted her to accept him.

Coming out of her reverie, she noticed signs pointing towards Old Orchard Beach. She turned onto Route 5 and headed east. She passed Wild Acres RV Resort. The sign caught her breath. That was a place Lilia had referenced in one of her letters. That was the very place where she and Billy were staying temporarily when Lilia met Jake at the beach.

She turned right on Temple Street and made another right when she reached Seaside Avenue. She imagined Lilia as a teenager riding her bike along the same route. The beautiful girl with the warm smile was so real to her at that moment. She parked on one of the smaller side streets on the south end of town, making a mental note that she'd parked on Oceana Ave so she could find her way back to her car. She grabbed her tote bag and headed to the sandy path at the end of the road.

She took off her shoes to feel the cool sand beneath her feet. Then she thought of the incident with Jake and the broken bottle and hastily put them back on. As she strolled along, Nina encountered very few people. Some kids were playing in the sand, and someone was collecting rocks or seashells, but those who might have ventured to the beach for a holiday appeared to have departed. It seemed as if, with the summer people gone, the town had settled into a more sedate routine.

She passed several motels that could have been the place Jake's mother managed, but she knew that finding it wouldn't help her solve the questions she had about Lilia and what became of her, David, and Elizabeth. Lilia's letters revealed that her contact with Jake's family ceased even before he was killed. The only family Lilia wrote about was her brother-in-law, Jesse.

Nina had walked for more than a half-mile along the shore when she saw an older woman poised at an easel. From behind, long, graying hair peeked out of a wide-brimmed straw hat. She wore an oversized men's plaid shirt and a paisley skirt. Her loose-fitting clothing seemed to be aimed for comfort. The woman held a paintbrush in one hand and a palette in the other and appeared to be painting the scene in front of her.

In several ways, she looked exactly how Nina envisioned Lilia would look if she were alive. She began to imagine a conversion with the woman. Perhaps it would start with a simple hello, and Nina would comment on her painting. After exchanging pleasantries, it would be easier to ask her about herself.

"I'm sorry to interrupt you, but you remind me of a friend," Nina would explain. *"Her name was Lilia Michaud."* That wasn't entirely accurate though. Lilia wasn't Nina's friend, no matter how invested Nina had become in her life.

"Sorry, dear, I've never met a Lilia, but there are certainly a lot of Michauds in Maine," the woman might say. *"What was her maiden name?"*

Nina startled. *What was Lilia's maiden name?*

"Uh, her husband, Jake Michaud, was killed in the war."

"Which war was that, dear? We've had more than our fair share."

"World War II. She lost him in 1944, I think." Nina grew flustered that even her imaginary conversation wasn't going well.

"Well, that was a long time ago," the woman might lament. *"This place has grown so much since those days. How old is your friend?"*

Nina considered, trying to remember Lilia's age and the years of the stories she related to the children. She did the math in her head and realized that if Lilia were alive, she would only be in her mid-fifties. Nina's eyes widened. She'd always thought of Lilia as a great deal older. Could she actually still be alive? Nina was so absorbed in thought, she didn't even realize the woman she was watching had gathered her easel and other belongings and was preparing to leave. When Nina finally noticed, her entire body stiffened, anticipating the practiced encounter. She froze in place, watching the woman move closer and closer to her. She wished she'd brought a book or some other prop to hide behind.

"Hello," the stranger nodded as she passed without stopping.

"Hi," Nina responded weakly, shifting her gaze to the sea.

Far in the distance, she spotted a small fishing boat navigating its way through the increasingly frothy white caps. It seemed to be headed towards the shore. She marveled at how those who navigated these types of vessels managed to endure the daily chores of making a living at the expense of the ocean. *Did they get used to the sea's antics and unpredictability, or did they confront each moment as it occurred? How did they ignore the rough waters that sometimes tried to eject them at a whim?* She watched as the boat came closer. Whoever was at the helm barely seemed to acknowledge the waves that crashed upon the rocks sending spouts of white, misty water high in the air above before being folded back into the sea. Nina shuddered. She knew of the tragedies that occurred, claiming the lives of even the most experienced sailors. *How was it possible to face the uncertainties of such a life? Did they know something that eluded her, a child who'd grown into a woman who was forever anxious and guarded?* She left the beach wondering how to cope with life's turmoil. Perhaps she should stop investing so much time in Lilia's life and start investing in her own.

Chapter Fifteen

When Nina arrived home from Old Orchard Beach she lay on the futon, thinking. She was unable to escape her pensive mood and eventually drifted off to a restless sleep.

She woke to an urgently persistent pounding noise. She thought she was dreaming but soon realized someone was indeed knocking on her apartment door. She stood. The throw rug beneath her feet was wet. She could hear water running, and as she approached the bathroom, she discovered the overflowing toilet.

The spare roll of toilet paper that usually sat on top of the tank had fallen into the bowl, forcing water to spill all over the bathroom. She stuck her hand into the bowl and removed the roll, tossing it into the waste can and shutting off the valve to the toilet.

The lip of the doorjamb in the small bathroom had kept much of the water contained. It had only spilled into her bedroom and living room. Instinctively, she knew the pounding on her door was because the water must have leaked into the apartment below.

Nina rushed downstairs. There was a young girl with a long

dark braid in her hair, the same girl she'd seen staring at her out the window earlier.

"I am so sorry! My bathroom flooded. Is your apartment ruined? How bad is it?" Nina asked frantically.

"It looks like it's raining inside."

"I'm really sorry. I can help you clean up. I just have to mop up my mess upstairs first."

"Okay. I want to get it cleaned up before Maddie gets home. She's kind of a neat freak!" she told Nina.

"What's your name?"

"Penny," she responded with hesitation.

"Well, Penny, I'll be down in a minute, if that's alright?"

"I'll get started. It's really not as bad as what you're probably dealing with," Penny assured her.

Back upstairs, Nina gathered as many towels as she could find and soaked up the water, wringing them out in the bathtub before reusing them again to absorb as much of the water as possible. A half-hour later, she finished the job.

Nina headed downstairs to help Penny. She knocked on the door and waited for a moment. Muffled voices came from inside.

Maddie stood with the door slightly ajar. "We're all set. It's all cleaned up," she told Nina brusquely.

"Are you sure? I'm happy to help," Nina told her and smiled.

"No, we're all set," she repeated and gently closed the door.

Nina stood there for a moment, completely baffled. Finally, she went back into her apartment, still mystified by Maddie's abrupt response. Nina knew there was possible damage to the ceiling, but she wasn't prepared to question her about it at that moment. One thing she did know, however, was that Maddie was hiding something, and it probably had to do with Penny.

NINA LOOKED at the clock and found it was nearly ten p.m. The last thing she ate was at breakfast with Ben, and she was starving. She warmed up some leftovers from the dinner she'd made for Julia's visit and carried it upstairs to sit on the futon while she ate.

Desperate to distract herself, Nina retrieved a letter from her nightstand that she'd meant to read earlier. It stood out from others because it was written on stationary far different than Lilia's, and it wasn't in an envelope.

She wrapped herself in her afghan and sat on the futon and began reading.

My Dearest Lilia,
I am able to write to you as our letters are no longer being censored. I wish I could tell you that my introduction to the E.T.O. was spectacular but that would be a lie. Even though months have passed, the memory of you as I left home the last time is seared into my heart. The only thing that keeps me going is my desire to hold you in my arms again.

You asked me to be frank about my experiences here. That is hard because I don't want to frighten you by the things I write. But I admit it is a relief to share these events with someone other than those also living through them because they are as disillusioned as I am.

Once we left the train depot in Maine, a ferry transported us to a place in New Jersey. We arrived in the early morning hours but it already felt like and eternity. It was knowing I might never see you again that made my heart so heavy.

We were brought to a peer in Manhattan then troops were loaded onto a ship. Men were crowded into compartments so tight we had to walk sideways to get from one end of the compartment to the other. Many of us were seasick the entire time crossing the ocean. I've had to tighten my belt buckle so much because I've lost so much weight in such a short time.

When we arrived in Europe, they loaded us into trains. Days later, we reached France, arriving at the port city of Le Harve. All around us the harbor there were ships that had sunk. The stench of death hung in the air.

We were all exhausted having spent about forty hours traveling without much sleep. The only thing that kept many of us going was the enthusiasm of those that cheered us as the trains passed by.

They piled us into trucks and we traveled throughout Belguim and then into Germany to a place called the Hurtgen Forest. This is where the blood-iest battles of the war were taking place.

I could hear artillery being shot all around us. Since my assignment was to carry heavy weapons, I knew I would be heading to the front lines.

As tired as I was it was another sleepless night knowing that in the morning we would be marched to the front lines the next day. I was terrified to see all the dead bodies of Germans all around us but worse were these wounded. I can't begin to describe what I saw with injuries so horrible I wanted to flee.

I thought it couldn't get any worse but I was naive. When we reached our unit it was nightfall. The moonless night meant we had to approach in complete darkness. As we settled into the empty foxholes the Jerries shot at us with long-range railroad guns oblit-erating every tree that once grew on the wooded hilltops.

The things I've witnessed here would appall you. We've been forced to do horrendous things. Even though we aim to capture our enemies we know it is kill or be killed. For me the most awful things is looking into the eyes of these young boys knowing they would kill me if I didn't kill them and watching as their life ended. I fear I'll never forget what I have seen or been forced to do.

When I hear artillery shells screech through the air I pray as I've never prayed before. I hear them in my sleep and even when I block my ears.

But that is nothing compared to the other insane things I've seen. The empty eyes of soldiers being led by the hand to the rear of the battle still haunts me. But these thoughts remind me daily of just how precious life is.

Lilia, our time together seems like a dream now. I'd gladly trade any part of civilian life for what I've experienced over here in the past eight months. This bloody war is hell on earth.

I could be home with you in Portland. Instead, I am surrounded by misery. The people here are tired and hungry. Young and old are dirty and starving. They beg for our scraps. For over half a decade now they have lived like this, while back at home, many take food and shelter for granted.

Soldiers give them things like choco-late bars but what good is that as they have abandoned hope and we have none to offer them.

I hope when you read these words, you will know I only write them to let you know my darling Lilia that it is your love that sustains me. Thoughts of holding you once again bring me to the other side of each day. The memory of your laughter and bright smile ease a life that has quickly grown weary and I am forever grateful I had the good sense to marry you.

Stay well my dearest and I will come home as soon as I'm able. Regardless of what happens, always remember that I will cherish you forever.

Your loving husband, Jacob

Nina was in tears by the time she finished reading Jake's letter. His anguish left her aching to reach through time and comfort Lilia, who must have been so despondent. She wiped her eyes and thought about the misery this twenty-two-year-old man had experienced. He wanted to live. His desire to come back home and experience once again the life and love he was forced to leave behind scorched her heart.

Nina found a tissue and blew her nose. She began rummaging

through the shoebox for the envelope so she could return the letter to its proper place. When she found it, she gasped. The postmark was hard to make out. All she could read was 1944 and the words "Service A.P.O." She stared at the middle of the envelope where Jake had written their address— the address where he and Lilia lived before he went off to war.

Chapter Sixteen

Nina paced the floor of her living room, trying to think of what to do. Back and forth, she went over and over again. Her agitated motions caused Cinnamon to reach out to play with the leg of her pants each time Nina passed her. Finally, she picked her up, kissed the top of her head, and returned her to the floor where Cinnamon resumed attacking her leg. Nina laughed. After she'd almost stepped on the kitten's paw a few times, she decided to go down to the kitchen and make herself a cup of tea.

While the water boiled, she sat clutching the envelope, rereading the four lines scrawled in the middle. She knew Lilia had likely moved long ago, but the connection to her past was more solid now, and Nina wanted to go to Portland as soon as she could.

The whistle from the kettle blew, and Nina moved to the stove in a trance. She watched the steam rise from her cup as her tea steeped, wondering what it would be like to meet Lilia face to face. She stared into the cup, wishing it would reveal her future, but all it offered was a faint, wavy reflection.

The ups and downs of the past few days made her head spin. She thought about trying to distract herself by listening to the radio, but instead, she reached over to pick up the book tucked away in the corner of the kitchen counter. She had no idea what this book *Carrie* was about, or if she'd even like it, but she was intrigued enough to turn to the first page.

Nina sat reading for the next few hours, glued to her seat. Her tea was long gone, and she had to use the bathroom, but she was so taken by the characters in King's story of Carrie White, a cowed teenage girl who possessed telekinetic powers, she was reluctant to get up and move.

The sound of Ben coming up the stairs broke the spell, and Nina put the book down. As she heard him arrive in the hallway, she opened the door wide before remembering that she had changed into her nightclothes.

"I've been hoping you'd come home soon."

"What's up? Is everything okay?" he asked.

"Better than okay. Can you come back once you've put your instrument away?"

"Sure. Now you have me wondering. Give me a minute," he said and walked down the hall.

Nina rushed upstairs and slipped into a pair of jeans and a sweater. Seconds after arriving back in the kitchen, there was a light knock on her door, and Ben entered without waiting for Nina to open it.

"Can I get you a cup of tea?" she asked.

Ben pulled a chair from the table and sat down. "Yes. So what has you grinning from ear to ear?"

"Look on the table." Nina gestured toward the envelope. Ben picked it up and studied it for a moment.

"Wow! This is right in the neighborhood of the Portland Symphony. Are you going to try to locate the place?"

"I am," Nina told him as she put a cup in front of him. "I'm thinking about heading to Portland tomorrow if I can get up the nerve. Do you want any milk or sugar?"

"No, this is fine. Jeez, I'd offer to tag along, but I have plans," Ben told her.

"I was hoping we could go together," Nina admitted. "But, I don't want to wait. Chances are, it might even be a parking lot by now.

"That address can't be too far from the symphony building because it's on Congress Street."

"Really?"

"It's a nice neighborhood to take a stroll. I'm sure you'll have no problem getting around."

Nina was quiet for a moment. "I could wait, but I think I will go tomorrow. After that, I have to start job hunting again, but I'll go out of my mind if I don't check this out first."

Ben picked up the book Nina had set on the table. "Are you reading this?" he asked.

"Yeah. I just started. It's pretty wild."

"I read it this spring when it first came out. Wild is right. I like the guy's style and have to admit there were times I couldn't put it down, but it was also really disturbing."

"I know. I'm wondering if I want to keep reading it, but I'm having a hard time stopping. I mean, that poor girl. And what a wretched mother! It made me realize how lucky I was to have been adopted by two loving people."

"I can't even imagine what that is like. Being adopted, that is. Are you still in touch with your aunts and uncles?"

Ben's comment reminded Nina of her childhood. She would often just sit on the couch reading or playing with whatever toy she brought along trying to stay out of their way.

"No, they were all much older than my mother. She was what they called a change-of-life baby. By the time I graduated from high school, most of them had died, or were old, or had moved away. Then there was this thing that happened even before my father died," she told him.

"What was that?"

"I had an uncle who was an alcoholic. Uncle Joe was sweet as pie most of the time, but often, he turned so nasty that parents started to refuse to visit other relatives if he was going to be there. It caused some really hard feelings," Nina said. "I remember my mother crying about my aunt Angie. She hated Joe and how he treated her sister."

"Your aunt stayed with him?" Ben asked.

"Yeah. After my cousins left home, the situation got worse. Angela was an excellent mother, but she was terrified of my uncle. Once, when I was about eight, my folks took me to a cookout at my aunt Stella's house, and Uncle Joe was there with Auntie Angela. At the time, I didn't understand what was happening. Joe started to yell at Angie, and my father defended her. Then Joe started calling Papa names and told him to mind his own business. Then my other uncle, who was married to Stella, chimed in and told Joe to leave. Angie didn't know what to do and started to cry, and all I remember was my mother started swearing at him in Italian. I'd never seen her so mad. My father had to practically hold her back."

"I can't say I've ever experienced anything like that, but I know it happens. It makes me appreciate my folks even more. I'm fortunate because they didn't freak out even after I told them I'm gay. I was so worried they would disown me, but they've been amazingly supportive. Maybe because they'd already lost Byron, they were determined not to lose me as well."

"It's beyond difficult to lose someone you love. I used to worry all the time that something would happen to my mother, especially after Papa died. Since my aunts and uncles weren't exactly in favor of them adopting me, I was afraid they would send me back to the orphanage."

They sat quietly for a few moments, and Nina let out a sigh. "I never realized this, but my folks missed out on a lot of family stuff because of Joe and how he felt about me," Nina told Ben. "Even though some of the others didn't approve of my parents adopting me, they at least respected my parents' decision—but not Joe. He made fun of me and thought I wouldn't know what he was saying because he spoke in Italian, but I knew. "I once asked my father what *brutti occhi erdi* meant, and he asked me where I heard that. So I told him that Uncle Joe called me that."

"I'm sorry, my Italian is rusty," Ben joked. "What does that mean?"

"Sorry. It means ugly green eyes. My father was so angry, but it wasn't the first time I'd overheard comments. Even my aunt Stella said, 'She looks like a Jerry or a Paddy.' I thought she was talking about my name and couldn't figure out why anyone would suggest to my parents that they should have named me Jerry or Patty. But when I was a teenager, I realized that Jerry was code for German, and it was Paddy, not Patty. They were trying to guess my ethnic background."

"That's sad," Ben told her, shaking his head. "You were a child that was loved and wanted by a couple. I'll never understand how anyone could find a way to sully that."

"That was mild compared to the jokes about my height and eye color. It was as if anyone that didn't have brown eyes was somehow evil. I used to wish for brown eyes all the time."

"Your eyes are beautiful! They're your most striking feature."

"Richard used to tell me that all the time when we first met. 'Your eyes are like the color of frost,' he used to tell me. At first, he seemed to mean it as a compliment but over time, he started making it sound like my eyes made me look cold and unfeeling. He said it often enough; it was like he thought I could simply change the color at will or something."

"The more I learn about him, the more I think you're fortunate that things ended. I know it's been painful, but people like that deliberately say things to make others feel bad about themselves. And they take advantage of their vulnerabilities." Ben reached out and took her hand and squeezed it. "But, families are strange, and sometimes, you just have to make your own family. Did you ever consider trying to find your other mother?"

"Not really. My mother told me my birth mother died in delivery, and my father was young and couldn't take care of me, so I was put in St. Anne's Orphanage when I was about six months old."

Nina was touched by his kindness and smiled in appreciation.

She never thought much about her strange and complex family life, but for some reason, Ben seemed more like family than many of her aunts and uncles. He was right, she thought. *Sometimes you do just have to make your own family.*

Chapter Seventeen

Nina navigated her Beetle down Congress Street, clutching the paper in her hand where she'd scrawled Lilia's Portland address. She gulped when she saw the sign: Munjoy Bakery. The hour-plus drive from Kittery seemed a total waste of her time and gas.

The parking lot on the east side of the building was almost full, but there was an available space between two other vehicles. She pulled in with the intention of turning around to return home. But, once she stopped her car, she sat staring at the brick wall of the building, immobilized by her disappointment.

The October sun reached inside the car's interior and began to displace the momentary fog that had beset her. Ben had told her that the Munjoy Hill neighborhood of Portland was a lovely area for a stroll. She turned off the engine and opened the car door, stretching her body after the long drive.

The salt air of the nearby ocean beckoned her east, and she walked one tentative step at a time, allowing her body to lead her. Finally, she walked as far as she could on Congress Street and reached the trail with a sign indicating the Eastern Promenade. The trail could be taken north or south along the shoreline and provided access to the sea.

Nina unzipped her jacket and let the breeze refresh her as she ambled along. When she reached the point where she had to determine which way to go, she paused. Looking north, there was a dock lined with dozens of colorful boats moored to their temporary home. An inviting beach with sand the color of golden caramel stretched to the south. Straight ahead, however, there was a rocky outcropping where flat stones formed a path towards the sea. Nina decided to move straight forward and explore whatever lay in that direction.

She reached a stone path made of sea-worn boulders. She climbed up on the one closest to her to give herself a better view. Flashes of light played off the surf, and graceful seagulls danced with the surf before catching a meal. The waters off Casco Bay were teaming with life that thrived in the salty brine.

She walked ahead, careful not to disturb the gray seals that rested on rocks. She stopped and stood not far from them. A large male raised his head momentarily as if to eye the intruder. Then, sensing no danger, he must have signaled to the others they should remain to bask in the sun.

Nina sat down on one of the flat boulders closest to the sea. She was uncharacteristically tempted to dangle her feet over the edge, but ultimately, she kept them tucked up close. Below her, she observed two large boulders embedded deep in the sand. They formed an immovable barrier for the sea life trapped in a shallow pool between them. A large swath of mussels with their violet-blue shells had attached themselves to the rocks while a horseshoe crab tried to move forward, lurching on a wet, sandy bed between two rocks, struggling to find its way to the sea. Several strands of seaweed floated on top of the pool, causing playful shadows to appear on the sand below. As they moved, Nina could see sand dollars that would be washed away with the next high tide that would overpower the fragile creatures trapped within the shallow enclosure.

Nina crossed her legs and leaned forward trying to mitigate the hardness and inflexibility of her chosen seat. She looked off to the south, noticing that the ocean ahead was dotted with small, lush islands miles from the shore. Their isolation from the mainland made her curious about whether they were inhabited. And if they were, did those who lived on those enclaves wish the sea that flowed between their lands could be bridged? Or were they happy to find their own way? Wherever she looked, the vast Gulf of Maine stretched before her. Whitecaps formed out in the ocean as the wind blew. Clouds were forming on the horizon. She smiled at the unpredictability of New England weather.

The rumbling in her belly told her she needed to find something to eat before long. She waited a while since she was acclimated to the warm air that balanced the coolness of the surface beneath her. But soon the hunger overtook her, and she got up to leave.

On her way back to her car, Nina felt foolish that she had forgotten that Lilia had sold their business after her uncle got ill. Of course, Lilia didn't live or work there anymore. She shook her head, wondering how she could have convinced herself that she would find Lilia that day.

As she approached the lot where she'd parked, wonderful aromas wafted through the air from the Munjoy Bakery, the same property where Lilia had had her restaurant. The smells were familiar and comforting, as though they came from her own kitchen, inviting her to explore further.

Once inside, she surveyed the long row of display cases lined with a wide array of luscious goodies. Nina's mouth watered. She wasn't sure if she wanted something sweet or savory, but she knew the choice would be difficult no matter what.

She joined a line of people waiting to be served, so she had some time to think about her selection. By the time she'd almost reached the counter, she'd narrowed it down to either the cinnamon- and sugar-topped cardamom tea cake, a blueberry, lemon, and thyme muffin, or maple pecan schnecken. She was torn. She'd never had schnecken before, and it looked delicious. The perfectly round pastry was smaller than a sticky bun but somewhat similar. The pecans looked like they were glazed, perhaps with maple syrup, and that combination was mouthwatering. Yet adding thyme to blueberry and lemon was also intriguing. She'd never considered such a combination. She stood there lost in thought while the young woman behind the counter waited on the man in front of her.

"May I help you?" she asked him.

"I'll have two apple cider donuts, please," he told her. That was one of Nina's fall favorites.

When it was her turn to order, Nina said, "I'll have two apple cider donuts and one of the maple pecan schnecken," Nina blurted out. "Do you have coffee by any chance?" she asked, digging money out of her purse and handing it to her.

"No, I wish we did, but there's a great little diner right across the street on Merrill Street that serves coffee to go. It's close enough to walk to," she told Nina. "Turn right when you go out the door, and then take a left. It's two doors down on the left side of the street. Tell Lilia Bridget sent you,"

Nina froze. She turned back and stared at Bridget whose attention was already on the next customer in line. Nina hurried out of the bakery and headed towards her car. Her mind raced. It couldn't possibly be a coincidence. She took her bag of pastries and went towards her car. She wasn't sure whether to get back in or try to go to the diner.

She opened the door and sat in the driver's seat, trying to think. She mindlessly ate the donuts she had craved just moments ago. *Tell Lilia Bridget sent you.* That's what the young woman said. *It had to be her, didn't it?*

Now that she might actually meet her, what would she say? Would she panic and make a fool of herself as she did the other day at the beach, feeling helpless to get the words out? She sat in the safety of her car for a while. Finally, she decided she had to at least see if it was her.

Nina forced herself to get out. Once back on the street, she made a right, then a left turn as Bridget had instructed. She stopped when she spotted the entrance and stared at the sign for Dizzy's Dinner. Nina knew she had found her.

From the outside, Dizzy's Diner looked like a throwback to the American classic so popular decades before. Through the large glass windows, Nina could see the traditional Formica counter-tops, porcelain tiles, and black, leather-like booths, reminding her of one of her favorite diners in Worcester. The wood paneling was covered with pictures of various seafaring scenes, and the terrazzo floor was flecked with black, teal, and light blue, which matched the wall art colors.

As Nina entered, a small bell jingled announcing her arrival. The smells rivaled the bakery she had just left, and she found herself looking around in complete disbelief, unable to accept that she might actually meet Lilia herself.

A few patrons were sitting on the stools at the counter, and a couple sat in one of the booths. No one was behind the counter, and Nina wondered if she should take a booth or just approach the counter.

From the kitchen, Nina heard a woman's voice.

"Oh, Walter! You're awful. I will have to slap your hand if you don't stop!"

A beautiful woman in her mid-fifties stepped through the door. She had the same brilliant smile as in the photo, and Nina had no doubt that this was Lilia.

"May I help you?" Lilia said, looking at Nina.

"Can I get a coffee to go?"

"Of course." Lilia laughed. "Did Bridget send you?"

"Yes, but actually, I have a long drive back home. Maybe I could have it here instead," Nina said, stalling for time.

"Make yourself comfortable, and I'll bring it to your table," Lilia said, motioning to one of the booths.

Nina took one of the empty booths towards the back. She settled in and waited for Lilia to bring her coffee.

"So, where are you traveling from that you have such a long drive home?" Lilia asked as she placed a mug in front of Nina along with a small pitcher of cream.

"Kittery." Nina waited for a reaction.

Lilia filled the mug with the steaming, brown liquid. "Well, that's not too far, especially on a day like today. I'm sure it will be a lovely drive."

"Do you know the area?" Nina pressed.

"I'm familiar enough," Lilia told her. There was a sudden uproar in the kitchen. It sounded like something breaking, and Lilia excused herself quickly and went to see what had happened.

Nina told herself to take slow breaths as she waited for the chance to engage with Lilia again.

"Walter, what have you done, old man?" Lilia could be heard asking.

"Sorry, love. It was an accident. I didn't realize the handle was so hot."

"Here, let me help you clean it up. I guess we won't have a soup for our lunch special today. That's too bad because it sells so well." Lilia jokingly chastised him.

"I'll make it up to you later," he told her, and the two of them giggled.

Nina stayed glued to her seat, trying to think of a way to bring up Kittery and her reason for being there once again. She knew Lilia would have to interact with her again, either when she brought the check or when Nina went to the counter to pay. But these were the kind of moments that Nina often wrestled with—moments that left her immobilized.

For a brief moment, Nina thought about leaving some money on the table to cover the cost of her coffee and a small tip. But Lilia emerged from the kitchen and approached one of the other tables with a fresh pot of coffee before she returned to Nina's table.

"Can I warm that up for you?"

Nina covered the mug with her hands. "No thanks."

"Is something wrong with the coffee?"

"No! Not at all. It's perfect." Nina drew in a deep breath, not knowing what to say next. "Except—I didn't come here for coffee. I came here to see you," she blurted out.

"Me? Why would you come to see me?"

"I live in the same house you used to live in," Nina told her. "My ex-husband's aunt and uncle used to own it. Their name was Hirst."

"Oh, my goodness! I thought maybe the place had been torn down or something. No one seemed to want it. But why would that make you want to come to see me?" Lilia asked.

"Well, when I married their son several years ago, we bought it and renovated it."

"You said ex-husband. Did you divorce him?"

"Yes."

"Robert, no Richard, wasn't it? I only knew him as a teenager because they rarely visited Ida, even after Henry died. Well, surely you didn't come all the way to Portland to discuss your ex-husband."

"I've wanted to meet you for quite a while."

"Why is that?" Lilia was looking more and more puzzled.

"I found your letters and read them. Well, many of them anyway. I'm so sorry! To be honest, I thought you had passed away."

Lilia slid into the booth, taking a seat opposite Nina as she continued. "You see, when Richard and I divorced, the only way I could keep the house was to move up to the third-floor attic apartment. I discovered your letters by accident one day."

"Oh, dear! I had forgotten all about those; I left in a hurry." Lilia paused for a moment before asking, "You read all of them?"

Nina put her head down and folded her hands together.

Lilia patted Nina's hands and told her, "For such a long time, I hung onto the past and it made me miserable. Initially, I left them there because the Kings forced me to leave once they put Ida in a nursing home. But in some ways they did me a favor because it forced me to start over, so don't fret."

Nina lifted her eyes and gazed at Lilia intently. "But what about David and Elizabeth?" Nina asked urgently. "Don't you want them to have the letters?"

"Not really," Lilia told her.

"But what if you find them?" Nina implored her. "Don't you want them to read the letters for themselves?"

Lilia smiled. "One day, not long after Walter and I opened the diner, a handsome young man strolled in and hugged me as soon as he saw me. It was David. He lived in a small town west of Boston, and someone told him about a diner in Portland called Dizzy's. So that's how he found me."

"Oh! That's wonderful! But what about Elizabeth?" Nina said, wondering if it was impolite to ask.

"That wasn't possible. She was already gone when David found me."

"Gone?"

"Yes, Lizzy moved to England. But, Walter and I will be visiting her sometime next spring. She's a nurse and finds it hard to get away from work and her family."

"That's wonderful! Are you sure you don't mind that I read them? They kind of kept me busy and distracted from all the misery Richard put me through."

"Did you find the money?" Lilia asked her.

"Yeah. I did. I'm sorry. I spent some of it, but I can pay you back once I get on my feet again."

"My dear, that money is yours. I left it there. I hid it because I didn't want the Kings to find it."

"But it was more than three hundred dollars! That's a lot of money."

"Oh, you must have found the chest with my trinkets. Of course. I think I stuck that close to the shoeboxes. I was talking about the other box with Henry and Ida's money."

"What? I'm confused."

"Henry had squirreled away a lot of cash. They'd both lived through the Depression and were leery of banks. So they stashed money all over the house. Then, after Henry died, Ida told me about a safe in the carriage house. She had me get it and keep it in the main house for expenses. Much of that was gone by the time I left. But unless someone moved it, there was some money in a small safe that we kept on hand for emergencies."

Nina was astonished. "Don't you want it?" she asked.

"My uncle Billy left me more than enough both from my parents and money he'd put aside. Plus, I never considered that money mine."

Nina was shocked.

"I'm not sure what your experience was with them, but in my opinion, I thought they were awful people for the way they treated Ida," Lilia said. "I hope that doesn't offend you."

"No, it doesn't."

"They gave me no warning at all. One day they showed up and said they were putting Ida in a nursing home. Mr. King told me to gather my belongings and be ready to leave the next day. I had no car or place to go. So, I never told them about the safe and then I hid money in the third-floor attic. So, now—I guess it's all yours."

Nina didn't know what to say and was quiet for several moments.

"Can I ask you something? If you had that money from your uncle, why did you stay working for Ida?"

"In the beginning, I was waiting for the courts to probate the matter, and I needed something to do. I was so miserable about losing Jake and then the kids. I'd already sold the old restaurant after my uncle got ill. Things were pretty complicated, especially after he got sick," Lilia told her.

"I'm sure that's an understatement."

"I saw that the old couple needed me, and it was a place to live and work while things got sorted out. Then when Henry passed, I wanted to stay because I loved Ida. She was truly a beautiful soul."

The two spoke for a few more minutes before Lilia said, "I have to get back to the kitchen. Both of my waitresses are out for a while. The sweeties both had babies just weeks apart. But if you want, maybe the next time I have a day off, Walter and I could come for a visit."

"I would love that!"

"Here. Write down your phone number, and we'll take a drive down to Kittery one day soon," Lilia told her, handing her a pen and one of her checks from her pad. "Don't worry. The coffee is on the house." Lilia reached over to give her hand a quick squeeze, then she returned to the kitchen.

Chapter Eighteen

When Nina arrived home, she noticed Ben's car in the front driveway. She pulled in beside him and he greeted her with a big grin. "I feel like a traitor! I just shopped at King's," he said as he unloaded groceries from his car.

"That's alright." She grinned back at him. "It's a good place to get anything except bread or pastry."

"Did things go well?"

"I found her! The address on the letter is for a place that's now a bakery, but Lilia has a small diner just around the corner. I talked with her this morning, Ben! She's alive, and so are David and Elizabeth."

Nina helped Ben gather his groceries, and they headed upstairs to his apartment. Once inside, she handed him the various items while he put them away, and she brought him up to date as they worked.

"Lilia is amazing. We didn't get to talk a long time because she was a bit short-staffed, but I gave her my phone number, and she promised to call and maybe even come visit."

"I hope I get to meet her," Ben said.

"Wait, there's more. But before I tell you, I want to check on the kitties. How about you meet me at my place, and I'll make us some tea and tell you the rest."

"You're on," he said. "I'll be there in a few."

As Nina walked down the hall, she glanced over at the door to Maddie's apartment. She wondered briefly what was happening with Penny, the young girl who seemed so eager to help her mop up water just a day ago.

When Nina opened her door, she found the kittens cuddled up together on a chair in the kitchen. She put the kettle on for tea and heard Ben gently knock. "It's open," she called to him.

She grabbed milk from the fridge and placed a saucer down on the floor to entice the kittens to leave their spot. She picked up Ginger and snuggled her before placing her in front of the milk. Ben did the same with Cinnamon and sat quickly before either could return.

"What kind of tea would you like— regular or herbal?" she asked him.

"I'll take the herbal. I can't wait to hear more. It's amazing that you found her. I was convinced she was dead because she left all her stuff here."

"I guess when Mr. King decided to put Ida in a nursing home, he practically threw Lilia out. She didn't go into great detail, but he acted as though she was somehow taking advantage of Ida, and made her leave that very next day. But the letters aren't the only thing she left behind. Apparently, Henry had a habit of hiding money, and there's another strongbox in the attic crawl space that she refused to tell the Kings about."

"Doesn't she want it?" Ben asked in amazement.

"She said it doesn't belong to her, and since I bought the house and now own it apart from Richard, it's mine to keep. I'm starting to wonder if there might be other places where he stashed money. Maybe the carriage house contains more valuables. I have to wonder if Richard suspected that as well, and that's why he wanted the contents of the carriage house."

"But why didn't he try to get those things out before divorcing you?" Ben asked.

Nina stopped to think. "He probably never counted on me getting the house in the first place. He was really shocked when the judge ruled in my favor. It does make sense that he knew something because, on more than one occasion, Richard claimed he had "personal items" in there he wanted, like tools and such, so I just let him go in there and take things because I was so tired of arguing with him. Once, I watched him from the window in my apartment downstairs, and he came out without anything, looking pretty pissed." Nina paused to think for a minute. "You know, when I went in the carriage house a while back, one of the panes of glass to the back door was broken. I wonder if Richard did that when I was out."

"It wouldn't surprise me. Do you want some help retrieving the strongbox from upstairs? Now that you've told me, I can hardly wait to see what's inside."

"That would be wonderful. I'm not looking forward to crawling in there again, but from what Lilia indicated, it will be totally worth it. While I'm thinking about the bathroom, I don't know if I told you, but I accidentally flooded it the other day, and this girl Penny from the second floor, was the one to alert me to it. She's Maddie's sister, but something seems off. When I finished mopping up the water, I went down to help Penny, and Maddie answered the door. She was almost hostile and wouldn't accept my help. She practically slammed the door on me. I didn't even get a chance to see if there was damage to the ceiling."

"I'm not totally surprised. I don't know the whole story, but I had the day off and saw Maddie and a young girl get out of Maddie's car. She had her arm around her and kind of escorted her upstairs."

"Penny looks like she's only about fourteen or fifteen. I wonder why she isn't in school."

"I've wondered the same thing. I did hear them talking one day about a month ago while it was warm enough to have the windows open. I don't know if I heard it correctly because it was sometimes a bit muffled. And honestly, I wasn't trying to over-hear anything, but it's difficult when their apartment windows are close to mine. I think it has something to do with their father. All I'm sure of is that Maddie told Penny several times that she wouldn't let Penny go back there."

"That seems pretty serious," Nina agreed.

The two sat quietly for a moment, each in their own thoughts. When she finished her tea, Nina gently poked Ben's arm. "Before I try to get that strongbox, I'm going to put on an old sweatshirt I found earlier. I'll let you know when I'm ready."

Dressed in long pants, a sweatshirt, a knitted cap and gloves, Nina called Ben upstairs. She stood before him modeling her outfit.

"What do you think? Am I spider proof?"

"You look like you're dressed for combat." He laughed.

"I am! I must look ridiculous, but it's pretty nasty in there. I'm ready! Let's do it."

"What about the kittens?" Ben asked.

"Good thinking."

The two friends returned to the kitchen and managed to scoop up Cinnamon and Ginger and secure them in Nina's bedroom. In the bathroom, Nina removed the fabric curtain from the sink and crouched on all fours, then lowered herself to her belly.

"Well, here I go. If I don't come out soon, call someone to come get me, please," she teased.

"You bet," he promised.

Once inside the dark space, Nina let her eyes adjust for a moment looking for the silver-colored metal box. Off to the left, she spotted it among the dust and cobwebs. Doing her best not to let her fears overcome her, she inched herself forward on her hands and knees. As tempting as it was to look inside once she reached it, she grabbed it and began backing up to exit the space. She made sure nothing remained in the area to avoid climbing in again. She felt a sudden pain in her knee and let out a scream.

"What just happened?" Ben yelled, alarmed.

"I think I just got a splinter," she told him. "It really hurts."

"How close are you to the door? Can you make it?".

"I'm going to have to," she told him. "I can't stay in here."

Nina poked her head out and handed Ben the metal box, extracting herself from the crawl space. Then, pulling up her pant leg, she saw a long thin line of wood embedded below her knee cap. Tears welled in her eyes, and she looked up at Ben.

"Do you have some tweezers?" he asked her.

"Somewhere. I think they're in the medicine cabinet along with some hydrogen peroxide."

"Let's get that taken care of first."

Ben gathered the hydrogen peroxide, tweezers, and a bandage on a clean towel. He carefully washed and sterilized Nina's wound and the tweezers before attempting to pull the splinter out of her leg. Nina kept her eyes turned away and gritted her teeth. After several attempts, Ben finally managed to grab hold of its edge and pulled it out. She groaned loudly but allowed Ben to wash the area and put on a small bandage.

"Well, I hope whatever is in the strongbox is worth it," he told her, wiping a stray tear from her cheek.

After helping Nina to the couch, he disappeared into the bathroom to close the attic door before joining Nina again in the living room.

"Do you want me to let the kitties out of the bedroom or leave them in there?" he asked.

"They're not crying so let's leave them for a while," she said, rubbing her knee.

"Do you need a minute?" Ben asked her.

"I'm all set," Nina assured him. "You open it. I'm too nervous!"

Ben wiped a thick layer of dust off the box and lifted the cover.

"Well, this certainly looks worth getting a splinter for," Nina told him with a lopsided grin.

Inside the box were dozens of silver coins and odd-looking bills. Nina picked up one, and saw there was a buffalo on the front. The date indicated it was from 1901. Another had an American Indian on it, while others had various presidents and were more familiar to her. Nina's mouth went slack before she grinned at Ben.

He nudged her. "You know, it's not only the face value of these, but you're probably looking at things that have an antiquity value."

"I'm just baffled as to why Lilia didn't want all this," Nina remarked.

"Well, you said she seemed very happy and had inherited quite a bit of money from her uncle. So maybe she just didn't want to take it because it technically wasn't hers. And, let's not forget, there may be more hidden in other places. In any case, you no longer have to worry about your finances for a while."

"I guess not. I'm not sure what to do with this, but I think I'll take it all to the bank and get a safe deposit box. I'm uncomfortable even having it in the house. Would you come with me?" She asked, in a tone more pleading than she intended.

"If we can do it soon, I'd be happy to. I have a rehearsal later this afternoon, but why don't you get changed, and I'll meet you outside in half an hour."

"That's fabulous. Thanks, Ben. You're wonderful," she told him and gave him a quick hug, and tears once again began to flow. This time, however, it was for a completely different reason.

Chapter Nineteen

"Where do you bank?" Ben asked Nina when he got into her VW.

"In South Berwick."

"Why go all the way over there?" he asked, surprised.

"Because when I got divorced, I tried opening an account at the same bank in Kittery where Richard and I had an account for five years, and they gave me a lot of flack. I wanted to see if I could get a credit card for emergencies since I no longer had one after the divorce. They wouldn't even let me apply without a male co-signing on the account. I had to go as far as South Berwick to find a bank that didn't seem to care that I was a woman on my own."

"Well, if Ruth Bader Ginsburg has her way, all that will be part of the past soon," Ben told her.

"Who?" Nina asked, trying to focus on her driving.

"Never mind," Ben said.

BY THE TIME they got back from the bank Ben was running late for his rehearsal. Nina apologized profusely, but she was happy he had come along and helped her count the money and secure it in a safe deposit box. He hurried to get his instrument and left Nina, who was still glowing with excitement. The whole matter was totally unreal.

In total, there was $7,431.00 in both bills and coinage in the strongbox. However, as Ben told her, that might be an underestimate since many of the coins and bills were very old and could fetch more than their face value. She was uncertain how to deal with it and wondered if there was any legal issue with finding the money. Nina decided to call her lawyer in the morning to confirm that the money truly belonged to her. But now that it was all in the bank, she was relieved. Maybe soon, she'd have some real financial security.

She thought about calling Julia, but it wasn't just the overheard comments that still stung. It was the history between them that left Nina feeling as though Julia wasn't the type of friend Ben was, and she decided against it. At least for now. Then, she opened a can of tuna for the kittens and decided to treat herself to some Chinese takeout.

She saw Keith, her tenant on the first floor, pulling into the driveway on her way out. She pulled over to let him pass, but instead of going by, he rolled down his car window to talk to her. "Hi, Nina! I'm glad I've run into you." He spoke loudly over the noise of their car engines.

With both Keith and April leaving so early each morning, it was true that she rarely saw the couple since they came back from their honeymoon.

"I hope this isn't too much of a problem for you, but I've been offered a job as assistant principal at a school in Nashua. Unfortunately, it's a little too far to commute, so April and I will be moving. I won't be taking the position until after the Christmas break, but I wanted you to know as soon as possible."

"Oh! Well, congratulations on the job!"

"It's something I applied for a while back, and they called me out of the blue. I'm pleased about it, and so is April. She's wanted to move back that way, especially now that she's pregnant. Being close to her family will be nice."

"Keith, you're full of good news. I'm delighted that everything is falling into place for you. Don't worry about the apartment. I'm sure I can find a tenant," she said, trying to convince herself it was true.

"Well, if you need any help, I've had several people come by who love the place. Apartments are so hard to find in Kittery. I'm sure it will get snatched up the moment you advertise it."

"Yeah. I'll have to think about what to do, but the advanced notice is helpful. Tell April congratulations as well."

Nina sat in her car momentarily, wondering how to take the news. She had finally acclimated to her new apartment and wondered if it was wise to give up the extra rental income by moving back to the first floor even if she could afford it. As it was, she could probably charge a little more, and it would help with maintenance, taxes, and insurance. She was glad she had time to think about the matter and headed out to splurge on dinner. She made a mental note that she'd also have to hire someone to plow the driveway.

When she arrived, there was a short line at the take-out counter at Ming Garden, her favorite Chinese restaurant. She looked up at the menu posted on the wall, deciding what to order. She knew she wanted to get some extras in case Ben could join her after his rehearsal. It was the least she could do when she'd caused him to be late.

She wondered how difficult it would be to make some of these Chinese food dishes at home. None of it seemed wildly complicated. It was a matter of knowing what ingredients to use and what flavor combinations worked well together. She thought about her mother showing her how to make cannoli, which she mastered with practice and experimentation over time. The same was true for her work as a pastry chef. Nina worked tirelessly to perfect techniques and found ways to add unusual pairings to enhance other ingredients. It wasn't the complexities of her recipes that made the difference. It was how she used flavor profiles to bring out the best in each element of the dish, whether sweet or savory.

As she moved to the head of the line, she realized just how

much she missed her time in the kitchen, making inspired creations. Yet she couldn't see herself moving back downstairs and living alone in the enormous apartment or even using it for a business. Too many memories were associated with the space, and many of them made her angry or sad. It would be better to have a new place. But, first, she had to be sure the money from the attic was hers to spend.

Nina tacked a note on Ben's door inviting him to stop by for dinner when he got home. As she passed the door to Maddie's apartment, she heard arguing. She stopped and paused to listen for a moment.

"Mom, she's driving me crazy! I know she can't come home, but this isn't a solution either. Penny needs to be in school and with kids her own age," Maddie said in a pleading tone.

Nina wished she could hear what Maddie's mother was saying as she continued her end of the conversation. After a moment, Maddie sounded exasperated and she began speaking louder.

"I know. You've told me that before, Mom. I get it. But think of Penny and even me for a change, will you? He's a nasty drunk, and he'll never change no matter how many times he tells you he will. You were the one who took him back. You said she would be here for a week while you found a new place and it's been more than a month. I'm sorry, but something has to change even if I have to be the one to report him."

Nina tiptoed into her apartment but kept the door slightly ajar so that she could hear them. Someone was crying.

"Don't worry," she heard Maddie say. "I'm not going to make you go back and live in that house with that monster. I just told her that, so maybe she'll leave him."

"How can she do this?" Penny sobbed. "Why don't we matter?"

"I don't understand it either," Maddie told her. "But he has some kind of spell over her, and whenever he tells her it won't happen again, she believes him."

Nina heard someone opening the door in the downstairs foyer. She quickly closed her door, feeling guilty for eavesdropping. She knew it must be Ben, and she almost opened the door to pull him into the apartment so she could tell him what she overheard but decided against it.

She poured herself a glass of wine and was just about to begin opening the various containers that sat on her counter when she heard someone rap on her door. She opened it to find Ben standing in the hall with a bottle of wine.

"Well, hey there! I stopped on my way home to pick up something to help you celebrate! Seems like you have the same thing in mind," he said as he came in.

"Come in and close the door," Nina told him conspiratorially.

"Take the wine and let me put my cello away first. I'll be right back."

Nina got out some plates and utensils while waiting for Ben.

When he returned he asked, "What's going on?"

"I'm not sure," Nina began, "but I heard the two girls talking, and Maddie was arguing with her mom, yelling at her over the phone. I feel bad because I was listening in, but it's all so baffling. I realize I'm not exactly the easiest person to get to know, but Maddie seems wholly unapproachable. Maybe that's because she's got something going on. Like Lilia and Billy, sometimes things aren't exactly what they seem." Nina unpacked the rectangular take-out containers. "Anyway, I hope you're hungry. I bought some Chinese food."

"I am indeed, and thank you so much!"

"I wasn't sure what kind you like, so I got a little of everything," Nina told him, putting the containers on the table. "I'm so sorry I made you late for your rehearsal."

"No one seemed to mind because they were all tuning their instruments and gossiping about the new conductor coming on board soon. So what did you do with the rest of your day?"

"Well, I ran into Keith, and he told me he and April are moving out after Christmas," Nina told him between bites.

"Why is that?"

"He got a job in Nashua. And April is pregnant. I don't know them well, but I'm really happy for them. They seem like such a nice couple. But then again, people said that about Richard and me."

"Nothing is ever what it appears to be on the outside. We all have things we try to hide about ourselves and our relationships. I know my parents love and support me, but I doubt they've told many of their friends they have a gay son. When Byron died, they didn't even tell people how he died. Some of my relatives didn't seem to know at his funeral, and they were too embarrassed to ask questions."

"I'm sure it's tough to talk about but even harder to understand."

"I think because Byron and I were identical twins, everyone expected us to be exactly alike. But sometimes I felt like we didn't exist in the same universe, never mind being brothers. And at other times, it was like he was an extension of me. It's hard to explain. I still don't understand why he couldn't confide in me about what he was going through. So I was as surprised as anyone when we learned he'd taken his own life."

Nina was quiet for a while.

"There weren't any signs he was struggling with something?" she asked.

"None that we knew of. The only thing I could think of was that Byron was very impulsive and occasionally experimented with drugs. I have to wonder if something happened when he was in college. Unfortunately, I'll never know."

The two friends ate some more without talking further. Nina was pouring them some more wine when there was a knock at the door. Nina and Ben exchanged a look. Ben got up and cautiously opened the door to find Maddie standing there, sobbing.

Chapter Twenty

"Maddie! What's wrong?" Nina asked, getting up from the table.

"It's Penny! She won't stop crying. I don't know what to do," Maddie stammered.

"Where is she?"

"In my room," she said, leading the way.

They crossed the hall in seconds.

Nina could hear an anguished cry coming from the room Maddie approached. Nina followed her and found Penny sitting on the edge of the bed shaking violently. Sweat poured down the young girl's panicked face.

"I can't—breathe," Penny struggled to tell them.

"I'm going to grab some water and a cold cloth," Ben told them.

"Has this happened before?" Nina asked Maddie.

"Not that I know of."

"I think she might be hyperventilating. It happened to me a long time ago at my mother's funeral," Nina told her.

Ben came into the room with a glass of water and a wet tea towel. He watched as Penny gasped, clutching at her chest. Her eyes widened, and her face paled. She suddenly shook her hands in the air as though she couldn't feel them. Maddie watched in horror, unable to help her.

"Penny? I'm Nina. We met when you came to tell me I flooded your apartment. I want to help you, okay?"

Penny looked at her with wide eyes and nodded.

"I want you to do what I'm doing." Nina began modeling her breathing for Penny, who watched her intently.

Nina pursed her lips, looking like she was about to blow out the candles on a birthday cake. She breathed in slowly through her nose, exaggerating it for Penny's sake, repeating this for several minutes. After mimicking Nina's actions, Penny began to breathe normally, and the color returned to her face.

"It's okay. I think she'll be alright," Nina said, looking closely at Penny.

"I'm freezing," Penny said. Ben grabbed a blanket draped over a chair in the bedroom and offered it to her.

Nina noticed the apartment was chilly and went to see how high they had the thermostat set. She saw it was only set at sixty-five degrees and wondered why.

When she returned, Nina turned to Maddie. "What about you? Are you okay?"

Maddie turned towards Ben in an attempt to avoid Nina's question.

"Thank you so much. I really appreciate your help. I think she's okay now."

Nina was having none of it.

"Maddie? I asked you a question. Please, tell me. Are you okay?"

"Me? I'm fine," Maddie said. Then, turning away, she rushed out of the room.

Nina couldn't let it go. She followed Maddie into the other bedroom, leaving Ben with Penny. When she caught up to her, Nina found Maddie staring out the darkened window.

"Look. I know you don't know me at all. But something tells me things are pretty rough right now. What can I do to help?"

Maddie was silent for a long time. Nina knew it wouldn't help to rush her, so she stood silently waiting until the young woman finally turned around and spoke in a troubled tone.

"We could get in a lot of trouble if someone finds her. Well, if my dad finds her, that is. He could force her to go back home."

"So, your dad doesn't know where Penny is? Does he know where you are?"

"No. My mother calls me from a pay phone when she needs to contact me. We have a signal. My mom asked me to bring her here to keep her safe until she could leave my father. She's been threatening to do that for years. I thought she really meant it this time when she showed up this summer. But she went back home and didn't leave him. Suddenly, now my father is demanding to know where Penny is as if he finally noticed she's gone. He's threatening to report her missing to the police, and now my mother is panicking."

"I know this is really personal, and you do not have to tell me if you don't want to, but why did your mom bring Penny here? What was happening that she needed to get her to safety?"

Maddie let out a wail, and her voice choked with rage. "Because he is a monster, and she was afraid he would do to her what he used to do to me."

Ben and Penny rushed into the bedroom, but Nina waved them away. Maddie began pacing the floor. For a long time she seemed lost in another world. When she finally turned to Nina, she looked weary and frightened and spoke in a halting tone.

Nina held back tears as Maddie began recounting in vivid detail how her father began to exploit his daughter's naïveté with.

"When I was ten my father bought me the book *A Wrinkle in Time* for my birthday. I was so happy at first because he even offered to read it to me. You see he never did that before. He spent a lot of time with my brother Kevin, but Penny and I were never allowed to join them on their outings back then. So I figured he was trying to make up for it or something."

Maddie told Nina that when he began reading to her, she would snuggle close to him. The smell of his cologne and physical warmth was comforting to her. Each time they read he stroked her hair in a paternal manner. But over time, he began caressing her thigh and parts of her arm. It all seemed so innocent to the ten-year-old. Once they finished one book, he bought her another and another. He seemed to be more tender and loving towards his daughter each time. She cherished these moments together and looked forward to time alone with him.

"One night he was reading me a book called *Island of the Blue Dolphins,*" Maddie said quietly. "His breathing became heavy, and he took my hand and put it..." her voice drifted off. "He told me to rub him through his pants. I was terrified," she said bitterly. "He made me promise not to tell anyone about what had happened."

Maddie described how confused she was because her father said it was normal, but then she wondered why it was a secret at the same time. Nina fought her impulse to leave the room when Maddie told her that in her young mind, she thought maybe it was her fault and that somehow, she had encouraged him. She tried hard not to react when Maddie said that as she got older, her father became bolder. Tears streamed down Maddie's face as she told Nina about the first time he penetrated his her. She expressed the pain and bewilderment of the then thirteen-year-old girl being raped by her father.

After some time, Nina asked her, "What about your mother, Maddie? Didn't she do anything?"

"I always assumed she knew because my father told me that this was how fathers taught their daughters how to be intimate with a man. I only realized he was lying because right before I turned eighteen, I spent the summer with my grandparents since my grandpa had broken his leg and my grandma needed my help on their farm. My grandma took me to the library to get some-thing to read. I had figured out that my father was lying to me but while I was at the library, I did a little digging and that's when I realized what a monster he is. Then, at the end of the summer, my parents came to visit me at my grandparents' house. My father told my grandparents that since my grandfather was better, I had to go back home because school was starting. I begged my grandparents and my mother to let me stay and live with them. They all agreed to let me stay. I was surprised because my father didn't put up a fight. Instead, he waited until he and my mother were about to leave, then he came over to kiss me goodbye and whispered, 'You're not my only daughter.' So, I got my things and went back."

There were moments Nina didn't know how to respond to what Maddie told her. Her story made Nina's stomach turn but she forced herself to stay. She thought she'd heard the worst of it but Maddie continued.

"Everything got worse when I got back. My father has always been a heavy drinker, but he started drinking even more once I got home."

"But didn't your mother wonder why her husband disappeared into your bedroom?" Nina asked cautiously.

Maddie walked over to the window and peered out. "I've asked myself that a million times." She was silent for some time before turning back to Nina and with a tortured look in her eyes she said, "Right before my eighteenth birthday, I missed my period. That was when I told my mother because I was pregnant."

Nina crossed the room and wrapped her arms around her and let her cry. She didn't know what to say, but she had to let her know she and Penny were safe, and she would do what she could to protect them.

After some time, Maddie told Nina, "She took me to have an abortion and after I graduated, I left home and never looked back. I told my mother where I was, but he always managed to find me so I've had to move several times. That's when she helped me find this place. She said she was going to leave him and take Penny with her. She dropped Penny off to me this summer, but she never came back to stay. She promised to help me pay the rent and other expenses too but she never did that either."

Nina was dumbfounded how these two young girls had managed with all the heavy baggage they had experienced. Nina sat down on the bed and Maddie joined her. She leaned against Nina, who gently wrapped her arm around her shoulder. "I kind of blew up at my mom tonight when she called. I threatened to send Penny home if she didn't leave him. But I would never let her go back there. Penny overheard me and thought I was going to send her away. That's why she was crying. Please don't tell anyone," Maddie said, looking towards the door. "Penny doesn't know the whole story. She thinks it's all about his drinking. I've never told anyone else but my mother."

Nina stayed with Maddie and comforted her until the wee hours of the morning. When they finally left the room, they found Penny asleep on the couch and Ben snoring in a raggedy chair next to it. It was almost four in the morning.

Nina told Maddie she would stop by in the afternoon, and she woke Ben so the two of them could leave. Ben returned to Nina's apartment using the excuse he had left something there. When they were once again alone, he whispered something to her just in case there was a way Maddie and Penny could overhear.

"Those two are in dire straits. When I went in to get Penny some water, I looked through the cupboards for a glass. They have almost no food in either the cabinets or the fridge, unless you count cereal and peanut butter. I don't have a clue how they've been surviving."

Nina barely slept for the rest of the night. She vowed to herself to help the young girls and wondered how to approach them without seeming to be too intrusive. As she finally drifted off to sleep, she had a plan and hoped they would be open to going along.

Chapter Twenty-One

Nina felt something wet on her ear. It woke her from a sound sleep. It took a moment for her to realize Ginger was suckling on her earlobe as if she was nursing. The tiny kitten pumped her paws up and down, trying to release the milk she longed for.

"Aw, sweetie," Nina told the kitten, "That's never going to happen." She gently picked her up and moved her to the bottom of the bed. Ginger continued to knead the quilt.

The alarm clock on her nightstand read 7:42 a.m. She had set it for 8:30 a.m., but she decided to get up even though she was exhausted. Bits and pieces of the night before rattled her brain, and she recalled the idea she had to help the girls while also moving forward with her own goals. If they were willing, she would hire them to help her clean out the carriage house and other places on the property. Paying them to help her would provide extra spending money and keep Penny busy at the same time.

First, however, she wanted to check with her attorney to make sure there weren't any strings attached to the money she'd found. And then, she would have to see if the old bills and coins had additional value by locating an appraiser. In the meantime, she could invite the girls over for lunch and discuss the idea with them, keeping details of her attic discovery to herself, of course.

Nina went downstairs and took her Moka pot from the burner on the stove to make some espresso. While waiting, she pulled out the Vegetarian Epicure cookbook and began leafing through the pages looking for something interesting to make for lunch. She landed on page 248 and a recipe for polenta. It never occurred to her that one of her favorite childhood dishes was considered vegetarian. She had plenty of cornmeal on hand and decided it would be an easy meal to serve.

Nina was startled when she heard a soft tapping on her door. She opened it to find Ben standing in the hallway, looking unkempt but smiling. She let him in and motioned for him to take a seat.

"Oh, man. I could smell the coffee all the way into my apartment."

"Actually, I'm making espresso. Want some when it's done?"

"Yes, but only if I can add cream and lots of sugar."

"You can fix it however you want, bud. Did you sleep at all?"

"Not really. I closed my eyes and drifted off, but it wasn't a restful sleep. What a horrible situation," he said looking towards the door.

"I always thought that growing up with your birth parents was somehow better. But last night sure changed my mind on that one." Nina told Ben that the girls' father had abused Maddie from the time she was a young girl. She wondered how he would react if he knew all the details and hoped he wouldn't ask any more questions. She took the Moka pot off the stove and poured the dark liquid into the cups she'd put out.

"Thanks," Ben said.

"You know, as I was growing up, I thought I had some kind of invisible tattoo on my forehead that read, *adopted*. I was sure even those who didn't know my parents somehow still knew, and it always made me feel like an outsider of sorts. Even when I was older and my mother told me about being adopted, I always thought my biological father gave me up because he didn't want me. My mom tried to convince me it was because he couldn't care for me after his wife died in childbirth. And still, I couldn't imagine giving up a child. But somehow, hearing Maddie's story, I now realize that it was his gift to me and how much courage it took. My father must have loved me very much."

She sipped her espresso for a moment and enjoyed the comfortable silence.

"At least getting up this early gave me time to think about how I can help the girls," Nina said wistfully.

"What are you thinking?"

"I'm going to offer to hire Penny and Maddie to help me clean out the carriage house. That would help Maddie with the bills and keep Penny busy at the same time. I still have some money from what was in the wooden box. I don't even have to touch the money I found the other day."

"I think that's a great idea. But won't it be too cold out there to accomplish anything? They're forecasting a light snow this week."

"Great question. But there might be a way around that. There is a huge fireplace in the main room, and Keith and April never used the firewood I still have stacked near the covered porch. If you look at the building, you can see the chimney from the front of the carriage house. And there's a small wood stove on the second floor. I could have someone come check them to make sure they're safe. There's also a furnace next to the bathroom that I will have checked as soon as I can."

"You seem to have thought it all through. Are you still planning on talking with your attorney about the money?"

"I think it's a good idea, just in case. I left a message with my lawyer already, but I honestly don't see how anyone could claim it, as I own the property. But then again, I'm not a lawyer, so it's best to confirm that before I go and plan how to spend it."

"I still can't imagine anyone leaving all that in a box in the attic's crawl space, but stranger things have happened, I suppose."

"Well, like I told you, Lilia said they were really nasty to her. She seems like a real spitfire!"

"I guess, but it's not like the Kings need the money anyway," Ben added.

"They're not as well off as you might think. From some of the things Richard told me, his parents spend money like they're able to print it, and his father overextended himself financially by expanding the business before the recession hit hard. His stock portfolio took a major hit with the oil embargo, and his parents had to sell two of their smaller stores to a competitor. They even thought about selling the Kittery store, but apparently, my department turned the store around."

"Maybe that's why he was also so interested in this place. You said Richard seemed obsessed with money and believed Henry had hidden some, right?"

"I'm sure he suspected something, but I can't say for sure what he actually knew."

"I'd love to see his face if he ever found out," Ben told her.

"That's unlikely," Nina said confidently. "It would be too soon if I never talk to him again."

"THIS IS DELICIOUS," Maddie told Nina. "What's it called again?"

"Polenta."

"I've never even heard of it," Penny chimed in.

Nina was happy to introduce them. "What do you think, Penny? Do you like it?" she asked.

"Anything is better than chicken," she said, taking another bite.

"Remember when you put the egg in Kevin's shoe so you could try and hatch one?" Maddie said to Penny laughing.

Penny rolled her eyes and tried to ignore her sister. "Maddie loves to tell that same story over and over again. How do you make this stuff?"

"It's remarkably simple," Nina told her. "You just bring water and salt to a boil in a large saucepan, then slowly pour the polenta into the boiling water. The trick is to whisk it constantly until all the polenta is stirred in and there aren't any lumps. There are other ways to prepare it, but I wasn't sure you'd like it, so I kept it simple."

"I like it, and I'm going to learn to make it," Penny told her.

"I can show you," Nina said. "I'm not sure if you two know this, but I have a culinary background. As a matter of fact, I was the pastry chef at a restaurant in Massachusetts for years."

"A what background?" Penny crinkled her nose.

"That's a fancy way of saying I know how to cook."

"Really?" Penny exclaimed. "I love to cook, but I never thought a girl could be a chef."

"A girl can be anything," Nina assured her. "Do you still want to go to college, Maddie?"

"I don't think that's possible now. But, I do love plants and would still love to have a small farm like my grandparents have."

"Can't you go back there?"

"It would make it too easy for my father to find us. I love my grandparents, but they don't know anything about how my father is. It's too bad you can't get that greenhouse fixed up."

"Maddie could grow plants in there for you," Penny added.

"I never really thought about that old greenhouse. My ex-husband always talked about tearing it down and selling off some of the land if he could get the approval to divide the property. I don't know if it can be salvaged. What do you think, Maddie? Should we take a look?"

"It might be worth considering. Maybe you could put cold frames inside it in the winter."

"Cold what?" Nina asked her.

"Don't get Maddie started on this plant stuff. She'll talk your ears off," Penny told Nina.

Maddie ignored her younger sister and began to answer Nina's question with the enthusiasm of someone in love with their subject.

"My grandparents grow all kinds of vegetables in the winter

by using them. Cold frames can actually be made a couple of different ways, but the ones they have are made with bales of straw that surround the soil and plants to keep them warm. So, all winter long, they grow fresh veggies. They stick a bunch of old windows on top of the bales of straw to let the light in and keep out the cold."

"I can't even imagine that, but it sounds wonderful! If you want, we can look at the greenhouse together and see what could be done. But for now, I need help cleaning out the carriage house, and I'm hoping I could hire one or both of you to work with me on that?"

"I'd help for free!" Penny told her.

"No," Nina insisted. "I want to pay you both for any time you spend working. If there's one thing I learned working at the grocery store, paying your employees well makes for a better work environment. I had to beg to get raises for my staff, but everyone suddenly wanted to work in the bakery department once they got them!"

"Well, I work from 2 p.m. to 10 p.m. every day except Wednesdays and Thursdays, but I'd be happy to earn some extra money on my days off," Maddie told Nina.

"Well, I'll pay you $2.00 an hour. Does that work for you both?" Nina asked, already knowing the answer.

"It's more than I'm making right now!" Maddie told her.

"Then it's settled. Why don't we get to work tomorrow at 10 a.m.? You'll have to dress warm because I haven't had the heating system checked yet, but I really appreciate your help," Nina told the girls with a slight hitch in her voice. Just then the phone rang. From the kitchen, Nina heard Andrea leaving a message.

"I have an opening early this afternoon," her lawyer said. "Call me back if that works for you."

NINA HAD a few minutes before she needed to head downtown to meet with her attorney so she decided to take a short walk around her property again. She kept thinking about everything she didn't know about the very place she'd lived for years. In one of Lilia's letters, she wrote about picking some wild blueberries along the back perimeter of the yard and putting in an asparagus patch. She even had something called raised beds, and Nina was pretty sure that referred to some form of gardening, but she wasn't familiar enough with the term to know for sure. She chastised herself for not asking Maddie earlier, but there was time for that.

She was surprised that she'd never done this before, but realized Richard's evaluation of all things related to the property left her with the impression there was nothing outside the main building and the carriage house to consider of value. Her long hours at the grocery store began shortly after they were married, and she spent her free time either cooking, baking, or working on the renovations. Now that she alone owned the property, she decided it was essential to learn more about what could be done with the land and other buildings.

She got closer to the small greenhouse and wondered how many times she'd passed by it, barely noticing its existence. Now she saw that a few places most likely needed repair, but it was something else that might be salvaged.

She didn't want to be late for her appointment, so she didn't venture as far as the tree line where Lilia indicated the berry bushes would be. But she promised herself she would become familiar with all parts of the property once she completed the task of cleaning out the carriage house. The weather was too cold to do much in the way of gardening anyway. While it could be spring before any of this occurred, it gave her a real sense of purpose. The future seemed to hold infinite possibilities.

NINA CLIMBED the stairs to the second floor toward Andrea's office instead of taking the elevator. The last time she saw Andrea was shortly before she had decided to end her life. How long ago that all seemed now.

She made herself comfortable in the outer office, waiting just a few minutes before Andrea opened the door and motioned Nina inside while speaking to someone on the phone.

"Ma! I said I'd pick up the groceries on my way home. I'm sorry you're out of milk for your tea, but it's hardly an emergency. How about you try it with some lemon instead?" Andrea said, rolling her eyes at Nina.

"Ma. I have to go. No, really! I have to go. I'll be home about 5:30, and I promise I'll bring you a whole gallon of milk." Andrea hung up the phone.

"Well, Nina King! I don't know what you've been doing but keep doing it! You look wonderful."

Nina grinned. "DeMarco. I've decided to take back my maiden name."

"Good move," Andrea said. "No need to keep being reminded of the whole business. So what is going on?"

"I need to make sure I'm not doing anything I shouldn't be doing and needed to get your input before I move forward."

"Alright, now I'm intrigued. Ask away."

"Well, I came across a rather large sum of money squirreled away in the crawl space of the attic apartment. Not only was there over seven thousand dollars in a strong box, but it might also be even more valuable because the coins and bills are really old."

"Well, I'll be! That's fabulous! But I'm curious. What were you doing in the crawl space?" Andrea asked.

"It all started when one of the kittens I adopted wandered into the space and got stuck. I had to go in after her. The rest is a long story, but is there a problem with keeping the money?"

"This doesn't change anything regarding the division of the marital property. Those are the things the judge considered when we went to court. If your divorce wasn't finalized, it might have been considered something acquired after a decree of judicial separation. But remember, you got the house because the court considered all the factors when it decided how to divide marital property, including your and Richard's contributions during the marriage. Since your money was used to buy the property and complete the renovations, not to mention the fact you were also putting Richard through school, those things played a large part in why you ended up with the house. I'm sure Richard assumed that his family connections to the property would somehow override all that. Thankfully, here in Maine, the court will divide property equitably. Based on the Abstract of Divorce Decree, everything has been recorded and states that you are the official owner of the property."

"So, there's nothing Richard can do to claim this money?" Nina asked.

"Well, he can try. Men like Richard tend to think they're above the laws everyone else has to follow. But he'll be disappointed because the division of property can't be changed," Andrea assured her.

"You can understand why I'm concerned, though?"

"Richard has no claim to that money, and while I understand your concern, he doesn't have a leg to stand on legally. What are you going to do with the money?"

"Well, I want to renovate the old carriage house and perhaps use it for a business. I'm not sure how to determine the value of the money, though. Like I said, some of the coins and bills are really old."

"I'll give you the names of a few appraisers in the area. I'm so happy you found it before Richard did. Not that I can see him bothering to rescue a kitten." Andrea selected a sheet of paper from an organizer on her desk and handed it to Nina. "That reminds me. Did you ever change your will?"

"No, I never did," Nina told her.

"Well, obviously, we don't have time to address that today but let's get it taken care of as soon as we can," Andrea advised.

On her way back home, she thought about stopping at a payphone to call one of the appraisers on the shortlist Andrea had provided, but it began to cloud over, and she was anxious to get home. Besides, she wanted to empty the litterboxes and tidy her apartment. With her upcoming task of cleaning out the carriage house, she thought it might be best to attend to some housekeeping before she got too busy. Once all her chores were out of the way, business hours had ended. She would have to call the appraiser tomorrow.

She decided to take a long bath and put on some of her favorite music. She dug through a collection of records she'd retrieved from the basement and settled on some that were from her father's collection of favorites.

Having grown up in an Italian household, she was well versed in many Italian operas. On Sundays, her father would often blast works such as Monteverdi's *L'Orfeo* or Puccini's *La Bohème*. But it was Puccini's *Madame Butterfly* that captivated Nina the first time she heard it. For days after her Papa played it for the first time, she couldn't get the music of *Un Bel Dì* out of her head.

While Nina herself could barely carry a tune, she was moved to tears by the emotion Maria Callas stirred in her as she sang *One Fine Day*. Her father translated the words, and she listened with rapt attention as he told her of *Cio-Cio-san*, or Butterfly, as an American named Pinkerton called her. Butterfly waited patiently to see a puff of smoke on the far horizon from the ship that she hoped would appear in the harbor, bringing her lover back to her.

Richard hated it when she played almost any type of music, but he especially hated the operas she was fond of listening to. They even argued about it.

"You're not even Italian!" he told her as though that was the only reason one would listen to such music.

"Richard, that's nonsense. I grew up in an Italian household, and everything about my childhood was steeped in my parents' Italian heritage. I might not look Italian or have Italian blood, but that's my background. Why can't you understand that?"

Instead of trying to understand her musical preferences, he dug in his heels. "Well, the least you could do is spare me from listening to them when I'm at home, Nina. You get the house to yourself all the time. Can't I have some peace and quiet when I'm home? Is that too much to ask?"

The day after that argument, she found all of her recordings shoved inside a box on her side of the closet.

As the bath filled, Nina took her record player and moved it into the bathroom, placing it on the hamper. She put the record on the platter and set the tonearm at the beginning of the recording, so she didn't miss even a beat of the music.

She turned just in time to see Cinnamon jump on the edge of the bathtub. The kitten almost slid into it before Nina grabbed her. The lack of a radiator in the bathroom meant she would have to leave the door open so the heat from the living room would keep the bathroom warm. But she decided she'd better not, or she would have to shoo the kittens away every few minutes. Instead, she took Cinnamon out to the living room and closed the door to the bathroom door. Once the tub was full, she sank her body into the bath.

It seemed almost impossible to believe everything that had transpired recently. Still, even though the events of recent days were undoubtedly changing the course of her life for the positive, she had a sense of crushing anxiety that arose at the oddest times. Her mother used to tell her it was normal because it always seemed to happen just around the time she was due for her period. But Nina thought that was some old wives' tale because often she experienced it for much of the month. It was one of the reasons she'd started smoking at such a young age. She missed how cigarettes used to calm her. But Richard insisted she give them up, and she was glad she did, now finding it unimaginable to fill her apartment with the stale smell.

As she soaked in the tub, the tension in her muscles slipped away, and she vowed to stop avoiding this way of relaxing. Baths always seemed to help her sleep better too. Her unfocused mind drifted from subject to subject as Callas sang in the background. She was so caught up in the music surrounding her that she didn't hear the phone ring and someone leaving a message.

By the time she climbed out of the tub, Nina was ready to relax and get into bed. As she dried herself off, she looked out the tiny dormer window in the bathroom. She saw a car's headlights and assumed someone was turning around in the driveway of the property next door. But when the lights were extinguished and the car remained parked, an uneasy feeling came over her. She tried to shake it off and thought maybe a cup of herbal tea was in order before bed.

She turned the light on over the stove and placed the kettle on the burner. While the water heated, she sat at her kitchen table, trying to get a better view of the vacant house across the street since she could not think of a single reason someone would need be there at this time of night.

The screaming whistle of the tea kettle startled her, and she jumped up from her seat. She turned the burner off and made her tea, unable to oust the troubling thoughts. She was about to climb the stairs when she turned around and returned to the kitchen to shut the light off over the stove. Crossing the room, she could see the house across the street more clearly than she could before. For a reason she could not explain, Nina did something she often forgot to do most nights—she locked and bolted her door.

<h1 style="text-align:center">Chapter Twenty-Two</h1>

As she was just about to climb the stairs, Nina heard a light tapping on the door and Penny calling to her.

"Nina? Are you there?"

"Yes. Is everything alright?" she said, hurrying to unlock the door.

Penny strolled in and sat down at the table.

"I'm so bored. Even when Maddie's home, there's nothing to do except read. I never thought I'd see the day I wished I had homework."

"Would you like some tea?" Nina asked.

"Nah," Penny said, shaking her head. "I'm not a tea person at all. My mother is, but I never learned to like the stuff. Do you have any milk or hot cocoa?"

"I have milk. Would you like me to warm it for you and add some maple syrup? It's really yummy."

"Sure. I haven't had maple milk in a long time. I didn't interrupt anything, did I?"

"No, I just took a long bath and was planning to do some reading," Nina said.

"What are you reading? Is it something you think I'd like?"

"It was a book I saw when I was coming out of the library. It's called *Carrie*. The guy that wrote it is from Maine. I'm not finished yet, but when I am, you're welcome to borrow it, although honestly, there are parts of it that are pretty disturbing."

"I would love that. I've read everything Maddie has, twice or more. I can't go out because she forbids me to, and where would I go anyway? I'm so glad you offered me a job because maybe we could buy a TV or something. I never thought I would miss school, but it sure beats sitting around all day. I miss my mom and Charlie so much," Penny told her.

Nina was for a moment before she recalled that Charlie was Penny's dog. It made her realize how difficult it must be for someone Penny's age to be without companionship day in and day out. Nina had been lonely at night when her own mother had been at work, but at least school occupied much of her day. Maddie's full-time work schedule meant Penny was alone so much of the time.

"I'd be happy to get some books out of the library for you, and you're welcome to play with the kittens," Nina told her as she rose to warm some milk on the stove.

"Can I see them now? I mean after we have our drinks?" she begged.

"Sure. We can take the drinks upstairs if you want. It's much more comfortable and warmer up there," Nina told her.

Once the drinks were prepared, Nina led the way upstairs. Penny reached down and gathered up a kitten, cuddling it to her neck.

"That one is Cinnamon, and her sister Ginger is somewhere," Nina told her.

Penny was clearly an animal lover. While she was engaged with Cinnamon, Nina took a moment to listen to an unplayed message on her answering machine.

"Hi, Nina. It's Lilia. Walter and I won't be in tonight because he's taking me to the movies. So you don't have to call me back. We'd like to plan that visit to Kittery you and I spoke about, but I can call you again early tomorrow night. I'm looking forward to showing Walter where I used to live. I'll be in touch."

"Who is that?" Penny asked her as she looked around for Ginger.

It was strange to have someone there with her in the apartment. Only Nina and her furry companions had occupied the room, other than Ben and Julia. Penny seemed to fill the place with a different energy from the adults. Nina liked it.

"That was Lilia. She's kind of a friend. I just met her actually, but I know so much about her." Nina told her about how she discovered the letters and how her desire to return them led her to finding Lilia in Portland.

"That's wild. Can I see it? The attic, I mean," Penny asked.

"Yeah. It's right in the bathroom under the sink. It's easy to access when you know it's there," Nina added. "We just have to make sure the kittens don't get into it again because it's not the best place for them."

Penny peeked inside the bathroom to see the cubby, then returned and sat down again, apparently planning to stay longer.

"I'm not keeping you up, am I?" she asked.

"I had no real plans, so no. The excitement of my night was a bath, some tea, and finishing my book. Ben loaned me another book recently, but I've been so focused on reading Lilia's letters and this other one, I've had it for weeks and haven't even started it."

"He sure is nice. Rather cute too," Penny told her cheekily.

"Yes, he is. Nice and cute and a good friend too," Nina said, with emphasis on the word friend. "Oh, there you are," she said, thankful for the distraction as Ginger made an appearance. Penny went over to gather up Ginger while Nina collected their cups.

"I really appreciate your willingness to help me clean out the carriage house. Between your help and Lilia's, I'm sure I can turn this place around."

"What do you mean?" Penny asked.

"Well, once the carriage house is cleaned out, I can think of using it for something other than a place to store things. I'm not sure exactly what I'll do with it, but now I have possibilities at least. Since Lilia use to live here, she is much more familiar with the property as a whole than I am. I've rarely explored this place and, now that I own it, it would be nice to know what's here."

"I'm sure Maddie would help with anything garden-related," Penny assured her. "I always asked my parents for a pony each Christmas, but Maddie's dream is a big cactus or something."

Nina laughed at the ease with which Penny engaged in their conversation. It was nice to share unguarded moments with someone who seemed so comfortable in their own skin. As ten o'clock approached, Penny told her she had better get back to her apartment because she didn't want to alarm Maddie if she wasn't there when she got home from work.

"Maddie is such a worrywart," Penny told her.

"Well, she just wants to protect you, and that's because she loves you," Nina reminded her.

"She's my big sister, alright. And she never lets me forget it." Penny rolled her eyes.

Nina walked her downstairs and brought the empty cups with her, placing them in the sink. She opened the door for Penny, who gave her a spontaneous hug as she left. Nina was touched by the gesture. She watched the young girl disappear inside her apartment and was about to close her door, but she heard someone coming upstairs. She peeked around the corner and saw Ben.

"Well, this is nice having someone to greet me when I come home!" he said playfully.

Ginger scampered out into the hallway, and Nina ran after her as Ben reached the top of the staircase.

"She's quick! And boy, is she getting big." Ben leaned his cello case against the wall in the hallway, and Nina handed Ginger to him. They went into the kitchen and closed the door to her apartment.

"How is she doing?" Ben asked, nodding his head towards Maddie's and Penny's apartment.

"Tonight, she acted as if last night never happened," Nina responded. "I have to wonder if it's because she didn't go through what Maddie went through, or if it's her age that makes her seemingly immune to the horror of it all. It was nice to have her company for a while. I told her all about Lilia. Well, not everything, but some of the more interesting things."

"I feel like I know Lilia and don't know her all at once."

"Well, I reached out to her, and she called me back, but it must have been when I was in the tub. I hope to hear back from her soon," Nina told him.

"What happened at the lawyer's office?"

"According to Andrea, I don't have anything to worry about. She also gave me a few names of appraisers. I'm going to call them tomorrow. The girls are meeting me downstairs at 10 a.m. to start cleaning out the carriage house. That should keep us all busy for a while."

"Well, I'm going to say goodnight. I'll talk to you tomorrow," he said, handing Ginger back to Nina.

"Goodnight," she told him and watched as he gathered his cello and made his way down the hall to his apartment.

When Nina crawled into bed that night, it was close to midnight. She was tired in a good way. She lay there thinking about how her life had changed in the months since she'd moved up to the attic apartment. Nina was happy.

Chapter Twenty-Three

Nina left messages with several antique appraisers and a numismatist. Each responded quickly, and it was determined that it would be necessary to work with multiple appraisers since the items to appraise were so varied.

Mr. Jacobs, the numismatist she agreed to work with, was in Portland. He had a stellar reputation and had been in business for decades. He was very intrigued by what Nina told him over the phone about the coins and odd looking bills. She made an appointment for the next day, leaving the old coins and bills with him.

She tried several antique appraisers before finding one that would come to evaluate all the furniture and the items stored in the bays of the carriage house. She even thought about asking him how much she could get for the damn squirrel but resisted the impulse.

With that out of the way, the arduous task of preparing for the appraisers' visits began. Knowing that there was the potential for finding more things Henry had hidden throughout the carriage house, Nina was determined to sort items and clean up as much as possible before they came.

In the weeks that followed, this work consumed her. She

began by removing all the worn-out shades and cleaning the windows so she could see better. Then, with Maddie's and Penny's help, they removed the heavy cloths covering the furniture, cleaned the dirt and grime from both the main area and the room above, sorted through items they found, and created piles of things to toss, keep, or sell. Nina made sure she examined everything thoroughly but found nothing hidden.

Progress was sometimes slowed by the cold. As November arrived, they frequently had to take a break and return to the house to use the restroom or warm up. Each morning, the cement skies informed Nina the cold would only get worse. She was anxious for the chimney sweep she contacted to evaluate the fireplace and wood stove to determine if they were operational. Once he inspected them and she knew they were both safe to use, Nina ordered a few more cords of firewood to supplement what she already had for the downstairs apartment. It would have to do until she could eventually use the small furnace.

Nina was amazed at how lovely the room looked, in a rustic sort of way, with the floor-to-ceiling fireplace as its focal point. She planned to have the pink Mamie Eisenhower tiling removed from the kitchen and replaced with something more fitting. She wondered if it was possible to put a coat of paint over the tile in the meantime and if that would suffice.

She looked forward to selecting just the right elements for the renovations. It brought to mind several arguments she'd had with Richard over price and the aesthetic of her decisions when renovating the main house. It was liberating to decide how to proceed without having to justify every choice she made.

As things took shape, the thing that pleased her most wasn't the way the place looked, or even its tremendous potential for a food-related business. It was the way the girls were thriving with her attention and the extra money their work gave them. While Maddie was still a bit reserved, Penny made them both laugh regularly with her antics. It was as if Penny knew that laughter was the antidote both Nina and Maddie needed.

She had the plumbing and electricity inspected and, while

upgrades to these systems were suggested, they could be used in their current condition for the time being. Once the electrician determined the electrical system was safe to use, she contacted the electric company and had them come to turn on the power. Having lights and heat made it much easier to accomplish things, and the work began to go much faster. The only other major item she had to replace was the refrigerator, and she arranged to buy a used one then had it delivered. The kitchen stove still functioned well enough after a thorough cleaning.

After weeks of toil, the main room within the carriage house was ready for the appraiser's visit. Nina had decided to wait to tackle the items in the garage because it was simply too cold to manage. However, even without those items, she was thrilled to learn the contents of the main room would most likely yield more than enough to cover any repairs or renovations to the building, including replacing a few slates on the roof that needed to be repaired.

All in all, things looked very optimistic.

It was the first time in quite a while that Nina had had contact with so many people outside her immediate environment. Her mission kept her focused on the outcome, making it easier to get through encounters with strangers.

A FEW WEEKS BEFORE THANKSGIVING, Nina heard back from Albert Jacobs, the numismatist evaluating the collection of coins and paper money. He asked her to come to his office on Friday.

"I'm so excited to hear what he has to say," Ben told Nina when he popped over for some coffee that Friday morning.

Nina wasn't so sure. There was something in Mr. Jacob's voice that concerned her. She didn't know how to express her fear and not seem ridiculous, so she quietly sipped her coffee.

"Have you been in touch with Lilia?" Ben asked her.

"Not as much as I'd like. We haven't been able to arrange a time for her and Walter to visit yet. This project has consumed so much of my time, and theirs is occupied with the diner. But I thought about stopping in to see her when I'm in Portland today."

"I'm sure she'll be happy to see you."

"Would you like to see what the girls and I accomplished in the carriage house?" Nina asked.

"Yes, I would."

"I never even dared to imagine how nice it would look, but it's really a stunning room. We found a table and chairs that I've fallen in love with. It has wide teak planks and is somehow rustic and elegant all at the same time. The legs look hand-carved! The whole set sat piled up under the furniture covers, but with a little elbow grease, it simply shines."

"I can't wait to see it," Ben told her. "What time is your appointment today?"

"Mr. Jacobs asked me to be there at 11:00."

"I have to do some laundry before rehearsal today. Let me get that started and I'll be right over," Ben told her.

"NINA! This is so warm and inviting." Ben seemed astonished by the progress made. "I can see now why you wanted to possibly make this a place for your business. I agree the pink tiles have to go, but I think this will be wonderful once you have those replaced."

Nina beamed with pride and showed him the various items she'd found among the furniture hidden underneath the canvas tarps. There were paintings and old photos, pottery and enamelware, and household items she couldn't identify.

"Here's the table I like. I think it works for the room's style and will look great with the stone fireplace. What do you think?" Nina asked.

"I like it. I can imagine placing it in front of the fireplace."

Nina imagined the same. She was suddenly lost in thought about sitting in front of the fireplace, sharing a meal with the girls and Ben. Maybe she could even convince Lilia to come. She'd serve them something she hoped would please them. Maybe it would be something she'd made a thousand times or perhaps she'd try something new.

Ben cleared his throat to get her attention. "Well, I know you have to get to Portland. I'll stop by later to see how you made out, okay?"

Nina turned to her friend. "I'd like that," she smiled. "Otherwise, I might explode," Nina teased.

WHEN SHE ARRIVED at his office, Mr. Jacobs greeted her warmly.

"Have a seat, Mrs. King," he said, motioning to a chair in his office.

"Ms. DeMarco," Nina corrected wondering why he called her that since she had introduced herself using her maiden name.

"Yes, Ms. DeMarco. Sorry. I forgot. So, before we begin, I have a few pertinent questions I have to ask you regarding how you discovered these items."

"Is that customary?" Nina asked, getting nervous about this line of questioning.

"No. I'll explain in a moment," he assured her.

"Well, it's rather a long story," she began. Nina thought back to the night she tried to take her life. She couldn't ignore the facts that brought her to this moment any more than she could dismiss the impact of anything else that had happened before or after those moments. But she knew such details would most likely make her seem less credible, so she started with Cinnamon and Ginger.

"I adopted two kittens a while ago, and one of them found a

small cubby hole under the bathroom sink in the attic apartment where I now live. When I went in to get her, I discovered several shoeboxes full of letters and eventually another box with some mementos and some cash. I was able to locate the owner, a woman who once lived as a housekeeper in that apartment. She had left things behind when the King family put my ex-father-in-law's aunt into a nursing home and they insisted the housekeeper leave immediately. She never had a chance to retrieve the letters or anything else in that area of the attic apartment."

"So, you're telling me this woman is still alive?" Mr. Jacobs asked urgently.

"Yes, she's the one who told me that there was a strongbox in the corner of the attic that had belonged to the Hirsts. They were the relatives of my ex-husband who once owned the house. The housekeeper had stashed it there for safekeeping at Ida's request after her husband Henry died."

"So you had no knowledge of this strongbox before your divorce settlement with Mr. Richard King?" he asked.

"Not at all." Nina's voice began to rise. "How do you know I was married to Richard King? I never mentioned his name to you."

"Well, I'm not sure how this happened, but he contacted me. Apparently, he caught wind of your find and is claiming you knew about it before the settlement and that you fraudulently misrepresented your assets in the divorce. He's going to try and sue you over the matter because what you've found is worth more than several hundred thousand dollars."

"What? He's trying to sue me?" Nina said, instantly furious. "That's rich. It's so typical of... wait? Did you say several hundred thousand dollars?"

"I did indeed," Mr. Jacobs assured her. Nina looked at him with astonishment.

"Do you think this woman would be willing to testify to how you learned about the strongbox?" he asked.

"I can't say absolutely, but my guess would be yes. She actually owns a diner right here in Portland. I thought about going there for lunch to see if I could touch base with her over another matter."

"That's fortunate. What's the name of the place?"

"Dizzy's."

"Well, I'll be. I've eaten there often. They make excellent food. You could walk there from here. It's really close by," Mr. Jacobs said. "Why don't you continue to leave the items with me? You have the original receipt I gave you, and I've created a document listing all the items with their value. You can take it with you. I hope we can clear this matter up as soon as possible. I have someone who's very interested in the entire collection and would offer you a nice sum of money, but we must be assured that this won't become a legal headache."

Nina stared at the paper and the lines of items meticulously listed on the page. But the figure on the bottom was what really caught her eye. The collection was estimated at more than a quarter of a million dollars.

NINA WAS SHAKING by the time she left. She decided it was a good idea to walk to the diner to see if she could speak to Lilia right away. It began to sleet, and she hesitated for a moment before she continued. She hated driving in bad weather and worried that she hadn't put out extra food for the kittens when she left. She picked up her pace, continuing with her plans to visit Lilia, but decided to keep her visit short.

When she approached Merrill Street, she saw an ambulance parked in the middle of the block. The lights were flashing, but Nina couldn't see anyone near the vehicle. As she drew closer, paramedics rushed from the restaurant with a gurney. They lifted it into the ambulance, and shortly after that, Lilia hurried out and climbed in as well. The ambulance drove away, siren screaming. Without thinking, Nina strode into the diner.

A few customers were seated at tables, and a waitress was in tears.

"I'm sorry, Miss. We're going to close early," the woman explained.

"Hi, I'm a friend of Lilia's," Nina told her. "Did I just see her leaving in the ambulance?"

"Yes, with Walter. He collapsed," the young woman told her through a fresh stream of tears.

"Is there anything I can do?"

"I'm just trying to wrap things up for her before I go home."

"How can I help?"

"What's your name?" the waitress asked.

"Nina."

"I'm Dolly. I'll cash out the customers. Would you mind clearing the tables?"

"Sure."

Instinct took over as Nina stashed her purse and coat under the front counter. She rolled up the sleeves of her sweater and began clearing tables. She loaded plates, glasses, mugs, and silverware into gray plastic tubs and carried them into the kitchen. There was an empty rack near the dishwasher, and she placed the items in there before returning to continue clearing off more dirty tables.

When the last customer left, Nina helped Dolly put everything back in order.

"Do you know how to run the dishwasher, or maybe we should leave that?" Nina asked her.

"Not really. Lilia always does that. I'm not sure when she'll be back. I think they probably took Walter to Maine Medical. It's not too far, so maybe she'll stop here on her way home. What do you think? Should we leave it for her?"

"I rinsed the dishes really well, so they should be okay to leave," Nina assured her.

"This is just awful. Lilia has been trying to get Walter to retire for some time now," Dolly told her. "Just yesterday, she was teasing him. She said, 'Mr. Garrison, I'm ready to retire. When do you think you're going to let me?' I hope he will be okay, but it didn't look good when they put him in the ambulance. How do you know Lilia?"

"It's a long story, Dolly," Nina said with a slight smile. "I'll have to tell you sometime. Are you all set here?"

"Yes, I think so," she said, then followed Nina out and locked the diner door.

THE TRIP back to Kittery was harrowing. Nina's mind raced, worrying about Walter and Lilia. The additional stress of driving on icy roads made her regret her decision to take the highway. She thought it would be better plowed. Not long after she entered the roadway, she pulled over to the shoulder. The wiper's blades beat furiously, trying to keep pace with the sleet. All Nina could do was follow their motion, watching as they tried to drive back the icy mixture. She closed her eyes, trying to find anything to hang on to that would release her mind from the feeling of being paralyzed. The menace of threats both seen and unseen started to swallow her.

A tap on the window of her VW startled her out of her spiraling thoughts.

"Are you okay?" a woman asked. "Are you having car problems?"

Nina rolled down the car window. "No, I just needed a moment. I'm okay. Thanks for stopping," Nina said. Rolling up the window, she gave the woman a fake smile.

Nina looked in her rearview mirror and decided that she had to get back on the highway. She was desperate to avoid any further interaction with this stranger. Taking a deep breath, she turned on the radio, trying to drown out the thoughts leading to despair. Seeing that the sleet had abated, Nina got back on the road.

By the time she arrived home it was past three in the afternoon. She put some food out for the kittens, wrapped herself in her afghan and fell asleep on the futon couch.

The winds howled outside, and darkness had fallen when Nina woke. She went into her bedroom and looked out the window into the shadows of the night. She considered grabbing some pizza for dinner but realized her fortune wasn't as assured as she thought this morning when she visited Mr. Jacobs. She also didn't want to drive in the snow. While she was sure she could prove that she had no knowledge of the strongbox and its contents before her divorce, the uncertainty of the situation had her opting for a bowl of oatmeal and a cup of hot tea.

She sat in the kitchen, eating distractedly. She wondered how Walter was doing and if it was appropriate to reach out to Lilia or even visit him in the hospital. She was both hopeful and hopeless. She'd been spending money to renovate the carriage house, believing that the matter was settled and that worrying was unnecessary. But here she was yet again worrying about money. Nothing about the future was certain except that it could all be snatched away in a minute.

She could hear someone coming up the stairs and assumed it was Ben, having grown accustomed to his schedule and habits. She quickly turned off the kitchen light and sat in darkness. She could hear him pause at the door and tap lightly. When she failed to reply, she heard him continue to his apartment. Nina was unwilling to recount the day's events that had left her feeling completely despondent.

Chapter Twenty-Four

Having slept much of the late afternoon away, Nina found herself unable to fall asleep again. As she lay in bed, her mind churned. Seeing Lilia in the back of the ambulance brought back memories of her own mother, and of the day she cradled her father in her arms waiting for someone to arrive to help her try and save him.

Having finished Carrie, she picked up one of the books Ben had loaned her. It was called *The Golden Notebook* by an author unknown to her, Doris Lessing. So far, Nina could barely wrap her head around the words, but she continued reading.

Ideally, what should be said to every child, repeatedly, throughout his or her school life is something like this: 'You are in the process of being indoctrinated. We have not yet evolved a system of education that is not a system of indoctrination. We are sorry, but it is the best we can do. What you are being taught here is an amalgam of current prejudice and the choices of this particular culture. The slightest look at history will show how impermanent these must be. You are being taught by people who have been able to accommodate themselves to a regime of thought laid down by their predecessors. It is a self- perpetuating system. Those of you who are more robust and individual than others will be encour-

aged to leave and find ways of educating yourself — educating your own judgements. Those that stay must remember, always, and all the time, that they are being moulded and patterned to fit into the narrow and particular needs of this particular society.

The poor light in her bedroom tired her eyes. Nina put the book on the nightstand and lay there thinking. The passage made her think about her own life and how it molded her thoughts. All the things she valued had been defined by others. She imagined that if her parents were alive, she would be shunned if they knew she was associating with a gay man. Although Nina had never known a gay person, she knew from things her college friends had said that being gay was considered unacceptable by some. Ben had told her that if people knew about his homosexuality, he could lose his job. He told her of friends that had been harassed by police. But when he made these comments, it didn't register how difficult life must be, knowing that your very being was threatened by the status quo. How could someone so kind and caring as Ben be considered a threat to anyone?

She had once thought of Richard as a kind and gentle soul since he acted with kindness while they were dating and even for some of their marriage. The first time she had any inkling he was anything but the delightful man she thought him to be was about six months after they began dating. Richard took her to see the movie *Cactus Flower* and then out to a restaurant called Mi Casa. The night was engrained in her memory because it was a night of many firsts. For the first time, Richard spoke of a future together once he graduated from Boston University. As they strolled toward the restaurant, he was even more animated than usual, and he held her closely to him as they walked.

"I was waiting to tell you, but, what the heck, I can't wait," he gushed. "I got the results of my DAT! I passed with flying colors!"

"That's wonderful! Congratulations," Nina said, squeezing his hand as they walked. She was happy for him since she knew he was concerned about passing the dental admissions test that would allow him to be admitted to dental school.

"Well, this is certainly a night to celebrate."

"Where are we going? I thought the restaurant was on Highland." They were in her hometown of Worcester, where Richard came whenever they had a date.

"It is, but the restaurant doesn't have a liquor license. You have to bring your own booze," he told her. "I'm going to grab some rum or something."

By the time they arrived at the restaurant and were seated, Nina was famished. The waitress brought over a basket of tortilla chips and various sauces that Nina was excited to try.

"Don't fill up on those!" Richard admonished, slapping her hand away from the chip bowl. "I want you to try some of their mole poblano. I'll order it for both of us. It's quite filling, and I know you have a small appetite."

"I'm starving. I'll just have a few," she said, dipping a chip into one of the sauces.

Richard glowered at her, but he didn't say anything else. Instead, he asked the waitress to bring them glasses of Coke. Once the server brought them, he took a bottle of dark rum and added some to each glass.

"Don't put too much in mine, okay?" Nina told him. Nina grew up with wine being served at almost every meal, but her experience with hard liquor was relatively limited. In college, on the few times she didn't go home for the weekend, she'd shied away from the keg parties and the beer pong games Julia tried to get her to attend. However, she did venture into hard liquor at a frat party, and both she and Julia got rip-roaring drunk. Nina vomited for what seemed like days, and she had kept away from vodka and even orange juice ever since. However, the rum tasted good as she sipped her drink and munched on a few more tortilla chips.

As they waited for their meal, they talked about the movie. "What did you think? I was impressed by Goldie Hawn," Richard commented. "She was never my favorite on *Laugh-in*, but the chemistry between her and Matthau worked."

"It's awful that he would lie to her about his marriage. I can't imagine how he kept it all straight. It was weird that her character would try to commit suicide over her broken relationship with him," Nina replied. "To be honest, I'm not sure if I liked the movie or not."

Richard ignored Nina's critique of the movie. When the waitress delivered their meals, he ordered two more Cokes and poured a generous amount of rum in each glass. Then he began talking about what would happen now that he had successfully passed his exam.

Nina marveled at how he seemed to have his entire future mapped out. In the past, he'd often said things like, "I can't wait until you see the enormous tree my parents put up at Christmas," or, "I can't believe you never learned to swim. I'm going to have to teach you." That night, however, talk of the future included more than just Christmas with his family.

"What do you imagine I'll be doing while you're in dental school?" she asked playfully.

"Once I graduate from school," Richard told her, "maybe you can start your own bakery or something. You'll love it up there. I can't wait to move back."

"Oh! So you're saying, I'm moving to Maine?" Nina asked, astonished.

"Of course. I know it means giving up your job, but I'm sure we can find something for you to do at the grocery store," he told her. "My folks have a guest house we could move into."

Nina became more talkative and agreeable as they ate. But as the evening wore on, she had to focus hard on trying to cut the chicken into small chunks so she could move it up to her mouth slowly, making sure she didn't drop the pieces as she ate.

Her head was getting fuzzy, and she did nothing more to interject her own thoughts into the conversation. She wondered how she could navigate her way to the bathroom, as she wasn't sure she would be able to make it there without some assistance. Instead, she kept eating and drinking. Nina only vaguely remembered bits and pieces of the rest of the night.

She knew that once they got back to her apartment, she got

violently ill. But the thing that was etched in her memory was awakening the following day. It was close to noon when she woke up. She was late for work. Every part of her body ached, and she knew if she'd had anything left in her stomach, she would have vomited again. She called in sick, apologizing profusely. Then, she realized that Richard was still there. He'd never spent the night before. At first, she wondered if he'd done this because he was taking care of her. But then she remembered he had become very amorous and was kissing her even though she told him how awful she felt. He'd placed his hand between her thighs and spread her unclothed legs. The last thing she remembered was being very confused and disoriented. Later that morning, after he left, she noticed blood on her bedsheets. She was embarrassed at first thinking that it was from her menstrual cycle, as she had started her period. But there were times she wasn't so sure.

For weeks, she avoided seeing Richard. She had an uneasy feeling whenever she thought of him. But one night he showed up to surprise her with a bouquet of flowers, and soon he was once again in her life.

Nina wasn't sure what she'd experienced, if anything. Unlike some of her college friends, she was reticent to discuss sex. Her upbringing instilled in her a belief that only married people should have sex, even though she knew that was rather old-fashioned. She pretended to be so much more worldly than she was. Afraid her friends would mock her if she asked questions, she never told anyone. A few months later, Richard proposed marriage. Nina readily accepted, and before he started dental school, they got married and moved to Maine.

She had always avoided thinking about that questionable night; it made her too uncomfortable. Nina shifted her thoughts back to Lilia's poor husband, Walter. She hoped he would be alright. She picked up *The Golden Notebook* to read more, but instead, she closed her eyes and began to drift off.

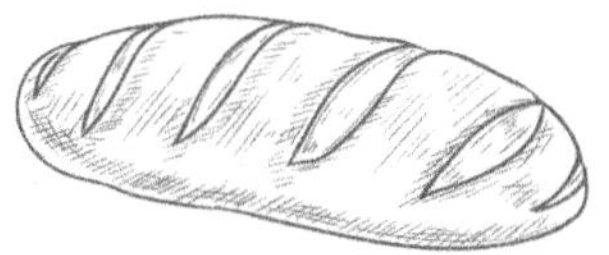

Chapter Twenty-Five

As soon as Nina woke the next morning, she called the hospital in Portland. The switchboard confirmed Walter had been admitted but would not provide any other information.

Determined to stay busy, she fed the kittens and put the Moka pot on the stove. She began trying to think of ways to keep herself distracted and found herself taking out her canister of flour because she had an urgent need to make bread.

Instead of a recipe, Nina drew from her years of experience as a baker. She knew that for the bread she had in mind, it was best to use water closer to room temperature, rather than warming it, because the cooler the water, the longer the dough would rise, increasing the bread's flavor. She was pleased to find she had plenty of unheated water in her tea kettle.

The container of cornmeal was still on her counter after using it to make the polenta. She decided it would be good to dust the pan with it to add more flavor and crunch to the bottom crust. Nina roughly mixed the ingredients together.

At first, the dough was very dry and seemed like it wouldn't come together. But as she used her hands to ensure all of the flour was incorporated, the dough became sticky. Since she had to let it rise for a few hours, she covered it with a tea towel and looked for another project to distract herself from thinking about Lilia and Walter.

Nina looked in her fridge and discovered she still had some Baileys. She wondered if she could use it to flavor some baked goods. Not sure how the liquid would impact a batter, she thought perhaps it would be best to use it to flavor something like a frosting. The idea refocused her attention, and soon she found herself making chocolate cupcakes and forgetting all about all the world around her.

When she finished making the bread and chocolate cupcakes, she made potato gnocchi from scratch. When that was done, the cupcakes had cooled enough to frost. She licked the spoon and smiled with delight, then carefully noted the amounts of Baileys and espresso that she had used in her frosting recipe so she could recreate it in the future. She couldn't wait to offer Ben and the two girls some of what she'd made. When Nina finally stopped, it was after noon and, in spite of her efforts at distraction, she knew she had to make the trip north.

Before she left, she packed up food to bring to Lilia. On her way out, she ran into Ben, who was bringing his laundry upstairs.

"I made a ton of food this morning, and if you want to stop by later, you're more than welcome to have some. I made these amazing cupcakes and frosted them with icing flavored with espresso and Baileys Irish Cream. They're delicious," Nina babbled.

"I can't wait to try them. I was actually coming up to see you. When I was doing my laundry, I noticed some water on the floor. You might have a problem with the hot water heater or something," he told her. "It doesn't seem horrible, but you should have someone look at it soon."

"Oh!" Nina said nodding. Then she realized Ben had no idea what had happened in the short time since she had seen him last. She became flustered and stared at Ben uncertain whether to tell him about Walter, address the problem in the basement, or report on the news from Mr. Jacobs. All these thoughts created a dam and Nina stood and stared at him unable to react.

"I should be home about six," Ben told her. "I'll come by as soon as I put my instruments away, and we'll take a look. It might be something straightforward to fix."

Nina finally managed to call after him. "Thanks, Ben," she said watching as the door closed behind him.

ARRIVING AT MAINE MEDICAL, Nina was directed to the intensive care unit. She saw Lilia sitting outside what she assumed was Walter's room with her head in her hands. Nina didn't need to ask how Walter was. She sat down quietly, took a tissue from her purse, and gave it to Lilia. After blowing her nose, Lilia melted into Nina's shoulder and wept.

After Lilia stopped sobbing, she said, "Charlotte and Dolly just left, and David's on his way. They were as shocked as I am. They loved Walter, too. Everyone did." Lilia stammered, "I don't know what I'm going to do now that he's gone." She began to cry again.

As Walter Garrison's body cooled in the hospital bed, Nina searched to find something to share with Lilia, but all she could do was listen. She knew firsthand that time doesn't heal all wounds, and there is no silver lining when death steals a loved one. Instead, it leaves a gaping hole that reopens at the most inconvenient times. *Moments like these create a trap that captures you until you find a way to crawl out,* Nina thought. So she remained silent because no matter how well-intended, Nina knew words would fail to comfort her friend.

WHEN LILIA WAS ready to go, she suggested they head to Dizzy's. Nina followed her there. When they arrived, the place seemed so lifeless. All the warmth the couple brought to the diner had been drained with the previous day's events. Nina made Lilia a cup of tea and brought it to the four-top table towards the back of the diner where she sat, then left for a moment to retrieve the food she had brought from home, still in her car. She shook off the chilled air and ignored the roiling charcoal clouds forming in the previously sunny sky.

Once back inside the dinner, she went into the kitchen, warmed up the gnocchi, and delivered it to the table, encouraging Lilia to eat. Sitting quietly across from her, Nina watched intently as Lilia brought the fork to her mouth in a robotic fashion.

Nina cleared the dishes when Lilia was finished eating and brought them to the kitchen. As she filled the sink with water to wash them, she heard a knock at the door. She peeked her head out of the kitchen door and saw Lilia get up.

Nina waved her arm. "Let me get it," she said, hurrying to open the door.

Nina found herself staring into the face of the adult David. She didn't introduce herself but moved aside as he passed her to rush to Lilia, who held out her arms.

"He's gone," she told him. "I never got a chance to say good-bye. He was fine yesterday morning, and now he's gone."

David bent down, wrapped his arms around Lilia, and let her cry. Tears welled in Nina's eyes, moved by David's tenderness.

When Lilia gained her composure, she introduced Nina to David.

"I feel as if I know you," Nina blurted out.

"Are you Walter's relative?" he asked.

"No," Nina said with hesitation. "I'm a friend of Lilia's."

David sat down opposite Lilia in the chair Nina had just vacated. Nina awkwardly retreated into the kitchen to provide Lilia and David time alone. She washed the dishes and busied herself, trying to avoid hearing their muffled conversation from the other room. After some time, Nina brought in the cupcakes she'd baked and placed them on the table in front of Lilia and David.

"Do either of you want something to drink? I'm going to make some tea."

"I'll take some more," Lilia told her. "David?"

With his mouth full of a cupcake, David nodded affirmatively before taking another huge bite. "I know the flavor, but it escapes me at the moment."

Nina smiled. "The cupcakes are chocolate, and the frosting has Baileys Irish cream and espresso mixed into it. I thought the combination might work well."

"It works better than well."

"Nina is a pastry chef. She used to work in Worcester. What was the name of the restaurant?" Lilia asked Nina.

"Angelo's," she responded, then turned to David. "Do you know that restaurant?"

"I'm afraid not. I don't get into Worcester much, although it's close enough. I live in a town east of there. Are you familiar with Natick?"

"I am," Nina told him. "My college roommate is from Natick and I worked at a restaurant in Wellesley years ago. What do you do?"

"I just graduated from law school. I'd like to be a public defender someday. But first, I have to pass the bar exam. So now I work as a clerk for a small firm in Newton."

"Speaking of lawyers," Nina said, "Lilia, at some point, I need to tell you what shenanigans Richard is up to regarding the contents of the strongbox."

"You can tell me now," Lilia said, reaching for a cupcake.

"Are you sure?"

Lilia nodded her head as she ate.

"I hired a local appraiser to evaluate what I'd found and somehow Richard caught wind of it. Now he's claiming that I had knowledge of the strongbox before our divorce and that I was hiding marital assets. He's threatening to sue me. Mr. Jacobs, the man handling the appraisal, asked me if you would be willing to confirm how and when I gained knowledge of it."

"This is certainly interesting," David said.

After assuring Nina she would be happy to cooperate, Lilia offered David a brief explanation while Nina returned to the kitchen to fetch the kettle.

Filling their mugs, Nina glanced out the diner's window and

noticed that rain that had begun to fall. It was already past 4:30 p.m., and she was exhausted from her unorthodox sleep schedule in recent days. She decided it would be best for her to leave.

"I need to head back to Kittery," she said. "But, Lilia, would you let me know what I can do to help? I'm available in any way you need me to be."

"I will. I promise," Lilia said through tears.

Getting up, David extended his hand. "Nina, it was so nice meeting you. I wish it was under different circumstances."

Nina smiled warmly, shook his hand, and left the diner.

Once inside her VW, she sat for a few moments. She was actually looking forward to the quiet drive home, even in the rain.

NINA HEARD a knock on her door shortly after she arrived home.

"It's open," she said.

Ben entered the kitchen and sat down at the table.

"He didn't make it."

"Who didn't make it?"

"That's right—you don't know. After I went to see Mr. Jacobs about the coin appraisal, I went to Dizzy's. Just before I got there an ambulance had arrived to take Walter to the hospital. He had a heart attack and died."

"Nina, that's awful! How is Lilia doing?"

"David drove up from Natick. When we left the hospital, Lilia and I went to Dizzy's because he was meeting her there. He's with her now."

"I had no idea," he said in shock.

"I was about to put the food away. Have you eaten?"

"No and I'm starving too."

"Let me fix you a plate."

"Thanks. I've been looking forward to one of those all day and am definitely interested in these," Ben told her, pointing to the remaining cupcakes on the counter. "Tell me what's David's like and then fill me in on what happened with the appraisal."

"He seems very nice. I was still thinking of him as the little boy from Lilia's letters. It was weird seeing this grown man who I'm guessing is around my age—maybe a bit older," she said as she warmed up some gnocchi. "He just graduated from law school and lives in Natick. That's where Julia is from. He seemed totally devoted to Lilia. She is going to help resolve the issue with the coins and my ex-husband."

"Slow down. You never told me what happened."

"That's right. Well, Richard is at it again. Mr. Jacobs, the appraiser, said somehow Richard learned about the money and is now claiming I knew about it all along."

"How would he have found out about it?"

"Mr. Jacobs doesn't know but my guess is that maybe one of the people he consulted with knows the Kings and passed along the information. Lilia said she's happy to confirm that she was the one that told me about the strongbox well after the divorce. So if Richard tries to continue with his stupid threats, he's in for a surprise," she assured him.

As Nina served Ben dinner and dessert, the two friends chatted until Nina began to yawn. Finally, Ben put the dishes in the sink and said goodnight.

Exhaustion overtook her, and Nina climbed the stairs with the two kittens trailing behind her. She climbed into bed, not bothering to change into her pajamas. It wasn't until morning that Nina realized she and Ben never went to check out the source of water on the floor of the basement.

Chapter Twenty-Six

The following day, Nina had a nagging feeling she'd forgotten something. As she brushed her teeth, she realized what it was. It was too early to ask Ben to accompany her to check out the source of the water on the floor in the basement, but she was hesitant to go down alone. After some thought, she decided to go despite her trepidation.

Stalling her descent into the bowels of the house, she went down to the kitchen to feed the kittens and began fiddling with the dials on the radio. She wanted to get a weather forecast, knowing she could be traveling back and forth to Portland a few times in coming days. She breathed a sigh of relief when she learned the weather was expected to remain sunny until Sunday.

She decided to have breakfast before going downstairs, so she got out some eggs and made an omelet. While it cooked, she prepared her Moka pot to make some espresso. Both her meal and the rich dark liquid in her coffee mug disappeared more slowly than usual.

As tired as she was, she knew she couldn't delay the inevitable any longer. When her breakfast was finished, she resigned herself to heading downstairs.

She'd been into the basement dozens of times before. But somehow, the added element of water being on the floor made it daunting. She wondered why. Was it the anticipated expense of a repair or merely the complexities of the unknown workings of the many systems that operated the very house she lived in that intimidated her? Fuse boxes, furnaces, pipes, and wires were mysteries to her. She wished she understood how they all worked, but she'd never learned, since Richard insisted he take care of anything remotely mechanical. All she knew how to do was to have someone else take care of the problem. Maybe, she thought, it was time to learn more about handling some things on her own. Before she could think any further, she heard some arguing across the hall.

The voices were muffled, and she couldn't make out what was being said, but she knew it came from Maddie and Penny. Nina wondered what was causing them to be angry with one another. She never had a sister or brother and couldn't imagine fighting the way they seemed to fight on occasion. She wondered how the two kept quiet before she got to know them because now Nina was well aware she had neighbors. Perhaps their age and circumstances added to the friction between them. Nothing had been resolved in the weeks since the row over their mother's call and her inability to leave her husband. Nina was ill-prepared to offer suggestions for problems like those the two young girls were coping with currently.

Suddenly, there was a loud knock on the door.

She heard Maddie saying, "Leave Nina alone."

Opening the door, Nina saw Penny standing there about to knock again. Her face was red. "Can I come in?" she asked, pushing past Nina and plopping down in a chair at the kitchen table. "I'm so mad right now. I swear to God I'm going to leave if she doesn't stop acting like such a jerk all the time."

Nina wasn't sure she wanted to get in the middle of their conflict and was trying to figure out a way to stay neutral when there was a light tap on the door.

"Nina? Can I come in?" Maddie called.

Nina opened the door, and Maddie entered, filling the tiny space with hostility.

"You can't just run away, Penny. What would that solve? I'm trying to keep you safe, and all you think about is having fun," Maddie told her.

"Going to school is having fun? I've been stuck in this apartment for months now, and if I ever get back to school, I'll be so behind! Getting my life back is not just about wanting to have fun."

"This didn't start with that, and you know it. You wanted to go to the movies. But I've told you before, every time we go out, there is more and more of a chance someone we know will see us. Dad's work brought him in contact with a lot of people. Don't you realize that? What if he finds you? He can't make me go back, but I'm sure he can make you go home."

"Maddie! All I wanted was to go somewhere for my birthday," Penny yelled. "You get to go off to work every day but I'm here going stir crazy. You have no idea what that's like!"

Maddie burst into tears and turned to leave but turned back to Penny instead.

"You have no idea what I went through. Don't you ever say that," she said and stormed out the door.

"Wait! I'm sorry," Penny said, rushing after her.

Nina wasn't sure if she should go after them or let them figure out a solution on their own. Moments later, a disheveled Ben stood in the hallway, half-dressed.

"What's going on?" he asked Nina.

"They're arguing," she told him.

"Yeah, I heard. They woke me up."

"I just made espresso. I can froth some milk if you want a cappuccino."

"That would be wonderful. I'm exhausted. Thanks for offering. I'll be back in a moment," Ben said, disappearing into his apartment.

Nina realized how much she'd come to rely on him. He offered a different perspective on situations, and she valued his friendship in ways she was only beginning to grasp. It was as if their developing relationship had started to encapsulate an unconditional alliance between one another as a way to empower and uplift each other.

In Nina's chosen career path, she rarely interacted with the women she worked with because they usually engaged in "front of house" activities like hosting and waiting tables. And the men she worked with rarely offered their friendship, so it left her feeling very isolated—she wasn't a part of the front or the back of the house. But she had observed the close-knit relationships many of her women co-workers had formed. Here in her own home, she had an opportunity to show Maddie and Penny how important they were to one another.

Even though both Maddie and Penny had some serious personal struggles that led them to argue or feel defeated, as sisters, they also helped one another in ways that they could never have done alone. Nina thought she should remind Penny that Maddie had her best interests at heart, even if that wasn't always evident.

Ben arrived back at Nina's apartment and sat down at the kitchen table, wrapping his hands tightly around the mug. He was reticent, and Nina was about to inquire about his reserved mood when Maddie returned to apologize for interrupting the morning.

"I am so sorry for all of Penny's drama. She's just upset because she wants to celebrate her birthday. I just don't know what to do. It's not like I want to keep her from having fun. Really, I don't. But I'm just afraid someone will see her and report back to my father and he'll find her."

"You know, Maddie. Penny might be in a better position than you think," Ben started. "It might be worth looking into what protections are in place for kids like her. We've all been assuming that she would be taken away from here or get in trouble. But she's surely not the first kid growing up in Maine that needed to leave home because of a bad situation."

"What do you mean?" Maddie asked him earnestly.

"It's worth getting some facts. I know you're doing the best you can to protect and provide for Penny. But imagine how much happier she would be if she could stay here and go to school without thinking she could be arrested or whatever the fear is," he told her.

"How do I do that?"

"I'm sure Nina and I can help you with that," he said and watched as Nina nodded her head in agreement.

"As a matter of fact, until we know what protections are in place for her, there might also be a way we can help celebrate her birthday without a risk of being seen," Nina added.

Ben cocked his head.

"We can take a page from Lilia's Uncle Billy and just have them dress as boys," she told them.

They all grinned at the thought. "Can we go tell her?" Maddie asked.

"Sure," Nina told her. Ben grabbed his mug, and they crossed the hall.

Penny was over the moon when they explained their plan. After they left Maddie's apartment, Nina paused in the hallway.

"Would you be able to come to the basement and help me figure out what's leaking?"

Ben hesitated for a moment. "Sure. I'd forgotten all about that. Sorry. I've been a little distracted. I'm not sure I can help if it's anything too complicated since I can't stay long. I was heading back to Vermont for the day, and I'm already leaving later than I planned."

"Are you sure?"

"Yes. Let's just do it and get it over with. Grab a flashlight," he said, disappearing into the hallway.

Something seemed off, but Nina couldn't quite put her finger on this vague feeling she had about Ben's response. He smiled at her when she began following him, and Nina tried to push the thought aside that he was angry or upset with her for some reason.

Once in the basement, Nina chastised herself for not coming

earlier, as the water had accumulated near the washing machine and would need to be mopped up.

She watched as Ben poked around. "Well, it doesn't look like the hot water heater, so that's good."

He then looked in back of the machine. "It must have something to do with the washing machine, but I don't think it's a hose. Maybe it's coming from here," he said, bending down for a closer look. It seemed like whatever was wrong could be more complicated than Ben initially thought.

"It could be a clogged drain. Do you have a coat hanger close by?" Ben asked, turning to her.

"What?"

"A wire coat hanger—do you have one?"

Ben's request reached her brain, and Nina hurried off to a closet where she knew she could find a hanger and brought it back to him. She watched intently as he used the make-shift plumbing device to dislodge some debris. As he moved the wire, it appeared to break apart some gunk and fluid that was causing the problem. Within minutes, she could see there was no more resistance, and Ben turned and smiled at Nina, having unclogged the drainpipe. But as he handed her the hanger, pent-up tears had begun to stream down her face.

"Nina! What's wrong?" Ben said, exasperated.

She couldn't speak. She just stared at Ben.

Shaking his head, Ben placed the wire on an old table and began to leave.

"Ben—I—," and then Nina stopped. She tried to think of a way to explain herself but she couldn't. Words once again became her enemy. They hid just beneath the surface of her whirling mind, taunting her use of them at a time she needed them most. She tried to force them to exit her mouth in defense of the turmoil that had built up for days.

Her mind raced, and when she tried to process too many emotions all at once, she began to feel unsafe and out of control. Thoughts became entangled and overtook her ability to reason. She couldn't tell Ben why she reacted the way she did because she didn't know why herself. Ben left the basement abruptly and Nina rushed to follow him upstairs. On the landing of the first floor, he turned to her.

"I have to get some stuff from my car, and then I'm taking off," he told her.

"Okay," Nina mumbled. "Ben, are you alright?" she blurted out.

He turned and looked at her. "Me?" he said hesitantly. "I'm fine. I have to go. See ya," he said and left.

Nina paused, watching him leave before she climbed the stairs to her apartment.

FOR THE REST of the day, Nina kept to herself. By early evening, she'd cleaned every inch of her apartment, organized her kitchen, and read the local newspaper from headlines to classifieds. But she still couldn't get her mind off of Ben. She thought of everything she'd wanted to say down in the basement but couldn't. Unbridled emotions bubbled to the surface and sometimes escaped when she least expected. At other times, they were well concealed, even for long periods. The fluidness of these moments left her ill-prepared to cope with moments like the one she encountered with Ben earlier. She wished she understood why, but more importantly, she wondered why he seemed so annoyed.

Trying to keep her mind off Ben, she thought about calling Lilia since she hadn't heard from her. However, she knew there were probably many details that Lilia had to attend to on her own, so Nina continued to busy herself with reading. When her eyes were tired, she played with the kittens for a while until finally, she couldn't stand it anymore and decided to call Lilia after all.

Just as she was about to pick up the phone, it rang. She hoped to hear Lilia's voice on the other end, but it was Richard. She dropped the phone as though she'd picked up a hot pan and had burned herself. She forced herself to pick it up and speak to him, knowing that it was most likely inevitable.

"What do you want, Richard?" she asked.

"Hello to you too, Nina," he said.

"What do you want, Richard?" she repeated.

"My attorney told me that you have a witness willing to testify when and where you found the money in question. However, in the interest of making this all go more swiftly, I'd be happy to negotiate some sort of split so that we can move on from here without more legal intervention."

"Are you? You're willing to negotiate?" she asked sarcastically.

"I'm trying to be reasonable, Nina. I think it's only fair that I get some of the money that should have come to me in the first place."

"And why is that again?" she asked, wondering how he would try to explain it.

"Ida and Henry were part of my family, Nina. That house and all the things in it should have come to me. How the State of Maine saw it otherwise is beyond me, but that's water over the dam. But what you found should have been part of the marital assets, and I am only asking for my fair share."

"First of all, just because you were related to Ida and Henry doesn't mean you treated them like family. I'm fairly certain that the only reason you were ever interested in Ida's welfare towards the end of her life was that you suspected Henry might have hidden things here. You told me as much on many occasions."

"You only think you know about a real family, Nina. I can't expect you to understand."

"Oh, and are you telling me once again that my parents weren't my real parents because I was adopted? Don't bother to answer because I've heard it all before. And let me guess, Richard. If the situation were reversed and you got the house and found the strongbox on your own, you'd have been willing to give me my fair share?"

"What you continue to ignore, Nina, is that you are the interloper here. I'm just asking you to be reasonable. You never should have been awarded the property in the divorce settlement and whatever you found belongs more to me than it does to you."

"It belongs to you? Have you forgotten that we used money

from the insurance settlement to buy this house? Have you forgotten that money also paid for years of your education? Do you know how many hours I spent at the grocery store working for your parents that I was never paid for? Do you want to know how reasonable I'm going to be? I'm going to tell you for the last time if you need to speak to me, do it through my attorney. I won't let you badger me over this."

Nina slammed the phone into the cradle. It immediately rang again. Sure it was Richard, she refused to answer it again and just glared at the answering machine.

"Hi, Nina. It's Lilia. I just wanted to...."

Nina grabbed the receiver interrupting the message.

"Hi, Lilia. It's me. Sorry. What were you saying?" she asked, trying to sound normal.

"I wanted to tell you about my arrangements for Walter's funeral."

With her heart still pounding, Nina took down all the information and told Lilia she would come to Portland in the morning to help with the restaurant. But when she got off the phone, she was still fuming about Richard.

She went around and around with things she wished she had said to him this past year. He had no right to tell her what she did and didn't understand about family. As strange as it was, this small group of friends that had come into her life felt like family. She truly cared about them. They were all struggling in one way or another, but they wanted the best for her too. She wished she'd told Richard that Lilia treated Henry and Ida more like family than any of the Kings did. Lilia was their real family.

NINA TRIED to sleep that night, but thoughts of her argument with Richard and the unknown reasons for Ben's coldness left her restless. She retreated to the kitchen and sat at the table where she and Ben often shared coffee or a meal . She thought about pulling out some flour and doing some baking, but even that wasn't enough to calm her.

Over and over again, the two scenes played out in her mind. She was proud of the way she stood up to Richard and wondered why in that moment she'd finally found the courage to tell him off. Maybe it was because in part all the words and thoughts were already there. She's said them dozens of times in her mind. But with Ben, it was quite the opposite. She didn't know what to say because she didn't know or understand what triggered her emotions. She wished she could find the words to tell him about the uncategorized pain that invaded her life. There were times it permeated much of her day. But she couldn't tell him where it came from or what made it subside. He knew she battled with these unknown demons, and sometimes they threatened to spill over at the slightest provocation. But when and why they erupted was as much a mystery to her as it seemed to be to him.

She was startled when Ginger jumped up to climb onto the windowsill. Nina stroked her fur and noticed Ben's car was still absent from where he always parked in the front driveway. She wondered where he was. She ached to try and find a way back to the ease of their friendship.

Looking up at the radiant full moon, she was reminded of one of her favorite stories as a child, *The Day Boy, and the Night Girl*. The story reached into her heart and gave her a sense of possibility as she grew up. She had all but forgotten most of the passages she'd memorized as a young girl, though she had repeated them often when she was distraught. But one came to mind now: *You must learn to be strong in the dark as well as in the day, else you will always be only half brave.*

The fairytale was about a witch who had abducted two mothers about to give birth. Maybe because she was adopted, she was comforted by thinking that sometimes babies were taken from their mothers rather than a child being willingly given away. She had checked it out of the school library so frequently that her parents bought her a copy for her birthday.

After the children were born, the witch convinced the mothers their babies had died, but in reality, she had taken the babies and planned to raise them herself. The boy, Photogen, was raised to bask exclusively in the light of day. He was never allowed to see the night or experience pain or sorrow. As he matured, his self-esteem flourished, and he was filled with confidence. But the witch raised the baby girl, Nycteris, in constant darkness. The only light she ever saw originated from a small window where she could glimpse the moon. Yet she developed an inner strength that connected her to all that was around her.

Nina's favorite passage was about the lonely girl. *Her heart—like every heart, if only its fallen sides were cleared away—was an inexhaustible fountain of love: she loved everything she saw.* Then she recalled trying to explain to her folks why she laughed so loud when she first read the story in their living room so long ago. The passage described when the two teens finally met, and Nycteris, unfamiliar with humans other than women, had no idea what a boy was. When she met the distraught Photogen, who was lost in the dark of night, Nycteris told Photogen, "Oh, I see! . . . No, of course! You can't be a girl: girls are not afraid—without reason. I understand now: it is because you are not a girl that you are so frightened."

The thought made her smile, and Nina wondered what had become of this book from her childhood. It most likely had been under her childhood bed where all her other treasures had been stored before the fire. The thought erased all the pleasure of this distant memory.

Nina wanted to avoid these thoughts, so she filled the kettle with water to heat for tea. Despite the late hour, she was determined to wait up until she saw the headlights of Ben's car traveling down the long driveway.

Having fallen asleep, Nina woke to footsteps on the stairs. She shook away the fog and rushed to open the door to her apartment as Ben reached the top step. His face was full of sorrow. The two stood looking at one another for what seemed to be an eternity until Nina led him inside and guided him to a chair.

Without asking, she fixed him some tea and placed a cupcake in front of him. An attempt at a smile crossed his face, and Nina knew when he turned away and glanced out the window, that he was confronting something he was struggling to reveal.

She sat down at the table with him and took his hand.

"Well, you might have noticed, I wasn't at my best today," he said.

Nina squeezed his hand tighter and gave him an understanding smile.

"I thought I could get through it—especially after this morning. But then it got to me by the time we went into the basement. Today is the anniversary of Byron's death. Ten years ago, he took his life, yet it seems like it was yesterday. My parents had Mass said for him, and there was a small family memorial service where all the relatives came. Of course, they stared at me. It's always so uncomfortable because I sometimes wonder if they wished it was me instead of him."

Nina couldn't find the words necessary to express what was in her heart. So they sat in silence for a while, sipping their tea.

Finally, Ben spoke. "I'm sorry, Nina. I just couldn't understand why you were upset initially. It could have been the hot water heater or something far worse," he told her, running his fingers through his hair.

"I know," she said.

"I was baffled why you reacted that way since it turned out to be no big deal."

"It was a big deal to me, Ben. I've been spending a lot of money lately. Not knowing what the problem was made me really nervous. It just seems like everything will be fine one moment, and then something unexpected happens. But I wasn't crying because I was upset. I was crying because I was so relieved. It's hard to explain. I had pushed away all these concerns for days, but they were still there even when I wasn't focused on them. So, by the time we were in the basement, and the solution to the problem was simply a clogged drain, I was so thankful it wasn't anything more, I over reacted. My tears were as much of a surprise to me as they were to you."

"Well, you've had a lot of things happen to you. I'm sure

they've colored your outlook," he told her. "I know it's hard because we never know what's around the corner. But we all face dark moments in life, and we just have to use those moments to change our lives for the better."

"You are a wonderful person Ben. I can't imagine anyone thinking otherwise," Nina told him. She gave him a warm smile before she leaned over and kissed his cheek. "I don't know what Byron was like and why he ended his life. But I know that I will be forever grateful to you as a friend for helping to save mine. You, my friend, make me brave enough to want to live."

<h1 style="text-align:center">Chapter Twenty-Seven</h1>

Nina woke up in the morning with more determination than she'd felt in a long while. Shortly after nine she called Andrea Goodwin to tell her about Richard's call the night before.

"Do you think Lilia would be willing to sign an affidavit that could be presented in court should the matter get to that point?" Andrea asked.

"I'm hesitant to bring up the subject under the circumstances, but I'll try," Nina said.

"Don't forget, we have to make a new will."

"As soon as this whole thing with Lilia is over, I promise I'll take care of that."

Before leaving for Portland, she also put in a call to Mr. Jacobs. He confirmed that it would be best to allow her attorney to handle the matter and wait until it was resolved before recontacting the interested buyer. With those calls out of the way, Nina got ready to leave.

She placed an extra bowl of cat food out for the kittens in case she got back late and stopped by to see Maddie and Penny before she left.

"Our plans to help celebrate Penny's birthday will have to wait until next week, if that's okay. Walter's funeral is on Friday, and I'm going to try to help Lilia out before then."

"Can I help too?" Penny chimed in. "You know I'm a really hard worker."

"Let me run it by Lilia first, okay? She's probably dealing with a lot right now. I'm not even sure how long I'll be gone today, but I'll check in with you when I get home, all right?"

"All right," Penny said with a sigh.

THE WEATHER WAS beautiful when Nina left for Portland. The sunlight was so bright, she squinted until her eyes adjusted. As she walked to her car she breathed in deeply allowing the crisp fall air to fill her. A faint scent of the sea was always present but on this day, its salty bouquet was even more assertive.

A sparkling layer of frost covered the windshield of her car. She dug her scraper from the glove box and went to work to clear it. The harsh noise of each stroke seemed incongruent with the lyrical songs of the birds hovering in the trees and scattered around the property. She persisted so she could get on the road and be on her way to help Lilia.

Despite the circumstances, it made Nina feel good to be helping her new friend instead of being alone with her thoughts. Lilia had welcomed Nina into her world and made her feel like she was a part of something greater than herself. Lilia treated her as though they'd known one another for years, and yet, it was barely weeks. That acceptance and familiarity both surprised and delighted Nina. Somehow, connecting with her and the other people in her life made her feel safe and secure. She knew Ben was right. Whether simply sharing time and conversations with him, or helping Lilia, Maddie, or Penny, being involved gave her a sense that life was about more than her personal problems.

She wondered if this was what helped Maddie too. Her sense of responsibility to her younger sister took up much of Maddie's time and energy. She showed no reluctance whatsoever to devote herself to helping Penny. That made Nina instinctively trust her. She was so honest and lived accordingly without sacrificing her own integrity.

Was that what it was like to have a sister?

Maddie had repeatedly offered to help whenever Nina was ready to make progress on the greenhouse. It was as if she wanted nothing more than to share her skills and passion for growing things and to show others the benefits as well. Nina was in awe of this because regardless of all Maddie had endured, she still tried to help others.

Penny, too, was amazing. She tried so hard to see the goodness in Maddie in spite of how difficult it was to listen to her older sister sometimes. She complained about it occasionally, arguing and even fighting with Maddie when she got frustrated, but Nina knew her youth and boredom caused her to be impatient. She hoped Ben was right and there might be a way Penny could attend school or do something other than sit at home each day. That would reduce the friction between them. Nina knew Penny's isolation could create an echo chamber of negativity.

It pleased Nina that Penny was interested in learning how to cook. The idea that she, too, could concoct her own recipes seemed to inspire her, and that made Nina feel powerful. She relished the idea that what she knew could benefit the young girl and broaden Penny's view of the paths before her.

Nina grinned thinking about when Penny had asked her for her recipe to make the baked custard she'd put together and shared with them.

"I have to know how to make this. It's so good," she said, licking every bit off the spoon. "Then again, maybe you shouldn't tell me. I would eat this for breakfast, lunch, and dinner."

"Well, it's probably healthier than some of the cereals I've seen at the grocery store, but you'd probably get sick of it soon enough," Nina told her.

"Never!" Penny insisted.

NINA LOOKED FORWARD to helping plan a celebration for Penny's sixteenth birthday. She wasn't sure exactly what the plan was, but there was time to organize something enjoyable for all.

When she arrived in Portland, Nina went directly to the diner. She parked a few blocks away because there was no room in the lot behind the building nor in front. As Nina entered Dizzy's, she found the place packed. Many of those gathered were friends and customers. Some stood in small groups with their winter coats draped over their arms, coffee mugs in hand, chatting quietly. Others sat at tables engaged in earnest conversations. They were all there to support Lilia, who was a vital part of the community.

David was standing next to Lilia and two others that appeared to be a couple. He motioned to Nina when she stepped through the door. She approached cautiously as she didn't want to interrupt their conversation. Lilia put her arm around Nina's waist and continued talking to the man with whom she was having a conversation.

"Charlotte wants to take it over," Lilia was saying. "It might be difficult with a new baby, but, honestly, I can't think of anyone else I'd rather see have it." Catching Nina up on the conversation, Lilia explained, "I'm going to let Dizzy's go. Walter and I had discussed selling it, but it was hard to give up something we both loved, and which brought us together. I just can't see working here without him. It would be better to work out something with Charlotte and move on from the place," she said, looking straight at Nina.

Nina wasn't sure how to respond so she nodded in agreement.

"I think you need to take some time off," David said. "You could spend time with Lizzy and her family. She'd be so happy to have you. I wish I could go too. It would be great for us to be together again."

"Yes. That would be lovely," Lilia agreed. Turning to Nina, Lilia told her, "Lizzy will be coming over for Walter's funeral. It will be the first time I'll get to meet her husband and their children. I almost feel like they're my grandkids."

"They are," David piped in. "We always thought of you as our mother, Lilia," David told her. "Years and miles didn't change that."

Lilia dabbed her eyes. "Thank you, David. You both meant the world to me. You still do." She paused for a moment. "I think I need an excuse to go cry. I'll go make some more coffee," Lilia said and hurried off towards the kitchen.

Before Nina could react, a couple approached David.

"Nina, this is Doug and Anita Blackwell. They used to own Dizzy's before Lilia and Walter bought it," David told her.

Nina reached out and shook their hands.

"Nice to meet you both. I'm sure you're pleased with how well they took care of this place," Nina said.

"I'm half tempted to buy it back from her, but she seems determined to let it go to Charlotte," Anita told her.

"I'm sorry. Who is Charlotte again?" Nina asked David. "She's one of the waitresses who has worked here for years. She just had a baby a few months ago. Lilia gave her some time off so she could stay home. But apparently, once she's able, she wants to take over Dizzy's. I'm not sure exactly what the two discussed, but if I know Lilia, she will make it happen if that's what she wants."

"Well, that seems like a wonderful solution if Lilia wants to retire."

Lilia came up behind her. "Who said anything about retiring? After I do some traveling, I will need a new project to keep me busy. Who knows what I'll end up doing."

"Well, you could always come back to Kittery. I'm still not sure what I'm going to do with the carriage house yet, and I also have to figure out what to do with the apartment downstairs. My current tenant will be moving out after the New Year."

"That certainly opens up possibilities. I'm excited to see what you've done to the place. Do I have to invite myself, or are you going to extend an invitation?" Lilia asked.

"You are always welcome to come. As a matter of fact, I was

thinking that since Thanksgiving is right around the corner, why don't you plan on spending it with me if you don't already have plans? You're welcome to come too, David."

"That would be wonderful, except Walter and I are usually open for Thanksgiving. So many of our regulars count on it because they can't cook for themselves, or they want the company. Maybe we can do something earlier in the day and go to Kittery in the late afternoon. What do you think?"

"I like the idea very much," Nina said.

"Well, based on those cupcakes you brought the other day," David said, "I think I'd better seal the deal right now. So you can count me in."

"That will give me something to look forward to," Lilia told them.

When most people had left, Nina approached Lilia, who was fiddling with something inside her purse. She seemed to find what she was looking for and looked up at Nina as she slipped Walter's wedding ring on her finger.

"I don't want to lose this," she told her. "I still can't believe he's gone."

"How long were you two married?" Nina asked, unsure of what else to say.

"It would have been seven years in December. We had a Christmas wedding. Can you imagine that?"

"How did you meet?"

"We met right over there," Lilia told her, pointing to a booth in the diner's corner. He used to come in with his late wife when the Blackwells owned the restaurant. I worked here part-time back then. They were the ones that told me about his wife's horrible accident. After Nancy died, Walter would come in occasionally. He seemed so lonely. One day, we just started talking. Soon he was coming in every day and staying longer and longer. We were two lost souls that found each other."

"You've led an interesting life, Lilia." Nina told her. "I was captivated by the stories related in your letters, especially the ones about your escapades with your uncle. He must have been a wonderful man."

"He was. He literally saved me from a terrible life. I still shudder when I think of the wretched Mrs. Peck."

"Did you ever go back there? To California?"

"Yes, but not that part. Walter and I went out to see his daughter Marilyn and her husband Dan a few times, but they live in Southern California, and I was from way up north. My uncle handled selling my parents' property through his lawyer, so I never needed to go back."

"Your descriptions of what happened and how you crossed the country were fascinating. I can't imagine how difficult that must have been."

"Billy made it as if it were some kind of elaborate game, so I thought it was fun. He kept me amused almost the entire time. And of course, I was thrilled just to be getting away."

"What made you and Walter buy this place?"

"We found out the Blackwells were selling, and Walter loved to cook. He came up with the crazy idea of buying it. He wasn't the best cook, but he did try, and since we only served breakfast and lunch, it worked. Bless poor Walter, though. I don't know if he realized how much work it would be. He never complained, but there were times I sensed he would have been happier if he'd continued puttering around in the garden and taking short trips here and there. Now it's too late." Lilia dabbed her eyes.

"Well, he clearly loved you and wanted you to be happy."

"I know. Walter was the most generous soul I've ever met. I never had to ask him for anything. If I made dinner, he would clear the table and wash the dishes. There was never any discussion. He just did what had to be done."

"That is wonderful. I don't think Richard picked up a dish the entire time we were married, regardless of the fact I worked all day and still came home to make dinner. He made it seem as if it was beneath him."

"My ex-brother-in-law, Jesse, was that kind of man."

"Did he straighten out? Is that why he came and got them?"

"No. He didn't. After the kids' mother died, he married a woman named Tina. I never met her, but Elizabeth told me horror stories. Apparently, she told Jesse that they could get welfare money for the kids if he got them back. They only stayed with their father for about a year before being taken into protective custody. They were luckier than most, though. A family took both of them in until they aged out of the system. From what I understand, that's highly unusual. Both the kids are still close to the Grant family, especially David, as he was there longer."

"Well, I am becoming more aware of how imperfect the system is, as I have two young girls living in one of my apartments. One is of age, but the other is a minor who can't live with her parents anymore. I don't want to get into details right now, but Penny, the younger one, is bored to tears. So the next time I come here, would you mind if I bring her along?"

"Not at all."

"Penny is a great worker and needs to be around more people."

"I'm going to stay closed, but after Walter's funeral is over, I'll need help. Mostly just getting the place in shape for Charlotte. This place needs a thorough cleaning."

"That's something both Penny and I can help with, I'm sure."

"Thanks for your offer to host Thanksgiving. I'm looking forward to seeing what your next food venture will be."

"You will be one of the first to know once I figure it all out." Nina kissed Lilia's cheek.

Nina glanced around, looking to say goodbye to David as well. He was talking to someone across the room, but Nina managed to catch his eye. For a moment, she found herself unable to let go of his gaze when he smiled back at her. She waved goodbye and then turned quickly so he wouldn't see her blush. She hurried to her car, suddenly wistful that she was heading home.

Chapter Twenty-Eight

Nina arrived home shortly after four and was greeted by Penny, who opened her apartment door as Nina rounded the corner.

"What did she say? Can I come help next time?" she asked eagerly.

Nina forgot what Penny was talking about for a moment and stared blankly at her. Penny drooped and looked at her feet.

"Oh, sorry! Yes, she would love to have your help, but not until next week after the funeral. She has a lot on her right now." Penny continued to frown. "I know you want to help, and I really appreciate that, and Lilia will too, especially once she sees how hard you work. It's hard to be patient but just try a little longer. Trust me, we'll have so much work you'll wish you never asked," Nina teased.

"I doubt that. I'm so bored I would happily sit through a math class," Penny retorted.

"I can't imagine ever being that bored," Nina told her. "Hey, can you come in and help me now because I want to plan something special for your birthday dinner. Want to help me figure that out?" Nina asked.

"Sure," Penny told her, coming into the kitchen.

Nina put on the kettle for some tea.

"I have a few cupcakes left. Would you like one with a glass of milk?" she asked as Penny plopped down on a chair at the kitchen table.

"Yes. I'm hungry. I didn't have lunch because I'm going to grow feathers if I eat any more chicken, and all we have for sandwiches right now is peanut butter and jelly."

"What about the money you earned? Can you use some of that to buy yourself something you'd rather eat?"

"Maddie does all the shopping, and she's always trying to save money. She said we have to save it in case we have to hire a lawyer or if we need to get a different apartment. That's why she brings home all the leftover chicken at the end of her shift. The owner of the Golden Skillet lets the employees have one free meal on their shift, so she eats dinner there most nights."

"Maybe we need to figure out a way to use some of that chicken and make it tastier. Do you have any in your fridge now? I have an idea."

"Yeah?" Penny looked doubtful.

"What if we made some crepes and added the chicken to some kind of sauce? We can take off the breading and just use the meat. Do you like mushrooms?" Nina asked.

"I'm not a big fan, but I'll eat them. I'd eat cardboard if you put it in gravy," she joked.

Nina laughed. "Well, I'll keep that in mind if I have any old boxes I want to get rid of. Let me show you how to make crepes, and that way, you can surprise Maddie some night with your culinary skills."

"Where did you learn all this? From your mom?"

"My dad was the real chef in the family. He taught me to make a couple of dishes on my own, and when I would serve it to him, he'd act like he was eating food from the finest restaurant. He died when I was quite young, though, and after that, I made most of our meals because my mother had to work such long hours. But I didn't mind. I've always loved to cook, even as a tiny girl. I'm not sure if I ever wanted to do anything else, really."

"I like it too. My mom isn't the best cook, so I started

making dinner when I lived at home. It was really easy stuff, though. My best thing was pot roast. My dad would actually be nice when I'd fix it for dinner. That's just about my favorite meal."

"Pot roast, eh? Do you like to bake?" Nina asked.

"I've never really done much baking," Penny told her.

"Let's make some cookies later," Nina offered.

"I'd like that if you're sure I'm not in your way. Maddie told me not to bother you too much."

"I enjoy your company. I think Cinnamon and Ginger do too," she added when the two kittens appeared downstairs. Ginger strolled over to eat some kibble, but Cinnamon stopped and nuzzled Penny's pant leg.

"Can I pick her up?"

"I'm sure she'd love that."

Penny snuggled with the kitten, and Nina served Penny the milk and cupcakes and had one too. When they finished snacking, Nina gathered the ingredients for crepes that they could fill with a chicken and mushroom sauce. She was surprised but delighted at how enthusiastic Penny was to learn how to cook.

"Let's make the filling first, and then you can make the crepes on your own. I have a simple recipe you can use. Can you run to your apartment and grab the chicken?"

Nina took out some butter from her fridge and placed it on the counter with the canister of flour.

When Penny returned, Nina said, "The ratio of fat to flour is one-to-one when making a roux, another word for sauce. I'm using butter, but you can also use other types of fat. First, you heat whatever you're using for fat in a pan. I'm making a white roux. That means we won't brown the butter, otherwise it would create a kind of nutty flavor."

Penny looked over Nina's shoulder in awe, observing everything she did.

"Now we'll add the flour, but we have to keep whisking it so it doesn't burn. Here—you try."

Nina handed Penny the whisk and had her stir the flour and

butter until it was well combined before giving Penny the other ingredients to add to the pan.

"This is harder than it looks. I'm afraid I'm going to burn it."

"Just keep stirring, and it will be okay. Go around the edges, too."

When the filling was done, Nina shut off the burner and gave Penny a cookbook that had a simple crepe recipe.

"The most important thing is getting all the ingredients prepared so you're not searching for anything while trying to cook. There aren't that many things needed for crepes, but it still helps to have them all together before we start."

She heard Ben coming up the stairs and popped her head out the door.

"Howdy, neighbor! What's going on? Everything good?" he asked.

Penny called out to Ben, "Look what I'm doing! I'm making the batter for crepes. Want to come to dinner?"

"I would love to join you! I've never had crepes before," Ben told her.

Nina grinned at her young protégé. "Tell you what. If Ben wants to join us, you can finish making the batter, and then when we're all ready to eat, we can take it over to your apartment to make and assemble them with the filling, okay? That way we'll have room to spread out."

"Sounds good to me," Ben said. "Let me drop my stuff off, and I'll be right over."

Nina and Penny began transporting the stuff for dinner next door. They sat out plates and began assembling Penny's creation. Within moments, Ben joined them.

"It smells amazing," he said.

"All I did was show her the recipe," Nina said, "and she took it from there."

Ben stood inside the doorway, listening as Penny babbled.

"This is actually pretty good. I like that it makes it tolerable to eat all the chicken Maddie brings home. Not that I'd want to eat this every night. It's so funny because when I was little, I wanted a chicken as a pet. Whenever we went to visit my grandparent's farm, I used to beg them to let me take one home."

"I take it they never let you?" Ben asked.

"No. But I did try to get one by hatching eggs. I'd steal them from the egg carton and hide them all over, thinking they would hatch if I put them someplace warm. My brother Kevin got really upset with me because I'd hidden one in his shoe and he didn't see it before putting it on," Penny told them.

Nina still laughed although she'd heard the story before. "Oh! That's what Maddie was referring to the other day. Well, it must have been quite a surprise."

"She never let me forget it. Every time we had eggs for breakfast, she'd ask my mom if she got them from my brother's shoe." Penny told them, chortling. Her infectious laugh had Nina and Ben grinning at her antics.

"Hey, before I forget to tell you both," Ben said, swallowing a bite. "I've been making some calls about Penny and Maddie's situation, and I have some news. I was going to wait until Maddie could be here, but I can fill her in later. Penny, how would you like to be emancipated?"

"Emancipated? You mean like a slave?" Penny asked, perplexed.

"Well, that is something that did happen after the Civil War for those held in slavery, but emancipation isn't just strictly about enslavement. In your case, after you turn sixteen, you could petition the court to allow you to be what's called an emancipated minor."

"Are you sure?" Nina asked. "I've never heard of this before. How would it work?"

"I don't know exactly, but I plan to find out more. I think Penny just has to prove she can manage without her parents. In effect, it's just a legal process conducted through the court." Turning to Penny, Ben told her, "If you're able, you could be independent from your parents and even go to school here in Kittery."

Penny rushed over to Ben and hugged him tight around his

neck. For a moment she couldn't speak. Then with a choked voice, she whispered, "Thank you—so much."

BEN LEFT a little after nine o'clock, and Nina helped Penny clean up the kitchen. Then, the two sat on the couch chatting while waiting for Maddie to come home.

About 10:30, Penny got up and looked out the window.

"Is everything okay?" Nina asked her. "You seem upset."

"Maddie's usually home by now. Where is she?"

"I'm sure she's fine," Nina tried to assure her. "Maybe she had to get gas or stopped to pick up something on her way home."

"She would never do that. She gets really nervous about driving home at night, especially lately because she told me she thinks someone is watching her."

"Watching her?" Nina asked, growing concerned.

"Last week, she said, someone was on the other side of the bushes that line the parking lot where she works. I've never been to the place, so I'm not sure what she meant, but she said employees have to park in the back, and to get to her car, she has to walk past a row of bushes. She thought she heard someone there a few times, so now she waits until some of the others on the late shift are walking to their cars too."

"That's smart. Maybe it was an animal or something," Nina told her, trying hard not to transmit her own fear at this news.

"She did say the trash is back that way, and it could have been a raccoon or something, but it frightened her. Maybe she had to wait a little longer for someone to walk her to her car," Penny said.

"That's possible," Nina told her.

"Remember I told you she makes us save all the money we earn from working for you? That's why. We might have to move in a hurry."

A pause in their conversation had Nina thinking back to the car in the driveway of the vacant house across the road. Her thoughts were interrupted when they heard someone rushing up the stairs. Penny flew off the couch and opened the door, and Nina followed. Maddie's face was pale when she arrived on the landing.

"Are you alright?" Penny asked her big sister.

"No!" she told Penny, looking back over her shoulder as she rushed inside. Maddie hurried to lock the apartment door and stood staring at it before she responded further. "I'm sure it was Dad. I didn't see him, but somehow I just know it's him out there, and he's been watching me," she said.

"But how would he know where you work?" Nina asked getting up to calm her.

Without even removing her heavy jacket, Maddie began pacing the floor. "Don't you see? He's lived around here all his life and people know him! I bet someone saw me at work and mentioned it to him. So tomorrow I'm going to call my mother and see if she knows anything. I knew eventually he'd figure out some way to find us. He found me once before, and he's found me again. He told me he would never let me go." She crossed to the window of their apartment to search the darkness.

"Well, it might not matter," Penny told her. "I might be emancipated!"

"What?" Maddie asked, turning to look at her.

"Ben said he did some checking, and I could try and.... what exactly did he say I had to do?" Penny asked Nina.

"Ben said it might be possible for her to petition the courts to allow her to become an emancipated minor. Then she could go to school and live with you so you'd be free of your folks."

Maddie wrapped her arms around Penny and then stretched her arm out to include Nina, who didn't say anything more but stood in silence, holding the two girls as tightly as she could. Nina didn't want to spoil the moment and was reluctant to caution them that even if Penny were emancipated, it wouldn't necessarily prevent their father from continuing to harass them.

Chapter Twenty-Nine

The funeral home was packed by the time Nina arrived at Walter's wake. Standing there in the receiving line among others who were most likely family, friends, or colleagues left Nina feeling awkward. She decided to quickly pay her respects and return to Kittery.

Biting the loose skin on the bottom of her lip, she moved along with the others, waiting for her turn to express her condolences. There were several people in line smoking. The man in front of her had his cigarette so close to her she could breathe in the smoke as if she held one to her lips. The heady feeling made her long for just one puff. She wished she had a pack of Juicy Fruit, or better yet, that she could melt into the background.

She turned to avoid the smoke and caught herself watching David, who was engaged in conversation with those who greeted him in line. By the time she finally reached the receiving line, she expressed her sympathies and left, trying to avoid the pile up of what-ifs that often found their way into her head before she could stop them.

Getting into her car, she wondered if her abrupt departure was rude. She stared out the windshield, watching the night sky, which had begun to snow. The streetlight above illuminated each flake that hit the windshield. Their intricate beauty gave her pause. She watched them one after another as they began to accumulate, forming a thin layer that prevented her from seeing out.

She grabbed her ice scraper from inside her glove box and got out of the car to clear her windshield. Not far away, she heard the slow pace of Billy Swan's song, *I Can Help*, as a young couple exited a nearby bar.

They huddled together as they walked by her. The floral notes of the fragrance Charlie wafted on the air in their wake. Many of her coworkers wore that perfume when she worked at the grocery store. The cold night air stung, and by the time she got back into the car, her socks were damp from the snow that had entered her boots. But the melody and words reverberated in her mind, and she hummed as she started her car and drove back to Kittery, forgetting all about the questions she'd had just moments earlier.

WHEN SHE ARRIVED HOME, Nina was tired but wanted to stay awake since it was still early. So she lay down on the couch and picked up the Doris Lessing book she was reading, and turned to the page where she'd left off.

> *I'm going to make the obvious point that maybe the word neurotic means the condition of being highly conscious and developed. The essence of neurosis is conflict. But the essence of living now, fully, not blocking off to what goes on, is conflict. In fact, I've reached the stage where I look at people and say -- he or she, they are whole at all because they've chosen to block off at this stage or that. People stay sane by blocking off, by limiting themselves.*

The words struck a chord, and Nina wondered about Ben's reasons for giving her this particular book. It seemed like an odd choice, given all the books he had on his bookshelves. She put the book down and closed her eyes to rest, admitting to herself that there were times she believed she did little to contribute to the world.

WITH A GRUMBLING STOMACH, she turned her attention to making dinner and went downstairs to her kitchen. When she opened the door to the fridge to see what she had available, she was surprised to see the shelves were fairly empty. She hadn't done any shopping in days and had shared many meals with her friends. So she searched the cupboards to see what she had on hand. Reaching for some arborio rice, she thought of her mother, who insisted on making some type of risotto at least once week. Her instinct took over and she took the leftover chicken broth out of the fridge along with an onion and some parmesan cheese. She grabbed a bulb of garlic to use too, mincing it with the onion for a dish that had been such a large part of her youth.

As these cooked in the skillet, it reminded her of the moment just weeks ago when Ben told her how empty the girls' refrigerator was and how they both began to flourish as they began to learn how to create simple, inexpensive meals that would allow them to eat better. She smiled recalling the enormous pride she, herself, felt as a young child, carrying various meals to the table where both of her parents would gush over them as if they'd come from a high-end restaurant.

Nina poured herself a glass of wine and used the rest to add to the risotto that was now simmering in the pan. As it browned, she began to consider things from her past she had ignored. For many years, Nina could easily ignore the world around her by believing it didn't matter because it didn't impact her. After all, her life was relatively sedate and had seemed secure before her divorce.

Even after that illusion was shattered, she continued to shield herself from all the things that caused her to be overwhelmed. It was hard to watch the nightly news reports, especially when newscasters highlighted the body counts of soldiers to show who was winning the war. It was as if all those killed, injured, and missing bolstered justification of being in a war many Americans opposed.

Nina certainly couldn't ignore the price of gas, which had quadrupled in just a year. Yet thinking about it, she saw no evidence that the country was confronting the impact of t h e root cause of the oil embargo and the country's dependence on oil that cause the high inflation that now made financial matters so much worse.

These things hadn't mattered to her because she had convinced herself they weren't her problems. But when Nina thought about the world that Maddie and Penny would inherit, she began to wondered if there was anything she could do to make it a better place for them to live.

Nina finished cooking the risotto and added the parmesan cheese and a pinch of black pepper. She ladled some into a bowl and carried it to the table. She looked at her apartment door and wondered if she should see if Penny wanted to eat with her. She marveled at the thought that under her very roof were two young women who she might never have been privileged to know if it wasn't for an overflowing toilet.

Nina knew now that these young women were impacted by the decisions of those in power, who controlled so much of what was happening in the world. She determined to start becoming aware of the news, even if it often made her uncomfortable. There were still violent outbreaks in Boston over the court-ordered busing of students. Tuning it out as she often did wouldn't make it go away.

Whenever there were reports about the Kanawha County textbook controversy championed by Alice Moore, Nina felt powerless to do anything about it, so she turned the dial or turned the news off completely. But women like Moore, who argued that children should not learn about any history that even hinted at multiculturalism, wouldn't disappear because Nina didn't turn on the radio or watch the nightly news.

In the little seaside town of Kittery, it was easy to ignore what was happening in the nation. At one point, nothing seemed to impact her life beyond the people she had direct contact with personally or professionally. But she began wondering why she never connected national events to things that did affect the lives of the two young women she'd grown very fond of recently.

There were marches and protests by those opposed to war, those who wanted racial equality, and those who fought to give women the same rights as men. She recalled being home alone one evening in January of the previous year and watching as Cronkite announced on CBS that the Supreme Court had ruled in a landmark decision that made abortion legal. Now she wondered what had happened when Maddie's mother took her to have an abortion. It had certainly been illegal wherever Maddie's mother took her at that time. Did they have to make their way to Boston or another city? How did they find someone who would perform the abortion? Could Maddie's mother afford the cost to take her to the hospital or did they risk going to someone who used a rubber catheter attached to a coat hanger like Julia told her happened in Danielle's case? It made Nina realize that even if things happened in distant places, they did impact her because they potentially impacted others she cared about.

Growing up Catholic, Nina was taught that sex before marriage was wrong, and that abortion was also wrong. Simply put, it was a sin. These were things Nina had always believed as undeniable truths. Even when Julia told her about Danielle, she hid her disdain for the idea that Danielle would have needed to get an abortion, or that she'd risked her life to do so. In her mind, those were the consequences of immoral actions.

But hearing Maddie's story had changed Nina's mind. She still didn't necessarily agree with abortion. Nina simply thought that from now on, she would try to honor other women's rights to have a say in how or why they might choose to get one.

THE FUNERAL WOULD BE HELD on Friday morning at the State Street Church in East Portland, a few blocks away from the Portland Symphony Orchestra. Nina was relieved when Ben offered to drive her, even though it meant he would have to drive her back to Kittery and then return for practice later that night. His presence made her anticipation of the heavy emotional circumstances more bearable.

"The church is beautiful," Ben told her. "I sometimes go there to sit and think. They have a lot of wonderful musical events there, and they have a coffee house called "The Gate." Were Lilia and Walter active members?"

"I don't think so. I think she made arrangements there because she knew that they needed a large place to accommodate his friends and all the people who might want to pay their respects. Walter taught at Portland High for years, so she thought many of his former colleagues and students might come, not to mention their customers from Dizzy's. His daughter Marilyn and her family are with Lilia now, and Elizabeth is supposed to fly in for the funeral. It's strange that these people I only recently met are so important to me now that I'm attending a funeral. I'm not sure how to explain it. Lilia is just so warm. I wish I'd had a chance to get to know Walter. He sounds like such an amazing guy. I can only imagine the church will be packed."

"Is she holding a reception after the burial?" Ben asked.

"Yes, Lilia said the burial would be private because Walter and his late wife Nancy had purchased burial plots years ago. They never discussed his wishes after he and Lilia got married. But Lilia wanted to honor his daughter Marilyn and bury him with Nancy so her parents would be together."

"That is a complicated situation."

"Who knows what the future holds for her, so maybe it's for the best. She's still pretty young."

"I know. When you began reading Lilia's letters, I remember we thought she was really old and probably dead. It's hard to imagine her that way now. I'm also really surprised I've never ventured into Dizzy's. It's so close to where I work."

Ben seemed ready to leave, but Nina wasn't ready to be alone again and pressed to think of anything to keep their conversation going.

"Oh! I think I forgot to tell you. Guess who called the other day?"

"Who? Not Richard, I hope."

"I got a call from Julia. She wondered why I haven't been in touch. She asked me if I wanted to visit again, and I said not right now. I think I have to talk to her about what happened when she was here. If I want her in my life, I have to find a way past that and be honest with her."

"I think that's a very healthy approach, Ms. DeMarco. We all make mistakes, and confronting her rather than sweeping the matter under the rug is a much better idea."

"Yes, it is, but I'm not going there for a while. I have too much to confront at the moment!"

Chapter Thirty

Nina looked in the mirror. Light filtered through the small bathroom window, illuminating the space with a brightness not ordinarily available in other months.

The winter sun was graceful in its brilliance but not entirely forgiving. It cast shadows, making Nina's face seem ashen. She applied lipstick, thinking it might give her a bit more color. She wasn't fond of putting on make-up, as she thought it made her look ghoulish. Richard disputed this, but she wondered if he ever saw her how she really was rather than what he wished her to be. What he wanted from her was never clear. He used words of praise to describe her looks, her cooking—anything he found helpful, but he never seemed to find any words to praise Nina herself. It was as if she was an object that served a purpose in his life, but once it no longer functioned as he desired, he pushed it aside.

She realized Richard never loved her the way Walter loved Lilia. Maybe he found her intriguing, and she presented a challenge to a man who was used to dating whomever he wanted. But it no longer mattered. She grabbed a tissue and wiped the lipstick away.

WHEN NINA and Ben arrived in Portland for Walter's funeral, they found parking difficult around the towering Gothic-style church with a red freestone façade. They hurried towards the building, found seats in the back row, and sat down with minutes to spare before the service started.

The music reminded Nina of all the things she once loved about attending Mass when she was younger. She'd been far removed from those traditions for many years but found the melodies that drifted down from the balcony soothing.

As Walter's casket was carried in, his family walked solemnly behind it. The pallbearers placed the casket in the front of the church. Once everyone was seated, the minister spoke the life of Walter Garrison.

"Over the course of his life, Walter Garrison was known by thousands of people. As many of you know, he taught history for years at Portland High and acted as an assistant coach for their football team, the school's beloved Bulldogs. Walter encouraged students to learn history to have a better understanding of the world and to play sports to have a better understanding of one another. Yet his legacy at Portland High reached far beyond his years of teaching. When he retired to care for his wife Nancy, he showed us the meaning of love and commitment in marriage. When Nancy passed, he told me his grief was complicated by knowing that she was no longer wasting away before his eyes. He didn't seem bitter or resentful that he'd lost the love of his life. He was merely sad and missed the life they had together.

"In those days, he found solace in the community that he was a part of for decades. It was the members of these various communities that helped him heal and move on from his grief. But perhaps no one helped him more than the woman who brought great joy to his final days, his new wife, Lilia. She, too, seemed to know everybody in the world, or at least in this part of the world.

"I will never forget driving back from picking up food for our soup kitchen. Walter had offered to go along and help. He was quieter than usual, and I asked if he was alright. Then he told me about a woman he met and how she opened his heart to loving someone again.

"At that time, my own spirituality was strained. The unrest in the world and in our country tested my resolve that the teachings of Christ could win over the hatred and bigotry that still blackened the hearts of those fighting against the rights of others. Sometimes my spirit was shaken to the core watching the violence that turned peaceful demonstrations in areas like Selma into places where men and women believed they were justified in the killing of Black civil rights activist, Jimmie Lee Jackson.

"But Walter's faith led me to realize I could not let hatred exhaust me. As Scripture tells us, 'His mercies are not spent. Every morning, they are renewed. Great is his faithfulness. I will always trust in him.' We must love unconditionally, and Walter Garrison was a prime example of giving of himself in a way that showed me how to trust in the goodness of people again.

"And so today, we celebrate the life of Walter Garrison, a man who was loved by many. And that is what has brought us all together. It is not his death that brings us here but the life and courage he displayed daily. In remembering Walter, let us pray for one another. Pray that a world without him does not see darkness but is granted light from the stars shining brighter as he joins the heavens.

"Please stand and raise your voices with me as we are blessed by our Lord Jesus Christ. May all the angels in heaven and on earth lead you to Christ our Savior. You are a sign of his presence to us. May the Lord grant you peace and hold you in his love forever. Amen."

AFTER THE SERVICE, many of the attendees gathered downstairs for a reception. People shared their stories of Walter and paid their respects to Lilia, Walter's daughter Marilyn, and various members of his extended family.

"That was a very moving eulogy," Nina commented. "I'm so sorry I never got to meet him. What a remarkable man."

Lilia dabbed tears away from her eyes. "Yes, I was so lucky we found one another. Nina, you've met David, but this is his sister, Elizabeth."

"Hello. You and your brother look so much alike! I would have recognized you even if Lilia hadn't told me who you are," Nina said, shaking Elizabeth's hand. "This is my friend, Ben Comstock. Ben is a musician with the Portland Symphony right around the corner."

David and then Elizabeth extended their welcome to Ben. "Are you from Portland?" David asked him.

"No, I grew up in Vermont, outside of Burlington. I came here for my job with the Symphony."

"What instrument do you play?" Elizabeth asked him. "Mainly the cello. But I'm trained on the violin and viola as well."

As they continued to converse, Nina wondered if she was being too chatty. She was often either tongue-tied or too verbose. When she spoke, there never seemed to be a happy medium, at least in her mind. Nina noticed others waiting to talk to them, so she tried to think of a way to extricate herself from the conversation, knowing Ben had to get her back home and then return to the area for a concert that evening anyway.

"Elizabeth, I'm not sure how long you'll be staying, but you're welcome to join us for dinner if you're here over the Thanksgiving holiday. Lilia and David are coming unless plans have changed," she said, looking David's way.

"No, we're looking forward to it. I'd love to get a look at those letters."

"I'd love to join you, but I have to get back home," Elizabeth said. "I hope to see you again though."

"Me too," Nina told her.

Chapter Thirty-One

On Monday, Nina got up early to start preparing for Penny's birthday celebration. She had just put a carrot cake in the oven and had started making the frosting when there was a knock on her door.

"It's open," she called.

"It's me, Maddie. Can I come in?"

"Of course, you can," Nina told her.

Maddie entered holding a paper bag. She stood shyly in the kitchen waiting to be asked to sit. "Ben just took Penny to the courthouse to file some paperwork. I can't believe she might be able to become an emancipated minor. That will make her so happy."

"I'm sure it will," Nina said.

"Can I hang out here with you? I want to wrap her presents but I don't feel like being alone."

"Sure. I'm happy to have your company. What did you tell your boss when you called in?"

"I just said I'm sick. And I am sick," she told Nina. "Sick of working with idiots that treat me like I'm incompetent. The new guy told me how to run the fry machine the other day, something I've been doing for more than a year. He's been there less than a month. He told me I was doing it wrong, then he burned a whole batch of chicken. The manager pretty much told him, 'oh, well.' Man, I would have been fired if I did that."

"I have no doubt about that," Nina said, thinking back to the time she got fired from Ai Fiori's. Her thoughts suddenly veered into disturbing memories and a day she lost her job.

That day was unusual because Nina had arrived much earlier than her normal work schedule, trying to avoid some of her kitchen colleagues. Weeks before, she'd overheard some of them discussing her behind her back. She was always under the impression they at least respected her talent for making the complicated desserts for the upscale clientele at Ai Fiori's. But then she heard them describe her as high-strung and neurotic, a perfectionist, and a dumb blonde all in the same conversation. They always spoke in Italian because they assumed others didn't speak the language. But Nina knew enough to understand what was said. She decided it was best to ignore them.

Weeks later, one of the line cooks called in at the last minute, and the restaurant's owner, Mr. Marchesi asked Nina to fill in. But after witnessing some tactics they used to get food out of the kitchen, she finally had had enough and complained.

She knocked on the door of his office and said, "Mr. Marchesi, what your kitchen staff does sometimes is not just disgusting, it's dangerous. Someone could end up with food poisoning."

He just looked at her and said, "Miss DeMarco, many of these men have been my employees for years, some coming straight over from Italy. They're like family to me. I've tolerated your inability to get along for some time now because of your superb culinary skills. But this is forcing me to terminate your employment. I'll mail you your paycheck. Please close the door on your way out." And just like that, Nina was out of a job.

Completely beside herself, all she wanted to do was go home and see her mother. She left Wellesley not knowing she wouldn't be returning for weeks.

When she got close to her childhood home on Shrewsbury Street, firetrucks roared behind her. Nina pulled over to let them by. She decided it might be best to shop before she arrived home and stopped at the market to pick up some groceries. When she finished and drove closer to home, she had to park a few blocks over because something was happening up ahead. She walked a few blocks towards home where she saw a crowd of people in front of the building where she grew up. It was engulfed in flames. She dropped the grocery sacks as she realized her mother was most likely trapped inside. Nina shuddered trying to force the thoughts from her mind.s

"Can I lick the spoon when you're done?" Maddie asked. Her question brought Nina back to the moment and she looked down at the bowl of frosting.

"Sure," she told Maddie who seemed unaware that Nina hadn't been paying attention to what she'd been telling her.

"I can't wait to see the look on Penny's face when she opens this," Maddie said, attempting to show Nina the gag gift she'd purchased for Penny. Maddie held up a package of days of the week underwear.

It reminded Nina of the look on Richard's face when she gave him a gag gift of a pet rock on his birthday right before they were married. His parents had given him a Corum Feather Watch and, unable to compete with such extravagance, she got him some tickets to see the Celtics. He didn't seem to appreciate either of her presents and he acted embarrassed that she didn't offer something more since he knew by then she had plenty of money in her savings account.

"I hope she likes her real present. I used some of the money we earned from helping you for her present, but it was more money than I've ever paid for a game before."

Nina glanced over her shoulder trying to shake off the distant memory. "What did you get her?" she asked, turning back to finish making the frosting.

"It's some game a few of the people at work play. It's called *Dungeons & Dragons*. Penny loves to read, and this kind of reminded me of her favorite book, *The Lord of the Rings*. I hope I got it right. She's looking forward to going back to school, and this might help her make friends because she could talk about it to other kids."

Maddie went on telling her all about the many reasons she thought Penny would like the present, as if she were trying to justify purchasing it.

Nina wanted to avoid telling Maddie that she and Ben had chipped in to purchase something special for Penny's birthday, so she tried changing the subject.

"Well, I hope she likes the pot roast I'm making for dinner. She said it's her favorite. The carrot cake should be ready to take out soon. When do you think they'll be coming back?"

"I guess it depends on what happens in court. Ben had no idea how many papers they'd have to fill out."

"How he's found time to do all of this is beyond me," Nina told her. "He's quietly taken control of the matter, hasn't he?"

"I'll say. He hasn't discussed all the details with me, but I think that's because he is assuming Penny will keep me informed. What time are we leaving for the movies?" Maddie asked her.

"Ben suggested we go to a matinee, so we need to arrive in Portsmouth around noon. Penny asked to go to Dairy Queen for lunch, and after that, we'll head to the movies. How does that sound?"

"Great! I'm glad you suggested we wear caps and put our hair up to disguise ourselves. It's kind of fun, but then maybe I also won't have to worry about someone from work noticing me either," Maddie told her. "My red hair is hard to miss."

"It's one of the reasons we decided going into New Hampshire might be a better than doing something locally. The latest show is at one o'clock, so we should have plenty of time to eat and get there on time."

"Penny is going to love a juicy burger for a change, but she'll also be thrilled to have pot roast for dinner. Hey, is something burning?" Maddie asked.

Nina stood frozen in the moment. Her eyes widened in terror and her face turned pale as the smell of smoke leaked into the room. Maddie watched her in utter confusion. Not waiting for

Nina to act, Maddie got up from the table and grabbed Nina's oven mitts and opened the door. A small amount of batter from the carrot cake had spilled onto the bottom of the oven causing the smell. She grabbed a spatula, scraped it up, and closed the oven door.

"Are you alright?" Maddie asked Nina.

Sweat glistened on Nina forehead, and she was at a loss for what to say. Her frenzied mind had her looking for an escape route while her young friend took control and resolved the problem. Words couldn't express the wave of thoughts and emotions that had overcome her, so she simply crossed the room and gave Maddie a quick hug.

"I'm fine. Thanks," she whispered.

Nina took the cake out of the oven, and when it was completely cooled, she began to frost it.

"Can you show me how to do that sometime? You're showing Penny how to cook, and I can't have her always telling me about new things I haven't had a chance to learn," Maddie told her.

"Of course. I'd be happy to show you. Let me finish frosting the cake and then, if we have time before Ben gets back with Penny, would you like to make some bread?"

"That would be terrific," Maddie replied.

Nina looked over and smiled at her young friend.

"IT'S NOT FAIR! How can you two eat all that? I'd be sick to my stomach," Ben told Maddie and Penny as they gulped down huge double burgers, fries, and milkshakes. The sisters slurped their drinks to tease him. Finally, Penny surprised herself with an enormous belch, and they all laughed.

The festive mood made the afternoon go quickly. *Benji,* the movie they chose to see, was a huge hit. They all loved the stray dog who lived in an abandoned house on the outskirts of a small town. When the father sent Benji away, Nina found herself in tears. But the heartwarming story ended happily, and Nina came out of the movie humming the theme song, "I Feel Love."

Both girls wore old jackets that Ben had loaned them. Even with oversized jackets and hair tucked under hats, the girls' disguises wouldn't have fooled anyone who looked closely. Their petite frames and how they carried themselves indicated they were indeed girls. Nina wondered why she ever thought they would be safer dressed as boys. Lilia's escape from Mrs. Peck had definitely played a part in her thinking, but Maddie and Penny were a lot older than Lilia had been at the time.

BEN WALKED AHEAD with Maddie back to the car. He wanted to fill her in on what happened at court. Penny chatted with Nina as they followed.

"Can we please go back home now to open presents?" Penny asked.

"I think that's a great idea. Maybe we can have dinner in the carriage house. It's nice and cozy now that it's all cleaned out," Nina told her.

"That sounds like fun. We can grab the food and eat it in front of the fireplace," Penny suggested.

"Would you like that?" Nina asked.

"I'd love that. I can't wait to see what Maddie got me. She's been so secretive. It's probably something boring. She's always too practical."

"Let's not forget, she's had to be. But it sounds like everything is moving in the right direction," Nina reminded her.

"Just think, soon I'll have a lot more freedom. Maybe I can even get a small job after school. I can't wait. You both have been so nice to help us out," she told Nina.

"I'm happy to do it, and I think I can say Ben is too."

Nina was touched as Penny moved closer to her as they walked. She threaded her arm through Nina's, who instinctively kissed the top of Penny's head, something her mother had done when they walked this way. She was grateful these two young women had each other and that somehow, the four of them had formed a type of kinship, despite not being related. Maybe, Nina thought, family really is more about love and commitment to one another than anything else.

WHEN THEY GOT BACK to the house, Nina asked Ben to let them out in the back. As he rounded the corner of the driveway, he saw that Keith and April were blocking them from going further. Keith got out of the truck and approached Ben's car.

"Hey, Ben. Do you mind waiting a sec for me to move my truck?" Keith told him.

"Sure," Ben told him.

Keith went around to the passenger's side door and held it open for his wife, April. They joined hands as they made their way towards the house and disappeared into the back entrance.

"Who's that?" Penny asked.

"They live on the first floor, in my old apartment," Nina told her. "You've never seen them before?"

"No, I can only see the back of the house from the windows in our apartment."

"Yes, they normally park around front, and they keep pretty much to themselves. They're moving out soon. Keith got a new job."

"When are they leaving?" Ben asked Nina.

"By the end of December," she replied. "I have to decide what to do with the apartment after that."

While they were waiting for Keith to return, Nina thought again about how isolated and lonely Penny had been. She knew how much she'd miss them if they moved out and how helping them brought so much satisfaction to her life.

Moments later, Keith returned to the driveway and chatted with them.

"Thanks for waiting. I didn't have a chance to put sand down on the front steps, so I wanted to help her in," he told him.

"No worries," Ben told him.

"I bought some more and will make sure the front is taken care of, too," Keith offered.

"Thanks, Keith. I'll be having some company here for Thanksgiving. If we get snow, would you be able to clear spaces for a few extra cars when you plow?" Nina asked him. "We're having dinner in the carriage house."

"Of course. April has been dying to see what you've done to the place. Maybe the next time you're headed there, you could give us a peek?" he asked.

"We'll be having dinner in there soon, as a matter of fact. I made plenty of food, and you're welcome to join us if you're both up to it."

"I'm sure she'd like that," Keith told her.

"WE DON'T NEED THESE ANYMORE," Maddie said as they arrived at the landing at the top of the second floor. She took off Ben's oversized jacket. "I'll get my coat and be right back to help," she told them.

"Me too," Penny said, giving Ben back his coat.

"I'll go put these away," he told Nina. "I think it was really unnecessary after all, but the idea was not a bad one. I'll be happy once they don't have to worry about their father anymore."

Nina went into her apartment and found Ginger and Cinnamon curled up together on the kitchen table.

"Sisters," she thought, before luring them to the floor with a dish of milk.

BY THE TIME the others returned, she had placed everything they needed to bring to the carriage house on the counter. Ben brought over a grocery sack full of soft drinks he bought and offered to take more items with his spare hand. The girls each grabbed some of the food too, and Nina collected the remaining bag full of food from the table, and they all made their way out to the carriage house.

Once inside, Nina turned on the oven. Maddie had returned to her apartment to get Penny's gift, which left Penny looking around, scouting for presents. She seemed anxious that nothing was apparent.

Ben offered to start a fire, while Penny helped Nina in the kitchen.

"It will take some time for the pot roast and vegetables to cook, but I can't imagine you're hungry. You and Maddie had a pretty big lunch!" Nina teased her.

"I'm already hungry. I can't believe you made fresh bread. It looks so good," Penny told Nina, eyeing the loaves still in the pan.

"Let's save those for dinner. But I can get some cheese and crackers if you want me to," Nina offered.

"Yes, please!"

Nina looked over at Ben, and the two exchanged looks. There was an unspoken understanding that he should watch Penny so their birthday surprise wouldn't be ruined. Nina hurried off to put together the snacks. As she rounded the corner at the top of the stairs, Maddie was coming out of their apartment with her gifts for Penny. The look on her face revealed a sadness that wasn't evident before.

"Are you alright, Maddie?" she asked.

"My mom called to wish Penny a happy birthday. She went to stay with my grandparents, but now she's back in Maine with my dad again. She started crying. She's somewhere at a payphone and said he is a mess, so she's beside herself. I honestly wish she wouldn't call us anymore," Maddie said and began to cry.

"I don't know your mom or what's going on in her mind, but sometimes women find it really hard to break free even when their husbands are awful. I'm not sure why that's true, but the same thing happened to my aunt Angela even though my uncle Joe often beat her. Nothing anyone said could convince her to leave him. It happens, and it's their decision, I guess. But that doesn't mean you have to let your father or mother ruin your life. You and

Penny are breaking free of all that. I'm so proud of you," Nina told her and gave her a quick hug.

"You are?" Maddie asked her.

"Of course I am. I can't believe how strong and daring you are. I can't even imagine going through what you've been through and not wanting to just...." Nina stopped herself from revealing the way she reacted when life overwhelmed her to the point of despair. "I am very proud of you, Maddie, and you should be proud of yourself, too. Why don't you bring the presents down to the carriage house before Penny drives Ben nuts. I'm sure she's climbing the walls, she's so excited. I'll be down in a minute."

NINA WENT into her apartment to prepare the snacks, then decided to get a heavy sweater before heading back to the carriage house. She noticed the red light flashing on her answering machine and pressed the button.

"Hello, Nina. Mr. Jacobs here. Per Ms. Goodwin, the legal matter between yourself and your ex-husband has been resolved. Once I hear back from you, I will contact the buyer who expressed interest in your collection. Call me when you can."

The machine beeped, and Nina heard Andrea's voice.

"Hi, Nina. Call me when you can. I have some excellent news for you. If you don't reach me before five today, call me first thing in the morning." Looking at her watch, Nina decided it was too late to call either of them, but, along with the cheese and crackers, she picked up a bottle of wine, since now she had even more to celebrate.

Chapter Thirty-Two

"What took you so long?" Penny asked when Nina came through the door.

"Penny, that's rude! Just because it's your birthday doesn't mean you can act like a brat," Maddie chastised.

"Sorry, Nina. I'm just so excited. Can I grab those from you?" Penny offered. But instead of taking the cheese and crackers, she teasingly grabbed the bottle of wine and pretended to drink it.

"Don't even pretend, Penny. Just the thought of you drinking anything right now will make me upset," Maddie told her.

"Okay," she said and placed the wine on the counter.

"How about we get something to drink and a few snacks and then open Penny's presents?" Ben suggested.

"Sounds good to me," Maddie said. Penny was sulking, so she simply nodded and went to sit at the table by the fireplace.

"Alright, Penny! Since you're the birthday girl, you go first. What would you like to drink? I bought Coke, Mt. Dew, Dr. Pepper, and orange Fanta. All wonderfully refreshing," Ben told her.

"I love Dr. Pepper! Can I have that?" she asked.

"Sure. And you, Maddie?"

Maddie was melancholy but brightened at Ben's offer. "I'll take the same, thank you."

"Any for you, Ms. DeMarco?"

"Well, Mr. Comstock, I brought some wine. There's a lovely red that will go well with the pot roast. I think I'd like that. Would you care for some, or would you rather have a tonic?"

"I would love a glass of wine. Would you like me to open the bottle after I serve these beautiful young ladies?" Ben offered.

"That would be wonderful. I'll put out the cheese and crackers before we start."

Ben approached the counter where Nina was getting glasses to serve the beverages. With both girls on the other side of the room, she quietly told him about the calls from her lawyer and the appraiser.

"That's wonderful news. This is cause for a double celebration. I'm sure you're relieved."

"I am. I wondered if, somehow, Richard would manage to win his case even though I was told he didn't have one. I can just imagine how furious he is. I'm not sure if we would have found the strongbox without Lilia's help, but if Richard and I were still married and we did find it, he would have had a lot more than he ended up with when he divorced me."

"He lost out on more than money, Nina. But from what you've told me, it seems like the only thing that really mattered to him was this property."

"Hey, what are you two talking about over there?" Penny called over.

"We're discussing how much you'll love your presents," Ben teased.

Once everyone had their drinks, Maddie handed Penny her presents. She had used the funny pages from the Boston Globe to wrap them. Penny tore through the first present to find a package of days of the week underwear.

Penny's shoulders slumped. She quickly turned her head trying to hide her disappointment.

"Thanks," she mumbled.

"Gotcha!" Maddie laughed. "Here's your real present!" she told Penny, then handed her another gift.

Penny gave her sister a crooked grin and took the gift. She slowly unwrapped it revealing the white boxed set of *Dungeons and Dragons.* Her eyes widened as she looked across at Maddie. She pulled out a booklet and started to read the cover aloud.

"*Men and Magic. Volume One of Three Booklets.*" She showed Ben and Nina the picture of a man dressed in medieval garb holding a sword.

"What do you think? Do you like it? All the kids I work with are playing it," Maddie told her anxiously.

"This is so neat! I've never heard of it before! How do you play it? Will you play it with me?"

Just then, there was a knock on the door to the carriage house, and Keith and April came in.

"Are we interrupting anything?" April asked.

"Not at all! We're celebrating Penny's birthday, and she's opening her presents. She turned sixteen the other day," Nina told them.

"Congratulations, Penny. I don't think we've met. I'm Keith, and this is April, my wife," he said, moving into the room.

"And this is Maddie, Penny's sister. They live in the other second-floor apartment."

"Maddie, I've seen you around a few times when I lived on the third floor."

"Yes, you look familiar too."

"It's a shame we didn't get to know you better. We're moving to New Hampshire soon. I'm taking a position at a school in Nashua," he explained.

"My folks are thrilled since I come from that area," April told them. "I'm not due until May, but that will give me a chance to get settled long before the baby comes."

"You're having a baby?" Penny piped up.

"Yes, I'm really excited to be a mom. I hate to give up my job, but maybe I can go back to nursing someday."

"Do you work for a doctor locally?" Ben asked.

"I did, but Dr. Wilcox retired, so I took a job in York at the hospital."

Nina immediately looked away flustered when she realized April worked at the hospital where Ben had taken her in August. April didn't seem awkward towards Nina, and she breathed a sigh of relief when April changed the subject.

"This is magnificent! It's so much larger than it looks from outside."

"Let me get you something to drink, and you can join us near the fireplace. It's warmer over here," Ben said. "What can I get you?"

"I'll have a small glass of wine if it's no trouble. What about you, honey?" Keith said, turning to April.

"Make mine a soda. Can I have some of the Fanta?" she asked, looking at the bottles that were still on the counter.

"Coming right up."

Keith and April moved across the room and sat down at the table in front of the fireplace.

"Don't let us stop you from your celebration," Keith told them. "What is that you have, Penny?"

"Maddie bought me a new game. It's called *Dungeons and Dragons.*"

"I've heard of this. Some of the kids at school are talking about it. It sounds like fun."

"I agree, although one of the nurses I worked with is having a fit because her son is playing with his friends, and she's all up in arms thinking it's some kind of devil worship," April told them.

"What? Can I see that, Penny?" Keith asked.

"It's nothing like that!" Ben told them. "Some of the other musicians I work with play it too, and that hogwash is being used to stir up controversy. From what I'm told, it's a pretty cooperative game compared to, say, Monopoly, that we all grew up with. No bankrupting other players or sending them to jail for landing on the wrong space. My colleagues have told me that it's a game built on teamwork. You can't win unless you're working together."

"I don't know much about it either," Maddie said, "but some of the kids I work with play it too. So that's why I bought it for Penny. They love it and said it's a lot of fun. You kind of get to be anyone you want in the game, and the girl characters can be warriors or anything else they choose to be. So you all go on this adventure together, and even if your character dies, you can experience a totally different way of life while you're playing."

"What else did you get me, Maddie?" Penny asked.

"Well, that's it for my presents, but I know Nina and Ben got you something, although they wouldn't tell me what. Maybe they thought I couldn't keep a secret," she teased.

"Let me check the roast first, and then we'll get Penny's other present," Nina said.

After Nina checked on the food, Ben joined her over by the bathroom.

When they disappeared, Penny said, "Hey, where are you going?"

Moments later, the two brought a bicycle out of the bathroom. Penny's eyes were wide with surprise.

"Is that for me?" she asked, struggling to speak.

"Yes, it is," Nina said. "It's from Ben and me. But Maddie was the one who mentioned how much you like to ride. Do you like it?"

Penny didn't respond. Instead, she just rushed over to them and hugged them. She turned to Maddie and mouthed "thank you" before burying her face in Nina's shoulder.

Chapter Thirty-Three

For the next few days, everything seemed to be falling into place. Finally, Nina reached both Andrea Goodwin and Albert Jacobs about the sale of the collection she'd found. The buyer was ecstatic about being able to purchase the entire lot it as soon as he could.

On the day before Thanksgiving, Nina took Maddie and Penny with her to Portland to help Lilia make the pies she now planned to donate for the Thanksgiving meal prepared by the volunteers at the State Street Church, where Walter's funeral was held. They would be hosting the event usually held at Dizzy's, and many had volunteered to support those who were alone or in need of a hot meal.

On the way to Portland, Maddie caught Nina up on a discussion she'd recently had with Ben.

"He suggested I apply to a community college," Maddie said hesitantly.

"Maddie, that's a wonderful idea! What do you think you'll study?" Nina asked her.

"He recommended I try to complete what he called my general education credits before deciding what degree to pursue. But honestly, I know I want to do something with plants."

"Boy, what a surprise!" Penny piped up.

"Oh, hush," Maddie teased. "I'd really like to go in the spring, but I doubt I can afford it." She sighed.

"I'd be happy to help, Maddie," Nina offered.

"You would?" Maddie replied with shock.

"Yes. I would."

They had reached Portland, and Nina pulled into a parking lot close to Dizzy's. When she stopped her VW, Maddie reached over and hugged Nina's neck and hurriedly got out of the car, too overwhelmed to speak.

Several other women joined them, including Charlotte, who would soon be the new owner of the diner. They spent hours making and cooking pies, and by the time they left in the late afternoon, Nina wasn't sure she had the energy to cook a full Thanksgiving dinner the next day.

"Don't worry," Penny told her when she expressed her concern. "We're here to help."

It was a reminder of how different this Thanksgiving would be from the years she was married to Richard when Nina had always been expected to prepare the meal on her own. On most holidays, she would be entirely exhausted by the end of the day. Having everyone's help would make tomorrow easier and more enjoyable.

ONCE HOME, she bid the girls a goodnight. After feeding the kittens, all she wanted to do was relax in a warm bath. She wanted to leave the door open so the heat from the living room would keep the bathroom warmer. She hoped Cinnamon and Ginger would cooperate this time so she could enjoy some music without having to crowd the record player into the small space.

She placed it on the hamper and selected *Turandot,* the opera by Giacomo Puccini, to ease her weariness. While the opera recording with Joan Sutherland and Luciano Pavarotti was now wildly popular, she still preferred the recording she grew up with, with Erich Leinsdorf conducting. She knew the voices of Birgit Nilsson, Jussi Björling, Renata Tebaldi, and Giorgio Tozzi would transport her to a place far away from Kittery, Maine.

As Björling sang *Nessun Dorma*, she thought about all the times she'd danced with her father as a child around their tiny kitchen. She would place her feet on his as he moved with ease and grace, avoiding the tables and chairs that took up much of the room. He held her tight and sang to her in Italian, but her mind always heard the words in English.

Nessun dorma *None shall sleep,*
Nessun dorma*! None shall sleep!*
Tu pure, o Principessa, *Even you, oh Princess,*
Nella tua fredda stanza*, In your cold room,*
Guardi le stelle che tremano, *Look at the stars that tremble*
D'amore e di speranza! *Of love and hope!*
Ma il mio mistero è chiuso *in me, But my mystery is closed in me*
Il nome mio nessun saprà! *No one will know my name!*
No, no, sulla tua bocca lo dirò *No, no, I'll say it on your mouth*
Quando la luce splenderà! *When the light shines!*
Ed il mio bacio scioglierà *And my kiss will melt*
Il silenzio che ti fa mia! *The silence that makes you mine!*
Il nome suo nessun saprà *No one will know his name* E noi dovrem, ahimè! Morir! Morir! *And we must, alas! Die! Die!*
Dilegua, o notte! Tramontate, stelle! *Vanish, O night! Set, stars!* Tramontate, stelle! All'alba vincerò! *Set, stars! I'll win at dawn!* Vincerò! Vincerò! *I will win! I will win!*

The warmth of the water lulled her to sleep. She dreamt that she was about to board a plane. The stewardess had her arms across her chest and refused to allow Nina on board. She was hurt and confused. She felt a strange sensation and found herself wrapped in a metal case with wings. She was frightened and tried to escape. The metal surrounding her began to melt, and she somehow knew she could fly.

She found herself pushing past the woman and entering the cockpit. Suddenly, her entire body filled the room. Her eyes were the windows on the plane, covered in a layer of frost, which sparkled in the sunlight. Thin feathery lines spread out in all directions. She paused to examine its beauty.

In order, to get a clear view of the area in front of her, she needed to remove the icy blanket. Once the task was done, she saw an entire field of flowers of all colors covered in a sparkling layer of dew. She was energized and bursting with strength. She took off and hovered at street level, interacting with cars and other vehicles. She came to a four-way stop sign and, after assessing the situation, continued to go straight ahead before climbing far above the landscape.

Far ahead of her, Nina could see a bank of clouds. She approached it with caution. Her mother's face appeared. She was mouthing something that Nina couldn't understand. She drew closer so she could learn what she was saying but when she reached her, her mother faded away.

Nina looked down. She was now miles above the earth, and she could feel herself free falling. She reached into a pocket in pulled out a balloon. Blowing hard, she expanded it far beyond its capacity, yet it continued to grow larger. She began to float until she could see a large field of fluffy snow. She let go of the balloon and landed. As far as she could see, she was surrounded by the snow. When she reached out her hand to touch it, it was warm and soft, like cotton balls. She walked through a field and saw Lilia motioning to her from the other side.

SHE WOKE up when she heard the scratching sound of the record needle that had reached the last bit of music on the first side of the album. Fearful of damaging the turntable with splashes of bathwater, she carefully got out of the tub, lifted the arm off the album, and shut the record player off to dry herself and get into her pajamas.

Suddenly she heard a creak on the staircase. She froze, then grabbed a towel and clutched it to her, trying to remember if she had locked the downstairs door—something she often forgot to do. Someone was in the living room, walking across it as quietly as possible. Nina shut and locked the bathroom door.

She looked around for anything she had close by to protect herself. Unfortunately, there was nothing large or heavy to dissuade an attacker. With only moments to decide what to do, she grabbed the can of Lysol spray from the cabinet.. She aimed it at the door and heard a light rap.

"Nina, it's Penny. I think my father is here. I'm scared!"

Nina opened the door and found the young girl trembling.

"I locked the door to your kitchen and put a chair in front of it, but I don't know what else to do," she told Nina between sobs.

"Why do you think your father is here?" Nina asked her, slipping on her robe.

"I heard a car pull in back and looked out the window. A man got out and was looking around. It's so dark it's hard to see, but it must be him."

"You did the right thing even if you scared me to death," Nina said. "I'll be back in a moment."

Nina threw on some clothing and came out of her bedroom in minutes.

"Where's Maddie?" Nina asked her.

"She got called into work," Penny told her.

"Well, I can't see anything from my apartment, and I don't want to take a chance he's entered the building. If he came around to the front, I would imagine he could get in easily because the door is never locked. But since you saw the car in the back, it's hard to say where he could be. So, I'm just going to call the police and see if they can come to check it out."

Nina placed a call and explained that someone might be trying to break into the property. She and Penny waited anxiously for them to arrive. When the Kittery police announced themselves at her apartment door, Nina told Penny to stay upstairs and went to the kitchen, removed the chair Penny had placed in front of it and unlocked and opened the door.

"Hello," Nina greeted them.

"Are you Miss DeMarco?" the man asked as he stood there with a pad of paper and flashlight. A younger man stood off to the side.

"Yes. Did you find anything?"

"Other than a set of tire tracks, there was nothing. There's a car out back, though who's to say if the tracks are from the Bug parked there."

"That's my car. There was definitely another car back there. I saw it," she lied. "My tenants park in the front of the house, so I think it could have been my ex-husband. He's been giving me some problems since our divorce, and I thought maybe he was trying to get into the carriage house back there."

"Well, Miss, we don't get involved in domestic affairs. I can check the doors to that building if you want, but if someone was here, they're gone by now."

"I would appreciate that. Thanks for your help," Nina told him as they left.

As Nina went upstairs, she wondered if it actually was Richard. It seemed like something he would do, especially after learning that he'd lost any legal claim he thought he might have to the money she'd found. She started to go upstairs and found Penny sitting on the top step so she could listen to the conversation.

"Why did you tell him it could have been your ex-husband?" she asked.

"Well, I didn't want to explain anything about you and Maddie, and honestly, since you didn't see much, it could have been Richard. He's been really difficult to deal with since our divorce, and the latest blow might have caused him to come by."

"No. It was my father. I know it was."

"Maybe you're right. I hope not, but I suppose we have to be more careful until you get through with the whole emancipation thing."

Penny nodded.

"Let's go downstairs, and I'll make you some maple milk."

The two went into Nina's kitchen, where she again locked and bolted the door.

Chapter Thirty-Four

It was hard to get to sleep after Penny left. Nina had insisted she stay until Maddie was safely home. But long after Maddie arrived, the three of them sat huddled at Nina's kitchen table, speculating whether the man was their father, even after Nina insisted it could have been Richard.

The girls had returned to their apartment by the time Ben arrived home, and Nina had a chance to fill him in on what had transpired. He too was concerned but wasn't sure how to evaluate the situation. He suggested Nina hire a locksmith after the holiday, and they should all start locking the front door to the foyer as they entered or left the building. Nina agreed and bid him a good night.

IN THE MORNING, she was exhausted by the strain of an emotional night, but the promise of a lovely Thanksgiving boosted her spirits. She grabbed her record player and a few albums and went down to the carriage house hoping the music would revive her. As she approached the building, she noticed that all the downstairs windows of the carriage house were covered in a layer of frost. It perplexed her because she'd never seen them collect the beautiful layer of icy wizardry before. The color almost matched the tarnished copper gutters that surrounded the house. *The color of frost.* Richard's words came back to her unbidden, and she pushed them away.

When she reached the back door, she realized that the door to the carriage house was slightly ajar. The cold air outside must have caused the moisture from the warmer air inside to conjure the magical look to the windows of the stone structure. Nina wondered if the police had checked it after all. She thought about calling them but wasn't sure what she would ask. She had forgotten to write down the names of the two officers who arrived at her door last night.

Nina nervously looked around. The last time she'd been in here was two days ago when she brought over all the groceries to prepare for today's meal. Penny had offered to help. Perhaps she hadn't closed the door properly when they left.

Out of the corner of her eye, she spotted something shiny. There, next to a small clump of weeds lining the slate walkway, was Richard's Corum Feather watch. Nina would have recognized it even without turning it over to see his initials, RBK.

So, it was him! Nina thought. "What a dick!" she said out loud, picking up the watch and placing it in her pocket.

What did he think he would accomplish by breaking into the carriage house? Did he know she had cleaned it out? Was he the one sitting in his car late at night watching the house? Nina was furious at the thought that he couldn't let go. She considered calling the police to report him for trespassing.

Knowing that Maddie and Penny were becoming increasingly nervous, especially with the incident the night before, she wondered if she should tell them about what she'd found, just to assure them that it must have been Richard after all.

They've already been through so much. If they knew it was just Richard lurking around, maybe they would feel better.

As Nina stepped through the door, she was frustrated with

how cold it was inside. Seeing nothing out of place though, she relaxed, believing no harm had been done.

She placed her turntable on the counter and plugged it in. She brought some of the albums Ben had loaned her, knowing they would most likely be more in keeping with what Maddie and Penny would want to listen to.

She marveled that this place that once lacked purpose had been brought back to life. The carriage house had transitioned from a place crowded with things that had outlived their usefulness to an exquisite space to gather with friends and loved ones. From the inside, the frost on the windows looked magical, simple water vapor become solid and beautiful. She almost wished she could capture it someway because she knew that once she turned up the thermostat, it would begin to disappear.

She was so caught up in the moment, she didn't hear Ben enter the room. When he cleared his throat, Nina spun around, then breathed a sigh of relief.

"I'm really sorry if I scared you. I'm usually so loud people know I'm coming a mile away," he said placing a charcuterie board on the counter.

She smiled when she thought of these people who would be arriving and sharing the special day.

"I'm glad you came alone, although I imagine the girls will be here soon. I have something to show you," Nina told him.

"You're always full of surprises," Ben joked as he walked towards her.

Nina took Richard's watch out of her pants pocket and held it out towards Ben.

"Whose is this? It's beautiful," he said taking it from her.

"Turn it over."

"Richard's?"

"None other. His parents gave him this for his birthday years ago."

"Where did you find it?"

"Not far from the back door. Looks like he was our trespasser after all."

"Are you sure he dropped it there last night? Is it possible he lost it some other time?"

"I doubt it. I've been in here dozens of times and never noticed it before. That is no coincidence, and I'm tempted to turn him in."

"Are you going to return it?" Ben asked.

"You know, it never occurred to me to keep it," she said with a grin. "No, I don't want it. It's probably worth a lot of money but it's not mine. If I kept it, I'd be stooping to his level. Maybe if I give it back he'll leave me alone. I just want him out of my life. I'm debating whether I tell Maddie and Penny about it since they were frightened out of their minds last night."

"Well, maybe you tell them but don't give them the sense that it's outside the realm of possibility it was their father. You don't want to give them a false sense of security either."

"Good point."

"What's a good point?" Penny asked coming through the door with her sister.

"I'll tell you in a minute. Let's get this place warmed up first. Ben could you start a fire?"

"Sure."

"Maddie, why don't you and Penny put on some music and then join me in the kitchen to get things started?" Penny rushed ahead of her sister and began going through the albums Nina brought.

Nina planned on serving some of the foods her family had served at Thanksgiving, alongside more traditional American dishes. Since Lilia was bringing a turkey sometime in the early afternoon, Nina decided to make an eggplant *involtini,* her version of mashed potatoes, and a risotto made with butternut squash. David was bringing a selection of wines, and Ben's charcuterie board would be served as an appetizer. Both Maddie and Penny offered to help Nina make some ricotta pies and some pumpkin cannoli for dessert. Nina hoped it would all come together so they could eat sometime in the late afternoon or early evening.

"You have some weird music here," Penny called to Nina. "The only groups I like are the Beatles and Creedence Clearwater Revival. Can I put one of them on?"

"Of course," Nina told her, thinking perhaps she should have brought a wider selection of music or asked Ben to bring some albums with him.

For some reason, Penny put CCR's *Willy and the Poor Boys* album on the second side, and "Fortunate Son" blasted throughout the room.

"Hey, turn it down just a bit, okay?" Nina asked her over the music.

Penny either ignored her or didn't hear the request as she danced around the room to the rhythmic beat of the drum. She held her arms above her head and swayed gracefully, entranced by the music.

Maddie shook her head at her sister and went over and turned the music down before she joined Nina.

Penny eventually went to help Nina and Maddie, but by then they had already wrapped individual discs of pie dough in parchment paper to refrigerate. For the next few hours, they all worked while the music in the background provided a way to express the many emotions flooding the room.

With more prep work to be done, Ben jokingly put on the Beatles' album *Help*. Nina laughed at the appropriateness of his choice.

Once tasks were completed, Ben joined Penny and Maddie who stood in the middle of the room, belting out the Beatles' songs. They all fumbled the lyrics but enjoyed the entertaining way Ben accompanied them.

Nina had never heard Ben sing before and was struck by his pleasing baritone voice. When the album reached the next to the last song, Ben was quite animated, and they all enjoyed a laugh with his dramatic interpretation of the ballad, "Yesterday."

He took Maddie's hand and danced her around the room and crooned in her ear.

"Why did you go?" Ben sang.

Maddie played along and shrugged her shoulders.

"Did I say something wrong?" Ben teased and pretended to cry. Penny joined in by wiping his fake tears. Their antics didn't stop when the next song and last one on the album turned out to be "Dizzy Miss Lizzy," something Nina had completely forgotten about. She looked at her watch and realized the morning had flown by and that Lilia would be there soon.

When she arrived, they helped her unload her car. Nina suggested they all break for a light lunch featuring the beef barley soup Lilia brought.

"I can't believe how different this looks," Lilia said. "Putting the table in front of the fireplace was a great idea. Was that something that you found in here, or did you purchase it for that purpose?"

"It was here all the time, under one of the canvas cloths used to protect the furniture. All the other stuff went to an auction house, but I had to keep this piece. I will eventually do the same with the other things in the garage bays, but I want to have a better look at what's there since we both know Henry had a way of hiding things," Nina told her with a wink.

"Aw, be honest. You're just afraid of the squirrels," Ben joked.

"Well, buster, let's see how you like having one fly at your head," Nina teased. "By the way, Lilia, that other matter between Richard and me has been completely resolved. I can't thank you enough for helping to clarify how I found the things, not to mention telling me about them in the first place."

"That's wonderful to hear," Lilia told her.

Nina walked behind Maddie and put her arm around her shoulder.

"As a matter of fact, now that things are close to being settled, I'm going to help Maddie go to college full-time so she doesn't have to work and go to school." Maddie smiled at her. "And Penny, this goes for you too," Nina told her. "You know—when you're ready."

Before they sat down to eat, David knocked on the carriage

house door. Nina was at the stove warming the soup, so Ben answered the door.

"Here, let me help you with those," he said and reached for one of David's bags.

"Hi, David! You're just in time for lunch. Lilia brought some soup." Nina told him warmly.

David moved further into the room and crossed to where Lilia was sitting to kiss her cheek.

"David, this is Maddie, and this is Penny." Lilia gestured toward the girls. "They came up to Dizzy's to help us bake the pies for the church. Let me tell you, they were so helpful. I would have hired them on the spot if I planned to keep the diner." Lilia winked at them.

"It's nice to meet you both," David said, taking off his coat and hanging it on the coat rack in the corner. "This is stunning, Nina. My aunt often told me about this place, but I had no idea it was quite this grand until I pulled into the driveway."

"I wish I could show you both the first-floor apartment and how it was renovated," Nina said, "but the tenants are gone for the holiday. They'll be moving out after Christmas, so maybe we can do something for New Year's Day if you're up for it."

"I'm afraid you'll have to count me out," Lilia told her. "I'm going to finish packing up the diner, and in a few weeks, I'm heading over to spend time with Elizabeth and her family. If there is one thing Walter's passing taught me, it's that life is unpredictable, and I want to meet her husband and their children."

"Well, I don't have any plans, so unless I'd be a third wheel, I'd be happy to spend New Year's Day here," David said, looking from Nina to Ben.

Nina realized David might be assuming there was a romantic connection between her and Ben. She found herself urgently wanting to correct the notion.

"I'm meeting up with some of my friends after the New Year's Eve concert, so I can't be here either," Ben told him.

"Well, Nina, it might be just you and me," David said, looking her way. Nina smiled and nodded before turning back to the soup on the stove.

"We could come!" Penny piped up.

Maddie gave Penny a withering look that told her it might be best to be quiet.

AFTER LUNCH, Nina retrieved the letters from her apartment and brought them to the carriage house. Lilia, David and Ben sat around the table looking through them. Nina, Maddie, and Penny rolled out the dough for pies and listened as the others discussed the letters.

"I must have been wildly bored to have written all this. These are like finding a time capsule! Did you read all of them?" she called over to Nina.

"No. Not even close. I was just hoping to find you so I could return them. I do have some favorites, though. Especially the ones about Uncle Billy. Your adventures with him had me laughing on a lot of occasions."

"Can I ask you something rather personal?" Ben asked, leaning in to speak to Lilia quietly. "Nina often recapped the letters she'd read but one thing always made me curious. Was there a reason Billy was alienated from his family for so long?"

Lilia looked questioningly into Ben's eyes. It took a moment but she slowly found the words to answer him.

"I suppose you might have picked up on the fact that Billy and I moved quite a lot. I always thought it was because he was afraid the authorities might object to the way he took me from Mrs. Peck. But as I got older, I started to realize there was something more to it. So, I asked him." Lilia took a deep breath. "My father disowned him because he found out Billy was a homosexual. Since my grandmother lived with us, he prevented her from seeing him. The world was not friendly to men like my uncle.

Moving around was the only way he could protect the both of us. I hope this doesn't offend you," Lilia told him.

"Not in the least," Ben assured her.

David sat quietly reading more letters but suddenly laughed out loud.

"What's so funny?" Lilia asked, turning towards him.

"Look what I found," David said, showing her a piece of paper.

"Oh, my god! I'd forgotten all about that!"

"I never have. You had multiple copies posted around the apartment," David said, smiling.

"Well, keeping an eye on you and your sister while running a restaurant was challenging. I dare say it was effective." Lilia raised her brows.

"Family Rules," David read.

Always say please and thank you.
If you share with others,
they will share too.
Don't whine; it's annoying.
Always give us kisses before bedtime.
Tell the truth even if it might get you in trouble.
Do your chores.
Treat everyone the way you want to be treated.
Be kind.
Don't say mean and hurtful things.
Always love one another.
Enjoy a good laugh.
Remember how much you are loved
by Uncle Billy and me.

"That's really sweet!" Nina called over to them, listening from the kitchen.

"Well, should I remind you of your favorite phrase?" David teased Lilia.

"No, I remember it. It's still true. 'Life is not fair so get over it,'" Lilia told him, laughing.

"That wasn't all, though. She had us spend hours memorizing things like the states and their capitals, all the presidents, the Declaration of Independence, and even some poetry too," David added.

"And did that hurt you at all?" Lilia chided.

"Not in the least. I can still recite some of it."

"Really?" Nina asked him. "Like what?"

"My favorite has always been Desiderata," he told her. Then David began to recite the Max Ehrmann, poem.

> Go placidly amid the noise and the haste, and
> remember what peace there may be in silence.
> As far as possible, without surrender, be on
> good terms with all persons.
> Speak your truth quietly and clearly; and listen to
> others, even to the dull and the ignorant; they
> too have their story.
> Avoid loud and aggressive persons; they are vexa-
> tious to the spirit.
> If you compare yourself with others, you may
> become vain or bitter, for always there will be
> greater and lesser persons than yourself.
> Enjoy your achievements as well as your plans.
> Keep interested in your own career, however
> humble; it is a real possession in the changing
> fortunes of time.
> Exercise caution in your business affairs, for the
> world is full of trickery. But let this not blind
> you to what virtue there is; many persons
> strive for high ideals, and everywhere life is
> full of heroism.
> Be yourself. Especially do not feign affection.
> Neither be cynical about love; for in the face

of all aridity and disenchantment, it is as
     perennial as the grass.
Take kindly the counsel of the years, gracefully
     surrendering the things of youth.
Nurture strength of spirit to shield you in sudden
     misfortune. But do not distress yourself with
     dark imaginings. Many fears are born of
     fatigue and loneliness.
Beyond a wholesome discipline, be gentle with
     yourself. You are a child of the universe no less
     than the trees and the stars; you have a right to
     be here.
And whether or not it is clear to you, no doubt
     the universe is unfolding as it should.
Therefore, be at peace with God, whatever you
     conceive Him to be. And whatever your
     labors and aspirations, in the noisy confusion
     of life, keep peace in your soul. With all its
     sham, drudgery, and broken dreams, it is still a
     beautiful world. Be cheerful. Strive to be
     happy.

"That is lovely," Nina told him. "I've never heard that before!"

"For much of my childhood, I thought it was from the Bible because Lilia had us say it every night before we went to bed. But then she told us her uncle taught it to her, and she thought it was a wonderful reminder of how to live a good life," David told them.

"Well, it seems to have worked," Nina replied.

David smiled at Lilia, who bent over and kissed his cheek.

THE AFTERNOON PROGRESSED with sharing stories, playing music, and cards around the table. When everything was ready, Nina set the table with linen, the formal china she removed from the basement, and a Thanksgiving-themed centerpiece Maddie made. When dinner was served, Lilia commented on the excellent combination of different traditions, and everyone ate more than they intended.

"What are these called again?" Maddie asked Nina.

"They're called arancini," Nina replied. "They're really easy to make. I can show you sometime."

"You're a marvelous cook, Nina," Lilia told her. "If I was keeping the diner, I would be begging you to come work with me."

"Well, when you get back from visiting Elizabeth, I might be begging you to do the same," Nina told her with a smile.

"Have you decided what you're going to do now that financial matters have been resolved?" Lilia asked.

"Not exactly, but I do have some ideas. Until I know more about what I can and can't do with this property, I'm going to wait to decide anything. And, who knows, now that I have the resources, life might take me in a totally different direction."

The festivities wound down shortly before 8 p.m.. With everything cleaned up, David went out to warm up Lilia's car while she continued chatting with Nina. When he came back in, he expressed his concern about her driving the hour north on her own since she wasn't used to driving at night anymore.

"Don't worry about me. I'll stay off the highway, and I'll call you when I get home and leave a message since you have a much longer drive than I do," Lilia reminded him.

"I have tomorrow off. Maybe I should head to Portland and sleep in the guest room."

"I wouldn't mind the company," Lilia told him cheerfully. "He's such a pushover. Always has been." She winked at Nina.

Ben and the girls also said goodnight, and he walked them to their apartment. Nina stayed behind to tidy up some more. She dried most of the dishes but left the utensils and other cutlery in the drainer to put away in the morning. Finally, she blew out the candles that lined the table and stood before the glow of the fireplace, truly happy with her place in the world.

She grabbed her coat, shut off the lights, and walked towards the door. Then she remembered leaving the milk she'd need for the kitties in the fridge and went to retrieve it. She bent over to reach inside and heard someone behind her.

Nina turned, thinking Ben had come back. She began to smile at his thoughtfulness. She turned. The distorted face of a man with a red beard leered at her. She almost fainted at the sight of the carving knife he held—the very knife David had used hours before.

His stealth movements left her with no way to escape. There was nothing to hide behind—no time to protect herself—no one else was going to save her. She was alone.

The man brought his arm up, and he lurched forward. "Leave my daughters alone. They're mine," he hissed through clenched teeth.

The blade of his knife penetrated Nina's shoulder. She wondered, *why didn't it hurt?* Then he brought it down on her again. This time, the pain left her breathless as the white hot edge cut through her skin.

When he aimed to strike again, Nina tried to fight back. She twisted her body and jerked her head up as hard as she could, hitting him in the face. Her reaction stunned him.

Nina momentarily broke free and ran towards the door. He blocked her exit, but she dodged him and moved into the middle of the room trying to find a way around him. Her deep wounds and unsure movements caused her to stumble backwards allowing him to pin her against the wall. Once he immobilized her, he brought the knife down once again.

The anguished faces of those she loved flashed before her. Knowing one of them would most likely find her made her furious. When her attacker came closer, Nina dipped her body slightly and shot straight up, butting him in the head again before falling back on the floor. The unforeseen blow caused him to fall backward, and as he did, he tried to right himself. But he'd forgotten that he still had the knife in his hand. He looked directly at Nina and was in complete shock at seeing the same blade he'd used to attack her stuck in his thigh. Nina watched as blood gushed from his femoral artery. Then, he slumped to the floor.

Nina tried to get up, but she found her arms and legs wouldn't cooperate. As the blood ebbed from her body, she had little strength to even lift her eyelids. She feared that if she closed them even for a second, she would never open them again. Since her body was unwilling to cooperate with her mind, she rested her weary head on the unyielding floor of the carriage house.

She tilted it slightly straining to see why a cold breeze suddenly washed over her. Was this life leaving her body? She heard a wail but she could barely lift her heavy eyelids. Had Maddie entered the room? Was that Penny? Her eyes fluttered and Nina struggled to keep them open so she could plead for help.

Everything began growing dim. Nina thought back to the moments months ago when she desperately wanted to die. At that moment, she realized it was never about ending her life. It was always about ending the pain that invaded her mind and disrupted her sense of wellbeing.

She heard shouting—but the words themselves stopped having meaning. She finally closed her eyes trying to find the tiniest bit of comfort as she listened to a cacophony of desperate voices ringing out. While she faded, she marveled at their strength. Whoever it was, Nina was sure they had already endured more than their share of challenges. Now they were being called upon to save her. Moments later, she silently thanked them for their bravery, and mercifully, she passed out.

Epilogue

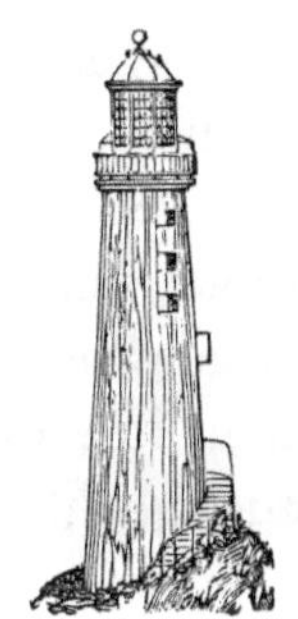

October 2018

Safe Harbour Foundation Headquarters, Pepperell Point Road, Kittery, Maine.

Nina stood at the back of the room, waiting to be called to the podium. She looked towards David, her husband, standing by her side. She reached out and gently took his hand, giving it a knowing squeeze. He was a good and kind man, and she was grateful for his love and support. But his presence could not forestall her diving into all the "what-if" moments inspired by being back in the place that was now the headquarters for the Safe Harbour Foundation. She tried to shake them off, but it was impossible to stop the memories from flooding back as she recalled the life that had unfolded within the many rooms of the house on Pepperell Point Road.

Her life had changed, even though she remained much the same inside. Nina couldn't help but connect almost everything good in her life to the struggles she endured here under this very roof. If Richard hadn't divorced her, she never would have found the letters and been able to renovate the carriage house. Even the brutal attack that almost took her life years ago had ultimately led her to this moment. The reality of death ultimately brought her back to life. It gave her the will to live and go on to find the strength to recover both mentally and physically.

After that, Maddie's and Penny's situation made her realize there must be others like them. So, she began exploring, using her resources to start Safe Harbour, which ultimately led her to spend long days working with David, who generously donated his legal skills and time. They fell in love over truly shared goals and dreams and had two wonderful children together and six beautiful grandchildren.

Their work had also led to finding her birth father, who read her story when the Globe interviewed her about Safe Harbour. She ended up discussing the stigma of adoption for some ethnic groups that existed at the time and still existed to a degree at the present. Her dad was a beacon of love and hope, as was Lilia, for all her pluckiness and inspiration.

They both inspired her in ways she couldn't fully explain. But she knew the love and support she'd received, especially as she recovered, led to a deep and fervent desire to provide others with the hope that had kept her from sinking into the quagmire she had once believed was inescapable.

She often questioned how she had managed to survive while Richard had died young and most likely alone. She'd seen him years ago when she and Julia were out shopping at the Natick Mall, and she almost didn't recognize him. She knew that he'd run afoul financially when his third wife divorced him, and he could not keep the chain of dental practices they'd started. Julia had pointed out the man who was once the love of her life as they passed him. Richard had been staring at something longingly through a store window. Nina asked Julia to hurry along, unwilling to spend even a moment saying hello. Not long after that, Nina learned he had died. While the obituary didn't disclose how, she couldn't help but recall the face of the broken man that reflected back from that window. All of these things were connected to her time within the walls of the house on Pepperell Point Road and the events that occurred here.

While she reminisced, she almost missed hearing them call her name.

"And without further ado," the chairwoman of Safe Harbour announced, "it is an honor and privilege to introduce the woman who started this foundation and its many programs. She has truly been a beacon in the fight to end violence against women for the past three decades: Mrs. Nina Michaud."

David squeezed her hand to get her attention. She mouthed a kiss and walked to the front of the room. There were dozens of people she knew who had gathered to support her. She would have recognized the woman that sat in the front row anywhere. Although her long red hair was now streaked with gray, she wore the same bright smile that she did the last time Nina saw her, bossing the crew around at one of the first vertical farms in Maine. Maddie turned in her seat and watched Nina walk down the aisle towards the podium and joined in the applause.

Nina had heard from Penny days before that she would have to miss the event because her daughter Abigail was due to deliver any day and she needed Penny's help minding her other grand-kids. She promised to get down to Worcester to see Nina and David in the spring. Nina knew it was a promise Penny intended to keep, but it would probably never happen.

Unfortunately, Ben and his husband Eric couldn't make it

either. They were both on tour and far from Kittery. Ben, however, had sent her a text that morning with a funny cat video and wished her the best of luck. She texted back with some silly emojis and a promise to get together once he was back in the States. She thought of the days she excitedly told him about Lilia's letters and all the questions she had about this mysterious woman that unknowingly played a significant role in her ability to move beyond her sorrow. She wished her mother-in-law could be there today but knew she would always be in her heart.

Nina stepped up to the podium and looked out. She hesitated momentarily at the weight of the message she was compelled to deliver. Finally, she breathed and spoke with a heavy heart but a grateful spirit.

"This is not the place I envisioned I'd be in my life when I sat in this very living room almost three decades ago. I thought I would be playing with grandchildren, and perhaps I would own a restaurant or bakery or maybe even be teaching something in the field of culinary arts. But like this room, my life was transformed. This room went from being a comfortable place to sit by the fire to enjoy a good book or a glass of wine to the place we used as the first office for the foundation when we opened. Now it provides seating for intimate gatherings when members of the foundation have urgent matters to discuss or something to celebrate.

"I stand before you today, grateful for all the ways in which I've been challenged to grow. So many of the lessons I've learned have come by way of painful encounters. There have been multiple occasions when these challenges threatened my well-being, if not my very existence. But I chose to fight, not always because I wanted to—but because I decided not to allow someone else to rob me of whatever life had to offer.

"Months ago, I sat in my living room at our home in Worcester. My newest granddaughter, Lilly, was sound asleep next to me. I looked down at her, and for a moment, I was so proud that we would be opening another center, this time in Springfield. I knew I was doing something to help make a better future for those I love and the world around me.

"But it occurred to me that it was not enough, even with more than thirty centers all over New England, each providing aid to women who have been abused or been victims of some kind of violence. All our efforts have been a reaction to the aftermath of what these people, mostly women, have endured. We haven't confronted the systemic problem of the root causes. We could never have enough shelters to end the violence or abuse because the problem is so much larger than the acts of individuals who harm us because they believe it is their right. If anything, violence and domestic abuse are on the rise. At that moment, I turned to my husband David, who was sitting by my side on the sofa, and said, 'This is insane. We're playing whack-a-mole by opening shelters. There has to be a better way to combat these issues at the root level.'

"David and I had long discussions over the next few weeks, and the result is that I've made a decision to resign as the head of the foundation." There we audible gasps in the room.

"As most of you know, David has been a representative for the State of Massachusetts for close to twenty years now. He has decided not to seek reelection so he can join me in our continued efforts to dismantle the systems that reinforce the power and control men have to legislate women's lives.

"My decision is based on a deep desire to understand what perpetuates this and to understand how can we take steps to stop its growth and spread. I don't need to tell any of you that women are losing ground in our fight merely to have the same rights as men here in the US.

"I keep asking myself, how did this happen? How do men hold onto the power that subverts equality? Not just for women but for people of color, those in the LGBTQ community, and other minorities. A partial answer came to me when I thought back to the time I spent recovering from the violent assault I experienced years ago. My recovery took years of therapy for both my physical and mental injuries. But during that time, I had a strong support group that helped me every step of the way. It was as if we were all recovering together. And in many ways, we were. While I was the one that was attacked, they all felt the pain and suffering to some extent. The assault was on *my* body, but the blade pierced the hearts of those around me.

"While it seems like an oversimplification of a way to address a monumental problem, we must find a way to work together: to unite as one in the same way other movements have united during periods of great civil unrest.

"In the many days and weeks after I decided to resign, David and I took a hard look at how society is structured to subvert equality. What leads to the inherent belief by some that men are by nature superior to women and that they have the absolute right to exert power and authority over them? We followed up with an extensive amount of research. Still, we are far from having all the answers.

"But the most glaring clue that we examined was the disparity in income and distribution of assets between men and women. In a day and age where money is used to literally buy political influence—when creating policies for a nation of people, those with the most money are almost guaranteed to win. That's what makes tackling this matter of utmost importance. We must understand that we cannot implement change effectively unless women have a global understanding that encourages their political participation.

"At this point, you might be asking yourself, what can you do? This is not something that can wait to be solved. Our planet is dying, and the way our political system, designed to serve those who profit from all its resources by oppressing others, solidifies power. We need bold action immediately. While that can lead many to feel so overwhelmed they become paralyzed, we can begin with the things we have control over. We can all speak up for both ourselves and others. We can't remain silent and hope this problem will just go away. We must use our voices.

"I'm not sure where this urgent mission will take me now. I just know that it is imperative to act now while we still have a chance to give women and other marginalized individuals a seat at the table. We can no longer wait for an invitation. We need to understand that we will never accomplish the change needed to effectively enact equality for women without global political participation.

"Shortly after this sudden epiphany, I ran across a speech from the actress Natalie Portman, at *Variety's* "Power of Women" event. She addressed women in her industry about how to take down the patriarchy so enshrined in our culture. While she was specifically talking about women working in filmmaking, what she said applies to all women in every walk of life. One of the most memorable things she said was, 'When you light another person's torch with your own, you don't lose your fire. Instead, what you do is make more light and more heat.'

"So our challenge is to spread our fire. Use the fire we've created with our foundation to light the fire of other women's torches. By doing this, we'll make more light and heat for everyone. Thank you for your years of support. I am very grateful to have been a part of the work and all we've accomplished."

Nina looked at David, still standing in the back of the room, and smiled as she left the podium. Then, with her head held high, Nina glanced around at the room and realized how much of the house embodied her life. Yes—it had been both a place of entrapment—and a place of refuge. It was the place where she died and was brought back to life. The struggles within these walls had tested her bravery and appeared to have forgiven her when she was ready to give up. Those who had helped her heal had gathered here. It was where she'd found a new love—both for herself and so many others. It was as if when she transformed, the house transformed with her. Or perhaps, it was the other way around? And she was willing to give it all up because she knew the chapters ahead had another destiny in mind if she were to find a more satisfying ending to her life's story.